Erie Tales:

Omnibus, Volume I

Presented by
The Great Lakes Association of Horror Writers

Edited by
Bob Strauss, Nicole Castle Kelly
& David C. Hayes

www.greatlakeshorror.com

Table of Contents

Saving Mr. Hockey
By Michael Cieslak...7
The Lonely Corridor
By Peggy Christie..29
Her Descent
By Peggy Christie..45
A Crowning Repast
By W. S. Cwik..47
Slaughter of the Doves53
By Mary Makrias..53
The Neighborhood Diner
By W. S. Cwik..63
Fear Cage
By Justin Holley..71
Hook
By Robert J. Christie...85
On The Island
By Michael Cieslak..93
Feed
By Peggy Christie..119
Find a Need and Fill It
By Peggy Christie..121
Beyond Dead
By Mary Makrias...133
Brains
By Michael Cieslak...141
Made In
By MontiLee Stormer...143
Reflections
By Mary Makrias...149

The Vessel
    By Colleen McEuen 165
The Stairwell
    By Michael Cieslak..181

Rosa, Rosa, Come Out of Your Room
    By Christopher Nadeau 191
Caliente
    By MontiLee Stormer 207
And on the Eighth Day He… Oops
    By Peggy Christie..213
Ragnarok Around the Clock
    By Michael Cieslak...227
Across the Pond
    By Christopher Nadeau 241
Poems From The End
Bloody Run
    By MontiLee Stormer 261
I've Got a Secret
    By Peggy Christie...263
Forgotten
    By John Pirog 267
The Woman Next Door
    By James Park..271
The Hike
    By Hall Jameson...285
Contributors...289

Saving Mr. Hockey

By Michael Cieslak

Davíd felt the familiar tension rising as the zombie shuffled closer. The narrow aisle slowed the creature's progress from its normal shamble to a crawl. The pace afforded David more than enough time to escape, yet he remained rooted to his seat. His stomach tightened and a cold sweat broke out across his forehead. It was a normal reaction, the standard response of the living when in close proximity to the once living. The reaction was made worse by the monster's nearness. Generally, people became aware of the undead before they could approach this close. The constant moaning or, more often, the smell of decay would warn potential victims before a zombie was within striking distance. Olfactory and oratory warnings had failed David this time.

The beast, which was slowly closing on David, had been a young man at the time of its death. Its skin had taken on the sickly gray-green pallor that was common to the undead, yet the flesh was still surprisingly taut. Zombies who reanimated after living long lives tended to decay faster. It had something to do with the elasticity of the skin and fat deposits. Overweight zombies did not last as long as thin ones. This zombie had patchy black hair matted close to its skull. It let out a low moan, an auditory early warning system, as it reached David.

When the zombie was almost upon him, David swung his feet to the right, pulling them out of the way of the push broom, which the zombie slid across the floor. The zombie moaned again and continued forward. It swept the area in front of the young executive. It glanced at David, but did not move towards him. He looked into the zombie's eyes. A gray film covered the pupils. David could find no spark of intelligence behind the cloudy orbs.

He watched as the zombie janitor moved past him and down the row. A small pile of discarded cups and wrappers preceded the zombie's broom. Within a few hours, the entire arena would be cleaned and ready for the crowds already forming outside. This would be accomplished by a small army of the undead. From where he was seated, David could see the swarm of cleaning corpses. Each section had at least one of the undead sweeping, straightening, or picking up refuse. Zombie labor was slow, but it was cheap. This was why it had been retained for so long at the Joe Louis Arena. The stadium was old. It was difficult to justify the high ticket prices, regardless of how well the Red Wings were playing. It was important for the organization to cut costs wherever it could.

This was the focus of the meeting David had attended a few weeks ago. It was that meeting which had started him thinking about the plan, which he would attempt later tonight. It was that plan which had him sitting in a nearly empty stadium, watching dozens of zombie janitors shuffle, sweep, and straighten.

* * *

The Meeting, two hours which had grown so important in David's mind that they warranted mental capital letters, had been weeks ago. It started with the announcement that Detroit's hockey team would be getting a new stadium. It ended with the announcement that served as the impetus for one of the craziest ideas David had ever had.

Most of The Meeting had droned on at a zombie's pace. Identical executives in expensive suits took turns offering their statistics, projections, and endless Power Point presentations. Discussions of concession revenue, skyboxes, and parking shared with the other sports teams' new stadiums buzzed around the room. Disjointed snippets from the meeting played themselves out in his mind. Isolated phrases echoed in his ears.

"Increased security means increased revenue."

"Imagine the publicity we will get when news of the mass hiring is announced."

"The new stadium will be a safe arena, a place for the movers and shakers to be seen. If this means that a bunch of rednecks with mullets have to watch the game at a bar while guzzling Molsons, so be it."

"The real fan is the one who can afford the ticket price."

When one of the speakers discussed plans for an additional stop on 'The Downtown Monorail' to accommodate the expected crowds, David stopped listening. No one from Detroit would refer to the People Mover as a monorail. Most would not bother to refer to it at all.

The drawn curtains and the lack of clocks made it impossible to determine how much time passed, but the meeting finally began to wind down. The lights rose, causing David to squint. There was a smattering of applause. A few questions were asked and fielded easily. Feeling that he should contribute somehow to the meeting, David raised his hand. After a nod from the speaker, he asked his question.

"What is the expected size of the undead labor force for the new stadium?"

Silence coalesced in the room like thickening fog. Alarmed looks flew around the mahogany table. The man in charge of the presentation glanced at his colleagues for help. His gaze came to rest on the person at the head of the table. David had no idea who this man was, but it was obvious that he was the real power in here. He oozed authority. His suit was cut just a little better, the cloth just a little more expensive than those worn by the other out of town yes-men. Unlike the others, he wore a solid gray tie, which brought out the blue-gray pinstripe in the suit. It would have matched the color of his eyes, had there been any animation in them. The tie was vibrant. His eyes were cold.

He nodded. The gesture both accepted responsibility for answering David's question and dismissed the man who had been giving the presentation. The icy eyes locked on David. The man's voice was deep, hard, and unforgiving.

"There will be no zombies at the new stadium."

David had realized then that the man speaking to him was the new head of the organization. The new Skyboxes, the sushi stands, the seat warmers, were all his idea. All of the changes, which would ensure that the new stadium was only a place for the elite, came directly from him.

He was the kind of person David hated.

This Suit did not become head of the organization because he loved the Red Wings. He did not even care about the game of hockey. He was simply in it for the bottom line. Numbers were what he cared about. Nothing David could say would change his position.

That did not stop him from one last appeal. Although it would probably amount to nothing, David felt that he had to try.

"I appreciate what you are doing for the organization. Increased revenue will definitely help the team. I just find that I have to ask what price are we willing to pay? What are we willing to give up to make a few more dollars? Are we willing to alienate part of our fan-base just to increase our profit margin?

"Zombies have been a part of hockey forever. I remember buying my first baseball souvenir from a non-living vendor. It was a cheap imitation jersey. This was before we sold authentic replication jerseys. I was eight years old. My uncle had managed to get tickets. Later he slipped me a twenty and told me to buy whatever I wanted. I remember my hand shaking, my heart pounding. Part of it was the thrill of the game, being there in the stadium, watching the steam of my breath. Another part was fear. I knew in the back of my mind that nothing could happen to me. The zombies were leashed and they were wearing their jaw clamps. Still, my heart pounded. I was excited and terrified."

David paused for a moment. He was suddenly aware of the other people in the room. Directly across from him, one of his coworkers was smiling, a tear welling in his eye. He nodded to David and the tear fell, making a dark stain on the Al the Octopus tie he wore. David pressed on.

"Are we going to deny that sense of wonder, that thrilling fear from a whole generation of hockey fans? Are we going to replace a tradition with dazzle? What you are talking about doing is like getting rid of that guy that used to dance while sweeping the bases during the seventh inning stretch at the old Tiger Stadium."

There was a moment of silence. There was a brief pause where David thought he just might have gotten through to the men at the other end of the table.

"What was that man's name?"

"Excuse me?" David swallowed hard.

"The sweeper, at the old stadium. What was his name?"

Too late, David realized that he had talked himself into a corner. He racked his brain for the name, but came up empty. He shook his head.

"Exactly my point. You do not know his name, and I bet that no one else in this room does either. He was once an extension of the team. Tiger fans could not imagine a baseball game without him. Now parents bring their children to baseball games and the kids get to ride the carousel. Sure, they might miss the old dancing sweeper, but that does not stop them from buying tickets.

"There is a place for traditions: the past. The old man may have been sentimental. Perhaps he just had a soft spot for the undead. Whatever the case, Mr. Pizza is no longer in control. There will be no zombies in the new stadium."

* * *

David stared out at the ice. Up where he was seated, he could barely hear the hum and whir of the Zambonis as they swept the ice. One Zamboni entered from each end of the rink. They circled the outside then began the careful pattern that would ensure a smooth skating surface. The drivers always ran the same routes. Repetitive manual tasks, which did not require problem-solving skills, were perfect work for zombies.

The seats began to fill with fans. Not many at first, just the die-hards who wanted to watch the teams warm up and perhaps catch a glimpse of the Zombonies.

Normally, zombies were not allowed to operate motor vehicles of any kind due to a few horrible accidents involving zombie gardeners on riding mowers. The NHL had received a special exemption from this law by simply going ahead and training the zombies, putting them on the ice in front of thousands of hockey fans, and then asking for permission.

The fans ate it up. It was a public relations dream. Everyone wanted to have their picture taken with one of the Zombonies, as they came to be called. There was no place where this was truer than in Detroit. As the fans flowed in, David watched the number one zombie attraction in all of hockey sweep the ice: Mr. Hockey himself.

Not the actual Mr. Hockey. Gordie Howe was still alive and making commercials. No one knew who had acquired this undead worker for the team. No one knew who first noticed the uncanny resemblance between the zombie and the hockey legend. However, the marketing executive who had seized the opportunity when it presented itself had retired at age forty-five and was living on a houseboat in the Florida Keys.

Mr. Hockey, the zombie, generated an enormous amount of revenue for the team. Tee shirts bearing his likeness were stocked in the gift shop next to rest of the merchandise. Authentic jerseys bearing the number 9 and the Mr. Hockey logo outsold many of the actual team player jerseys. He was a positive symbol, an icon of both the game and the city.

And he was going to be destroyed at the end of the week.

* * *

After The Meeting, there had been an official announcement regarding the new stadium. The groundbreaking had occurred, attended by a host of local celebrities and hangers-on. Work had already begun. The new home of the Red Wings would be in place for the next season.

There had been other revelations as well. A mass hiring had occurred. The entertainment group now employed a host of ticket takers, concession workers, ushers, and even maintenance workers. They were slowly being trained, or "acclimated into the new family," in the language of the new hire brochures. Editorials praised the organization for the group hiring: "Local sports team lowers local unemployment rate."

There were no headlines regarding the elimination of the zombies, which were currently occupying the positions. Internal memorandum referred to "the reduction in non-living personnel" and "the replacement of current workers by new hires." There was nothing, which overtly stated that the undead staff was to be eliminated. The suits all understood. This was going to happen, there was nothing that could be done to stop it, and smart employees would not discuss it.

The more he thought about it, the more David realized he had to do something. It simply was not right to dispose of people this way, even if they were dead. Granted, people had been disposing of the dead for the greater portion of human history, but things changed when the dead started to walk.

He did not consider himself an activist. He had never really given much thought to the "civil rights" of the undead. If anyone had asked him directly, he would have denied even thinking about the fair treatment of zombies. It was not that he thought they should be citizens. David just thought that it was not fair to destroy something that had been a loyal worker for years. It was like shooting a greyhound after it started to lose races.

He could not save them all. He realized that early on. It would be almost impossible to save even a small percentage of the nonliving personnel currently employed at the arena. He could, however, save one. It would be difficult, dangerous even. If he was caught, he could kiss his career goodbye. He would be lucky to avoid prosecution.

He knew that if he did not at least try, he would not be able to sleep at night. He had to do something, make some token effort. He decided that he would rescue one zombie from destruction. That rescue would be a symbol which would allow him to hold his head above the others he worked with who sat idly by and let the loyal employees die a second time.

What better symbol than the most recognized undead employee in the Motor City? David was going to save Mr. Hockey.

* * *

The Zambonis finished their dance and left the ice. Soon, the players would take the ice to begin their warm up. Fans, many of whom had been waiting in the cold for hours to see the skate-around, streamed in through the doors. David made his way back to the skybox reserved for members of the organization.

There were already a number of people in the reserved VIP box. They were all seated at the bar with their backs to the ice, watching television or talking on their cell phones. David's nod of greeting was ignored as he walked past them. He stepped out of the suite and took one of the reserved seats directly in front.

The game started. A few of the inhabitants of the skybox took seats near David. He paid little attention to them or to the game itself. Most of the people seated around him weren't watching the game either. They were talking to each other or on their ever-present cell phones. The only exception was a young blonde girl, part of the all important 'tween' demographic that the organization was trying to attract. She wore an Yzerman jersey, despite the captain's recent retirement. She spent most of the first period on her feet, cheering and watching the game through binoculars. For a change, David was as distracted as the VIPs that he despised. He made an effort to cheer when others did, but by the first intermission, he would not have known the score if not for the Jumbo-tron.

"Please direct your attention to the ice," the announcer's voice boomed. "Here come Mr. Hockey and Ted, your Detroit Red Wing Zombonies!"

A smattering of applause arose from the fans. A door at the far end of the rink opened and the two machines lumbered onto the ice. One made a quick right turn, the other headed for the opposite end.

A shiver went down David's spine. This was what he had come to see. The people around him did not realize it, but they were witnessing the second to last trip around the ice for the zombie known as Mr. Hockey.

"They are great, aren't they?"

David turned to the girl seated next to him. She held a pair of binoculars to her eyes, a wide grin on her face. He was struck suddenly by the need to tell someone about his plan. He did not need help, but he wanted someone else to know. He needed the approval of another person. He wanted someone to tell him that what he was doing was right, was brave...

...was not the most foolish thing they had every heard of.

"Do you want to take a look?"

David nodded, biting back the response which rose in his mind: *I will be seeing them close enough in a little while.* He took the binoculars and peered through them.

At first, he had a hard time focusing on what he was seeing. Then he realized that that he had failed to track the Zamboni's movements. It had turned. The flat, sparkling surface in the binoculars was the ice itself. He lowered the eyepieces for a moment, got a bead on the Zamboni, and raised them once again to his eyes.

David's head snapped back in alarm. The image, which grimaced out at him, was horrifying. He had focused not on "Mr. Hockey," who was smoothing the ice at the far end of the rink, but the other undead Zamboni driver. Its skin was a mottled gray. In places, the flesh had sloughed off all together revealing stringy gray musculature, which appeared both desiccated but strangely wet at the same time.

It had been a long time since David had seen a zombie in this condition. Reanimated workers were given regular treatments with a formaldehyde formula, which kept their bodies from breaking down. Allowing a zombie to decay was bad business practice. If the body reached the point where it was no longer mobile, the zombie would be useless.

Comprehension hit David like a blow to the back of the head. The company was not going to maintain the upkeep on its zombie employees if it was going to eliminate them. The Suits would think that would be a waste of money. Instead, they would continue to use the workers but do nothing to prevent their decay. When the zombies were no longer useful, living workers would replace them.

It made perfect sense from a business standpoint. It would even make it easier to destroy the undead when the time came. David winced. These actions were beyond indecent. It was simply inhumane to treat any creature this way, even if it was dead.

The young executive tried to spot "Mr. Hockey" through the binoculars, but was unable to get a clear view of it. There was no way to assess the damage, which the zombie had already sustained from this distance. He returned his gaze to the other zombie. It sat upright, grayish green hands gripping the steering wheel tightly. It was missing the last two fingers on its right hand. The lack of digits did not seem to affect its ability to guide the massive vehicle over the ice.

The red jersey hid most of the torso. It appeared to be fairly solid, but who knew? It could have been slowly liquefying, held together by nothing but the ribcage and wire. The shoulders, however, appeared solid. The muscles here had not decayed. Rising up from the shoulders was a matrix of heavy wire, which encased the zombie's head. It appeared as if the creature had a birdcage wired over its head. This outdated safety device ensured that no one could be bitten should the worker feel a bit peckish. These cages, which resembled some medieval torture device, had been widely replaced with other safety measures. Most zombies employed by the government wore a leather facemask known as a Hannibal, which obscured the lower half of the face. The military, which used zombies in a limited capacity, mostly to clear minefields, simply removed the lower jaw, making it impossible for the creatures to bite.

The National Hockey League wanted to give the illusion of danger. The leather restraints did not give this impression. Something which could be restrained by a mask, could not be all that worrisome. Conversely, nothing was more frightening to the public than the gaping maw of an undead creature without a jaw. It was also revolting, especially when the zombie was working one of the food service counters. The head cage was a happy medium. It provided a degree of protection while still giving the illusion of risk.

"Mr. Hockey" would be fitted with a similar cage. That, of course, would have to go. If "Mr. Hockey" were to survive in the wild, he would have to be able to fend for himself, as far as food was concerned.

* * *

The players retook the ice and the second period commenced. David was once again lost in his plan. In his distracted state, he did not even notice the quick succession of goals scored by the home team. It took him a moment to realize that the fans were not on their feet to salute the goals, but because they were making their way to the bathrooms and concession stands. The second intermission was starting and David had barely noticed the passing of time.

He mumbled an excuse and stood as well. He practically bolted through the skybox and into the corridor beyond. He had planned on being in place by the time the zombies finished their sweep of the ice. He was already behind schedule.

He forced himself to slow to a quick walk as he proceeded down the hallway to the gray security door. This would be the first hurdle. The floor plans he had studied for the better part of a week showed this as the most direct route to his goal. If this door was alarmed or locked, he would have to find another way to the sub-basement. This would mean walking past the fans milling about in lines for food, drinks, souvenirs or the restrooms. It would mean passing hundreds of potential witnesses.

David paused, his sweaty palm resting on the cool handle of the door. It turned easily. He eased it open. No alarms, no bells, no security guards yelling for him to stop. He crossed the threshold and was halfway down the first flight of stairs before the door closed behind him.

David vaulted down the four flights of stairs. He reached the bottom winded, sweating, and nervous. He closed his eyes, trying to project a map of the stadium's sub-levels onto his eyelids. If he got lost now, it was all over. He could wander for hours in the dark before finding his way back. By then the stadium would be locked, the zombies safely in their pens, and his plan would have to be abandoned.

After a few tentative steps to his right, David became more sure of himself. He navigated the maze-like corridors as swiftly as he dared given the sparse illumination thrown off by caged bulbs hanging from the ceiling. He passed hissing steam pipes, unmarked doors, and bare concrete floors.

He walked for ten minutes, threading his way past half-seen obstacles. As he walked, one sound differentiated itself from the others. What David first mistook for the hum of machinery took on an eerie, less mechanical tone. The pitch rose and fell, yet never left the lower end of the audible register. As he walked, the sound rose in volume. The small hairs on the back of David's arms rose and he shivered.

The corridor finally ended at a thick door made of reinforced steel. The sound was loudest here. It had ceased to be a single tone and had separated into many, similar tones: low moaning, constant and unending. He had reached the zombie pens.

The door opened easily and David's senses were blitzed. The moaning had been muffled by the door. Without the barrier, his ears were besieged by the sound of the undead. Their wails washed over him, a wave of sound. In the early days of the undead uprising, it had been this constant moaning which had caused people to abandon the safety of secure locations. It had driven them mad, driven them right into the waiting maws of the undead.

It was too dark to see but David knew that he was in the presence of a multitude of the undead. His sense of smell told him that there were many zombies hidden by the darkness beyond. It was the stench of the grave. The smell brought to mind scavenger beasts, beetles, and blowflies. He gagged on the noxious air.

His goal was on the other side of this room. In the plans, the pens were a rough circle. He could proceed straight through to the other side, but the thought of becoming turned around in the midst of the undead was horrible. His other option was to make his way along the outside of the room. He would pass three openings, each extending outward from the center like spokes from a wheel, before reaching the one he wanted. David steeled himself and began to inch his way along the wall.

He had reached the first opening without incident. He did not see the opening so much as feel it. The air was slightly cooler, slightly sweeter. It still held the fetid rank of the undead, but it no longer burned his nostrils. He remained in this refuge for a moment before pressing on.

Somewhere between the fist and second openings, the zombies became aware of his presence. The tone of their moans shifted, became louder, more urgent. David heard chains rattling, cage doors being shaken. Something threw itself against an unseen barrier a few yards from him. David strained to see into the room. He could make out dim shapes, but no details.

He passed the second opening without stopping. He no longer worried about his plan; he no longer cared about his job. He wanted only to get away from the moaning. He wanted only to escape from the smells of rot and decomposition. He wanted to run, but was afraid he would miss the opening and end up running in a circle, trapped within the room like a hamster on a wheel.

He trailed one hand along the wall as he moved quickly. He thought he heard movement under the moaning. A person? A human guard or zombie wrangler? One of the undead, escaped from a pen? His fingertips barely detected the shift from concrete to painted steel. If the door had not been cooler, he may have gone right past it as he feared. Fortunately, this door led to the ice rink itself and was cooled by the air on the other side.

He pushed it open and blinked in the harsh light. At the extreme periphery of his vision, he could see movement. He shook his head to clear his vision then jumped to the side. He ducked as an arm the width of a stout branch swung at his head. It missed him by inches. The hand hit the wall with a wet thud. The zombie to whom it was attached was in an advanced state of decay, too far gone to work in public.

David reached the horrible revelation that if the company was no longer working to preserve their undead employees, it was unlikely that they were feeding them. The human trying to slip out of the pen could be the first morsel of food any of these zombies had encountered in weeks.

The zombie, overbalanced by its wild swing, pushed away from the wall. It reoriented itself and started again for David. A ruin of blackish liquid seeped from the monster's empty eye sockets. Science had yet to determine exactly how the undead tracked their prey. They seemed to be able to track living flesh despite the lack of eyes to see, ears to hear, or lungs to draw in scents.

However they tracked their prey, this zombie had set its sights on David.

The door hissed closed, a pneumatic hinge forcing it shut. David shoved again at the door. It opened easily. He leapt through as the zombie lunged forward. It hit the door with a solid thump. David tried to close the door, but was unable to do so. The zombie managed to slip one hand into the crack between the door and the wall. David gave one desperate shove and the door slammed shut. The moan on the other side rose to a wail.

David glanced down and saw what appeared to be four fat worms on the concrete floor. His stomach roiled as he realized that the zombie had sacrificed the fingers of one hand in the fight. The digits squirmed on the ground. One writhed toward David's shoe. He yanked his foot back then brought it down with a grunt. He stamped the cement, squashing the fingers into gooey paste.

He leaned against the wall, panting. The idea of saving "Mr. Hockey" seemed insane, especially given what he had just done to one of his zombie brethren. David thought about abandoning the plan, but to turn back now meant re-crossing the zombie pens. He sighed and made his way up the hallway.

All of the halls leading to the zombie pens slanted downwards. This made it easier to corral the undead when their shifts were over, but made the walk up to the ice more of an effort.

David once again walked towards the audience. The second intermission was over. A roar arose from the crowd as some significant shift in play occurred. David realized dimly that he was probably missing a good game.

The air was also getting progressively cooler. The walls were painted white. Various pieces of equipment hung from hooks on the walls. David glanced at them as he walked past. His eye caught on one of the items that he thought he might need. It was a long pole with a loop of wire on one end: a zombie come-along. He grabbed it and kept walking.

The hall progressively widened, finally opening into a large, square room. There was a bank of service elevators against one wall, which led to the food service areas. Opposite these was a hall, which led to a ramp. At the top of the ramp was a large roll-up door.

A third hall led up to the ice. Parked here against the wall were the Zamboni machines. A few people encircled them. One had a come-along similar to the one which David held.

Instead of a loop, this one ended in a hook. The hook was fastened to a ring attached to the base of "Mr. Hockey's" sternum. He pulled and the zombie slipped off of the Zamboni and fell to the floor. The other men were occupied with unhooking the second zombie from the other Zamboni. A wheeled pallet waited for the driver.

David had not planned on encountering any living people. He paused for only a moment then strode forward, swinging the pole over his head. He brought it down hard on one of the men working on the second zombie. It caught him on the shoulder and sent him sprawling. The other two turned, startled. The one closest to "Mr. Hockey" reacted first. He let go of his come-along and snatched something from a holster at his waist. It was a small baton, similar to those used by the police. He depressed a button and blue sparks shuddered along its length.

Electricity would not kill the undead, but it would disrupt their mobility. David had no illusions as to what it would do to him. If the charge were enough to drop a zombie, it would be more than enough to stop his heart.

The man feinted forward, brandishing the stun-baton. David stabbed with the pole, but missed his assailant's arm. The heavy end of the comealong hit the floor beyond him. The man grinned and thrust at David, missing him narrowly. David backpedaled, dragging the pole with him. The wrangler stepped forward to attack again, his eyes filled with menace. The look quickly changed to one of surprise. His foot caught on the pole and he fell. He twisted, trying to regain his balance. He hit the concrete hard, both arms pinned below him. David stared as the man started to convulse. He turned away when he realized that his assailant had fallen on his own weapon. Smoke curled upwards and the air filled with the smell of ozone and burning flesh.

David turned back to the other Zamboni. One of the men, the one he had hit, had struggled to his feet. The other was racing up the ramp towards the ice. David let him go, concentrating on the one who remained. He was a squat, powerfully built man. Coarse hair covered arms crisscrossed with scars. The man grimaced at him in what may have been a smile then lunged.

David did not think so much as react. He brought the come-along up from the floor in an arc. "High sticking," he thought. The heavy pole connected with the side of the man's head. There was a loud crack. The short man dropped to the ground. His head bounced on the concrete with a hollow sound. Dark red liquid poured from his head. He spasmed once, then was still.

Bile burned in David's throat. He swallowed it back. He looked around the room. Four dead bodies. Two lying on the ground, one still bolted to a Zamboni, the other standing by the door. The last two regarded him with milky gray eyes. David gulped and approached "Mr. Hockey" slowly. The zombie tilted its head, regarding David like a curious dog might as the loop slipped over his head. There was a moment where it was completely still, then "Mr. Hockey" strained against the wire of its safety cage. A black tongue extended from its ruined lips and licked the gore from the end of the pole. David dropped the come-along and ran towards the rolling door.

A large red button sat half way up the wall. David hit it and the door ascended. To the right of the door was a pegboard covered with keys. David grabbed a ring at random. A shuffling, scraping sound caused David to turn. "Mr. Hockey" was moving towards him, the pole plowing across the floor ahead of the zombie. David grabbed the pole and swung it to keep the zombie as far away as possible. He got the beast in front of him. The two headed up the ramp and out the door.

Three plain white vans sat at the top of the ramp next to an idling ambulance. Although rarely used, there was always an emergency vehicle on hand during a game. Most times, it just sat there. When they did transport someone, it was more often a fan having chest pains.

"At the bottom of the ramp!" David hollered as he neared the vehicles. Two men were leaning against the side of the ambulance. One tall, one short, each smoking. Why was it that medical staff always smoked?

"There has been an accident," David said as he continued past the two. He received matching blank stares.

"People are hurt," he said slowly. "Much blood. Help them."

Mr. Hockey let out a low moan as if in agreement.

The message got through to the short one first. His eyebrows went up and the cigarette fell from his open mouth. The tall one was a little slower to respond, but at least he had the presence of mind to stub out his cigarette against the ambulance before darting inside the vehicle. The engine turned over and the ambulance headed back down the ramp.

Things were moving faster than David had expected. He had not counted on them reacting so quickly. Of course, he had not counted on the amount of bloodshed either. He had thought that someone might get hurt, but not dead. Two people, killed in order to save one undead. David fumbled with the keys. He finally found the one that unlocked the back of the first van. He opened the door and tried to maneuver the zombie inside. As he got around to where he could use the pole to push it in, the door swung shut. He managed to pin Mr. Hockey against the van door, but no better.

David held the zombie in place and looked around to the driver's side. Nothing. On the passenger side was another door. He smiled. He pulled with all his might, pivoting as he did. Mr. Hockey stumbled along at the end of the pole. David stepped quickly towards the back of the van, switching places with the zombie. It orbited David from the end of its wooden tether. David jumped into the van, pulling the pole behind him. He scrambled to the side door. It would not budge. He pulled on the handle, no movement. He felt the pole slipping from his sweaty hand. He fumbled around in the dark, finally finding the lock. The side door swung open.

David renewed his grip on the pole and yanked. He felt the zombie resist for a moment, then stumble to the back of the van. It reached its hands out towards the man who had just saved him. Panic and claustrophobia fought for the position of chief emotion and David resisted the urge to shove the thing away and bolt. Instead he pulled. The zombie stumbled forward again, its knees hitting the rear fender of the van. The cage on its head clanged against the roof. David pulled again, feeling something pop in his back. The cage snapped from the zombie's neck and flew back into the parking lot. Mr. Hockey fell forward into the van. It crawled towards David. He scrambled out the side door, tossing the pole back in. He slammed the door shut then ran around to slam the back door. He felt something crash into the door just after it shut.

People were shouting from the bottom of the ramp as David drove away, his prize safely caged in the storage area of the van.

* * *

The soon-to-be-abandoned stadium was located on the waterfront of the Detroit River, convenient to any number of freeways. The white van slipped into the northbound traffic on I-75. It passed through the revitalized areas, past the blighted neighborhoods that no one cared to revitalize, and across Eight Mile and into suburbia. Two hours later, even the northern suburbs were gone.

David had no plan for this part of the trip. He had simply intended to drive north until he was sure the area was unpopulated, drop off Mr. Hockey, then return, leaving the van in a parking lot with the keys in the ignition. This was the Motor City. Crime rates might be down in other cities, but not here. An abandoned vehicle would not last long.

This plan had hinged on stealth. In his mind, he had seen himself safely back home in his loft before anyone even discovered that Mr. Hockey was missing. David had not planned on the level of resistance that he had encountered.

Nor had he expected the resistance to die. By now, the State Police would be looking for the van. He had to get rid of it.

"I'm sorry, buddy," he said over his shoulder.

Mr. Hockey reacted to his voice by scratching at the heavy gauge mesh, which separated the cargo area from the front seats.

"I wanted to drop you off further away, where you wouldn't be caught. I wanted to leave you someplace nice, out in the country. I just can't take that risk now."

A blue and white sign announced an upcoming rest area. David took the ramp and was delighted to see that the lot was empty. He pulled past the lights, past where there would be security cameras, and pulled over. He left the motor running and stepped out.

He sat on the rear bumper, his head in his hands.

David wiped his eyes and stood. He steeled himself for what he would do next. He was going to open the back door and bolt for the open driver's door. As soon as Mr. Hockey crawled out of the van, David would drive away. He might not last a long time, this close to civilization, but at least he would last longer than he would back in the city.

As he flung open the back door, an unbidden thought exploded in David's mind.

What would the zombie live on out here? He had already seen two people die, how many others would he doom by unleashing this creature on them? At the arena, it was easy to forget that these were not tame creatures. How long would it live in the wild before resorting to its natural ways?

David slammed the back door closed again. He would have to think of something else. He could not...

...he opened the back door again and stared.

The cargo area was empty.

The sliding door was open.

David took an involuntary step backwards. He sucked in a lungful of air, his body going into 'fight' mode.

The air tasted like decay.

His breath was expelled in a ragged yell as rotted teeth closed on his neck. Somehow the creature had gotten out of the van while David was sitting there. Adaptable, able to learn simple tasks, that was why the zombies had been trained in the first place.

Blood erupted from his neck and shoulder. David tried to pull away, but the zombie held him tightly. Mr. Hockey pulled his head back and came away with a mouth full of jacket, shirt, undershirt, and shoulder. David's right arm went numb. He struggled in vain as Mr. Hockey lowered his head for another bite.

David coughed. Pink foam sprayed from his lips as his body went slack. His vision dimmed, going black on the edges. He had killed two people, and unleashed this zombie to hunt countless others. And, unless David got very lucky and had his spinal cord severed by one of Mr. Hockey's hickeys, he would be joining the zombie on that hunt.

The Lonely Corridor

By Peggy Christie

Nathaniel skipped down the street jingling the coins in his pocket. His mother had given him ten cents to spend at the candy store. He'd been particularly well behaved today, she said, and deserved a treat. He pulled his grandfather's watch from his pocket and noted the time. He only had an hour to horse around before he had to be back home. As he made his way down the main thoroughfare, he slowed to a walk so he could study the carriage factory.

He loved to sneak into the factory and watch them make carriage after carriage. The process fascinated him. There was a corridor that ran underground between the factory of Caleb's Carriages and its huge warehouse. Nathaniel always managed to sneak in the back door of the warehouse and quietly scurry down to the underground passageway unseen.

Today would be no exception. He made his way around to the back of the warehouse. He could hear the men grunting with the strain of moving cords of wood to the factory line. Kneeling behind a stack of wood panels, Nathaniel peeked around its edge to see if the coast was clear. No one was near the entrance to the corridor and it was just a few feet away. He dashed to the door and quickly, slipped behind it and down into the underground hallway.

At the bottom of a small flight of steps was another door that led into the hallway itself. Nathaniel pushed his way through and closed the door quietly behind him. The corridor stretched out in front of him for fifty feet, jogged to the right, continuing on again for another fifty feet where another door opened up on a flight of stairs that led into the factory.

Along the wall to his right were several doors spaced about fifteen feet apart. They each opened into a small closet or storage space. He could explore down here for hours, poking through each space, crammed with wood, tools, machine parts, and the occasional mouse.

Today, Nathaniel walked down to the second door and slipped into the storage space. In here, there were piles of cogs and wheels, drills, scraps of wood, belts and pulleys, chains, saws, and countless other used tools. He pulled the door closed behind him and set his eyes on an old hand drill and some wood scraps.

With the door closed, the room became warm rather quickly. Nathanial soon grew tired and fell asleep. Several hours later, he awoke, sweating and dizzy. He dreamt of being in a furnace, surrounded by heat and flames, trapped and unable to escape. When his head finally cleared, he realized the room was extremely warm and he was soaked in sweat. He reached for the doorknob and his hand sizzled on the hot metal. He pulled his hand back and screamed in pain and fear.

Scared now, he blew on his injured hand and wrapped the other in his shirttail. As soon as he managed to turn the knob, the door blew inward, sending Nathaniel sprawling on his back against the far wall. Bruised, but not seriously injured, he looked up. Fire licked along the doorjamb and ceiling. The brick wall directly opposite the storage room, however, was not engulfed in flames. Maybe if he managed to jump through the doorway and press himself against the brick wall, he might be able to escape the fire.

Mustering up all his eight-year old courage, he took a running jump at the doorway and sailed through the flames without incident. Moving quickly to avoid the parts of the floor that were burning, he hopped and jumped until he reached the door at the bottom of the warehouse steps. He tentatively tried the knob. It was warm, but not scalding - yet.

He turned and pushed but the door would not budge. He couldn't understand why they would lock it. Pushing and straining, he kept trying to open the door. With each effort, he sobbed and cried until he went mad with fear and began pounding on the door, screaming for help, knowing in his heart that no one would hear him.

He knew all the men up there had gotten to safety and were clear of the burning building. They wouldn't be listening for a little boy in the underground corridor even if they could hear him over the roar of the flames. He stopped pushing on the door and inched his way back down the brick wall. He made it as far as the first storage room when part of the ceiling above caved in and crashed through the floor in front of him.

Nathaniel jumped back, barely escaping being crushed by the falling debris. He was now trapped in the corner between the pile of burning debris and the locked doorway to the warehouse. The smoke started to pour over him and he coughed violently. He huddled down, pushing himself as far against the wall as he could, and cried softly.

The black smoke blocked out all the light and he could barely see his hand in front of his face. He wanted to go home now. He didn't want to be here by himself in the dark. He didn't want to die alone in the underground corridor. He wanted his mother

* * *

"God damnit, Randy. Do you think you could keep a steady beat sometime today?"

Bronin jabbed the neck of his bass guitar at the drummer for emphasis. Randy flipped him off.

"You're the one that's hung-over, Bronin. Are you sure you're not the fuck-up today?"

Bronin paused and smiled sheepishly. "Oh, yeah."

As the rhythm section of the rock group, Tripping Foul, had a good guffaw, Carl and Will, the guitarist and singer respectively, rolled their eyes. Will tapped the microphone.

"Uh, hello? When you two ladies are finished, we need to get back to rehearsal."

Bronin whined. "But, Will, we've been here for three hours already. I think my hand has gone numb."

"And if you were alone in your bedroom right now, I'd believe it," retorted Will. "But you're not. We've only got a month before the next gig. We've got to practice."

Carl slowly removed his guitar from over his shoulder. "Bronin's right, Will. I know you just want us to be prepared but we've been here all morning. Another five minutes or five hours won't do us any good today. Let's pack it up."

Will sighed. They were right. And even if they weren't, it was three against one. He clicked the power off on his microphone and wrapped up the cords and stand. He locked up his own guitar as the rest of the group packed up their gear for the day. Over the next half-hour, they hauled most of their equipment from the rehearsal space to their cars.

Will waved the other three off as he ran back into the building, realizing he left his coat inside. He jogged down a small flight of steps and through a narrow door, which opened onto fifty-foot long hallway. It angled to the right and continued forward for another fifty feet. The far end of the hall ended in another doorway, which led to another small flight of steps. Those steps led to the first floor lobby of the building above them.

There were several small rooms to his right and the second one was the band's rehearsal space. Will quickly recovered his jacket from the corner of the room. As he turned to leave, the door slammed shut. Frowning, he walked over to the door and tried the knob. Locked.

"Ha, ha, guys. Very funny. Open the door."

He leaned his ear against the door but heard nothing. A sudden wave of exhaustion washed over him. He tried the knob one more time but became too tired to really care if it opened or not. He slumped down onto the nearest chair and promptly fell asleep.

Will gasped and his eyes flew open. At first, he didn't realize where he was. As consciousness crawled upon him, he recognized the practice space. Rubbing his eyes, he stood and wiped the sweat from his brow. Sweat? Was the practice space always this warm and he just never noticed before?

Frowning, he grabbed the doorknob and jumped back in pain. It was scorching hot. His hand was already blistering. With his uninjured hand, he felt the wood of the door. It was hot. Wincing, he wrapped his jacket around his good hand and pried open the door. He quickly shielded his face, expecting a blast of heat from the fire that must be raging in the hallway.

Nothing. There were no flames, no heat, nothing. Carefully, Will poked his head out the door and looked up and down the corridor. The air was a little stuffy but nothing to indicate a fire burning anywhere nearby. He looked down at his burnt palm. Shivering with fear, he ran to the end of the hallway, threw open the door, dashed up the steps, and burst out into the alleyway behind the building.

Randy, Bronin, and Carl were still standing by their cars and talking. The all turned to stare at Will as he raced over to them. Pale faced and shaking, Will told them what had happened. Randy and Bronin looked at each other and then burst into laughter.

"Nice try, Will. That was your best story yet," Randy joked as he nudged Will in his ribs.

"He's just trying to get us back in there and then trap us into practicing some more. Get over it, Will. We're done for the day, okay?"

As Randy and Bronin joked, Carl looked down at Will's hand and frowned. Several blisters were ballooning with fluid already. He pointed to it while jabbing Randy in the shoulder.

"How do you explain that?"

Randy quickly stopped laughing. He grabbed Will's hand and pulled it up to his face for a closer inspection.

"Shit, Will. What did you do to yourself?"

"What did I...? Oh just forget it."

Exasperated, Will stalked off to his own car. Bronin and Randy shrugged in unison and sauntered back to their vehicles.

"I hope this doesn't fuck up his playing," Bronin muttered.

As the bassist and drummer drove off, Carl waved absently to them. He made pretense of arranging his equipment in the trunk so Bronin and Randy wouldn't see him staring off in the direction Will drove. He'd known Will long enough to know when he was shoveling manure and when he wasn't. Whatever had taken place, Carl could see that Will was honestly scared.

Something about Will's story nudged a small block of memory in Carl's brain. He'd heard a story like it before but he just couldn't remember where or when. Maybe he'd look into it over the weekend.

* * *

The following week they met again for another rehearsal. Will's hand was, miraculously, almost healed. There were only faint wrinkles and slight circular scars where the blisters had formed but even those were fading. Randy and Bronin ribbed him for pulling a fast one on them but Carl was silent. Will grumbled something about assholes anonymous and warmed up his guitar.

Afterwards, as everyone was packing up, Bronin stayed plugged in. He wanted to stay a little longer to work on the new songs. He kept tripping up during the chorus and speeding through the last few measures. Will mumbled a 'whatever' under his breath and raced out the door. He still seemed spooked from last week and wanted nothing more than to get the hell out of the rehearsal space. Randy and Bronin joked about it some more but Carl interrupted them.

"Don't you think it's strange, what happened to Will? I thought I'd heard about something similar happening years ago but I couldn't remember the details. So I was doing some research on the history of this city over the weekend. Pontiac had a huge fire downtown in 1840. Twenty-five buildings were destroyed."

Bronin and Randy exchanged looks.

"So?" the questioned in unison.

"So," continued Carl, "this entire block was destroyed. This building used to be a carriage factory. The corridor linked the Caleb family carriage factory to its warehouse. The brick out in the hallway is from the original structure. The factory, which was the building over us and to the north, was rebuilt. But the warehouse wasn't. That's why the corridor opens into an alleyway on one end and a building on the other."

Randy raised an eyebrow. "Again I say, so?"

"Well, don't you think it's odd that Will thought there was a fire here, burned his hand on the doorknob, only to discover nothing was amiss?"

Bronin looked at Randy. "Amiss? Did he just say, 'amiss'?" Randy held up his hands. "What are you saying, Carl? That Will had a run-in with a ghost fire from 1840?"

"Well, yeah, I guess."

"Carl, I think it's time you took up drinking."

"Randy, I'm serious."

"I can see that. That's why I suggest a diet heavy in depressants. Bronin, see ya later."

Randy grabbed his stick bag and headed down the hall. Carl looked to Bronin, who held up his hands, signifying the 'don't even start with me' gesture. Sighing, Carl grabbed his guitar and jogged after Randy. He caught up to him in the alleyway.

"Randy, wait a minute."

"Carl, if you've come to say good night, then I bid you the same. But if you've chased after me with more of this post-modern ghost story shit..."

"All I'm saying is something happened to Will. I don't know what exactly but I think it's worth investigating. You've got an uncle who works in the Hall of Records for Pontiac, right? Can't you ask him to do a little digging?"

"Have him dig into the records to find info on the 1840 fire because we think it came into the future and attacked our friend?"

"I don't know. Tell him you heard a story about the fire and were curious. Tell him you've heard ghost stories from the locals. Tell him anything. Just see what you can find out, please?"

Randy shook his head. Carl would do anything for his friends but right now he was creeping Randy out. He was Carl's friend, however, so he'd humor him. Besides, Carl's ideas were giving him the willies so if for no other reason, at least Randy could quell his own apprehension.

As Carl sped out of the parking lot and Randy headed for City Hall, Bronin stayed back at the rehearsal space and continued to practice. His fingers flew up and down the neck of his bass as he tapped out a complicated rhythm with his feet. He stumbled over a long set of sixteenth notes and came in late for the refrain. Cursing, he wiped the sweat from his forehead and began again.

Approaching the same set of notes, he furrowed his brow in concentration. Drops of sweat rolled into his eyes, the salt stinging them and blurring his vision. Frustrated, he pulled the bass over his head and rested it on the stand behind him. He grabbed the front of his shirt and wiped his face dry.

As he stared at his soaked shirt, wondering why it was so damned hot in the rehearsal space, he smelled something burning. He whipped his head around to look at his amp. It hummed quietly in the corner as it always did. He checked Will's and Carl's amps but they were off. He looked at the closed door and saw smoke curling underneath from the hallway.

Panicked, he ran to the door and laid his hand on the wood. It was warm. He touched the doorknob with a finger to test it and quickly pulled it back. The metal was scorching. He grabbed an end of his shirt, wrapped it around his hand, and twisted the knob carefully. Suddenly the door blew inward and he was thrown to the back of the room.

Stunned, a little bruised, but unharmed, Bronin shook his head to clear it. He looked up. Bright orange flames licked the doorjamb but the hallway floor and brick wall looked untouched - for now. He had to get the hell out of here before the smoke and flames overtook him. Maybe if he ran for the door he could jump through it and get to the brick wall unscathed.

Taking a deep breath, Bronin ran at the door. Just as he leapt through the opening, he saw a young boy pressed against the brick. He was feeling his way along the wall towards the doorway to the alley down the hall. He was dressed in wool knickers and a soot-covered dress shirt. His short blonde hair was ruffled with sweat.

Just before Bronin reached the wall, the boy turned. He screamed and covered his face with his arms as if they alone could protect his mind from the horrifying visage of the boy. He reached for Bronin, crying and whispering, and they both disappeared into the wall, leaving behind only a dark wet smudge on the crumbling bricks.

* * *

Randy drove his car into the parking lot of Pontiac's City Hall building. He walked up the entrance steps, shaking his head, hardly believing he was doing this. After passing through security, he headed for his uncle's office on the second floor.

He knocked on the door marked "Historical Records" and was answered with a gruff "What?" from within. Grinning, Randy pushed open the door.

"Now is that anyway to speak to family, Uncle Dave?"

Without looking up from his paperwork, he responded, "It's the only way."

Randy took a seat opposite his uncle's desk. He waited patiently until his uncle was ready for him. Scribbling out his signature for authorization on an order for a new filing cabinet, Randy's uncle finished with the form and looked up at his nephew, smiling.

"Now, as I was saying. What?"

Embarrassed, Randy looked at the floor. "I, uh. Well, I was wondering, um, that is, do you know..."

"For crying out loud, boy. What do you want? I'm up to my left nut in paperwork. I haven't got all day."

Randy sighed. "What do you know about the history of Pontiac?"

His uncle gaped at him. "Exactly where do you think I work, son? Circuit City?"

"What I mean is, do you know anything about the big fire here back in 1840?"

He frowned. "Of course. Why?"

"What can you tell me about it?"

"You mean besides things being on fire?"

"C'mon, Uncle Dave. I'm serious."

"Well, most of the main thoroughfare was destroyed. Twenty-five buildings in all. As a matter of fact, the building where you and your buddies practice in was built on the original foundation of the old Caleb carriage factory. Shame, really."

A tickle of fear crept up the nape of Randy's neck making the small hairs stand on end. "What do you mean?"

"Well, all the factory workers were able to get out before the building was destroyed by the fire. But part of the warehouse collapsed, blocking an entryway into the underground corridor that connected it to the main factory. Apparently, a young boy, a local merchant's son, was playing down there and got trapped. He died in the fire."

"Holy shit."

"Yep. They found him two days later in the corridor by the door that had been blocked by the ruins of the warehouse. More than likely he tried to get out that way but, obviously, he didn't make it."

"Holy shit."

"Uh, yeah. Apparently, part of the corridor's ceiling caved in, trapping him in the corner near the warehouse door. The bricks of the wall he leaned against basically became super-heated and... Well, let's just say that all that was left of the kid was pretty much a blackened skeleton."

Randy frowned. "Did they ever find out who the boy was?"

Uncle Dave scratched his head. "I believe so. His name was Nathaniel Brown. I remember reading something about the kid having his grandfather's pocket watch on him that day. For some reason, it wasn't completely destroyed by the heat. Maybe Nathaniel's body somehow protected it. There were only a few scratches on it and the monogram on the inside was untouched, which gave them proof beyond any doubt that it was Nathaniel. Sad that a little trinket of machinery survived but not the boy, huh?"

Randy stood slowly. He quietly thanked his uncle for his help and promised to call him later in the week. He left the office, gently closing the door behind him. He could still hear his uncle asking him if he was okay but he couldn't answer.

He walked in a daze only a few feet from his uncle's office when a hand on his arm stopped him. He jumped and looked up to see the custodian, Tom Dyer, frowning in concern at him. Tom was a tall wiry man in his mid-forties whose bright grey eyes matched his city overalls. Normally Randy liked to stop and chat with the janitor but today he just wanted to get out of this building.

"You okay, Randy?"

"Uh, yeah, Tom. I'm fine."

"Hey, I couldn't help but overhear what you and your uncle was talking about. You know, he didn't tell you everything."

Randy's face pinched in confusion. "What do you mean?"

"That building where the old carriage factory used to be? There's a corridor that runs underneath it and..."

"Yeah, Tom, I know. My friends and I rent a rehearsal space down there."

Tom's face blanched. He grabbed Randy's arm and squeezed with a strength that belied his scarecrow build. The panic in his voice was mirrored in his pinched features.

"It's not safe. Things happen, people get hurt. You boys have got to get out of there!"

Randy's face froze as the tingle of fear at the nape of his neck transformed into an icy hand that gripped his spinal cord and gave it a good jerk. Will's story. His hand. Uncle Dave's info on Nathaniel. Randy had stopped listening to Tom's rambling and tried to free himself from the janitor's death grip. But suddenly the man's words stopped him.

"Wait, Tom. What was that you said?"

"I said some people claim to feel the heat from the fire when they're in there. Some people say they can smell smoke or see the fire itself. Of course, those are the people that lived to tell their tales."

Randy couldn't speak. He couldn't believe what he was hearing. Tom continued. "You see, my great-great-grandfather was just a boy when the fire hit. He lived, of course, and he passed down stories through my family about how once they rebuilt the carriage factory, people started seeing things. Then they started disappearing."

"Why haven't I heard about any of this before?"

Tom smirked. "Because them bigwigs in real estate wouldn't be making no money if they told people looking to rent their property that there was a ghost running around their building, let alone one that kills 'em."

"Wait, wait. Do they see the fire or do they see ghosts?"

"Well, I supposed the fire is kinda like a ghost itself. It has appeared to people without the boy."

Randy gulped. "Do you mean Nathaniel?"

"Yep. Of course, I've only heard of one person who's seen the boy and lived to tell the tale. He's up in Northville in that loony bin. Mostly he just mumbles and drools as he bounces off them rubber walls. But every now and again the staff says he'll hunker down in a corner, grabbin' at the air and yellin' out Nathaniel's name."

"How do you know all this?"

Tom looked down at his shoes and kicked at the broom he was holding.

"Because, it's my brother in that nuthouse."

He looked up at Randy, his eyes wide with fear. "You boys get outta that place. It's not safe. It's not..."

Randy's own eyes mirrored Tom's horror but not from the story. He just remembered that Bronin stayed after rehearsal today to practice - alone. He thanked Tom absently as he pulled out his cell phone and dialed Bronin's number. No answer.

"Damn it!" Randy cursed under his breath. He ran for his car and dialed Carl's number. He picked up on the second ring.

"Carl? It's Randy. I think Bronin's in trouble. Meet me over at the rehearsal space. See if you can get a hold of Will, too. "

"Randy, what's going...?"

"Just do it, Carl. I found out a little info on our phantom fire. Turns out the fire isn't our only ghost. There's something else. Meet me over there!"

He punched the 'end' button and hopped into his car. He just hoped Carl, Will, and he could get to Bronin in time. As he pulled into the parking lot of the old building, Carl screeched around the corner and parked beside him. Randy frowned, confused as to how Carl got there so quickly.

"I stopped at the deli down the street for a quick bite. I was halfway through when you called. I got Will on the phone but he hung up before I could ask him to come back up here. What's going on?"

Randy filled him in on the back-story to the fire and the ghost. After explaining how Nathaniel died, Carl's face fell. He raced for the back door in the alley that led down to the corridor. Bursting through, he screamed for Bronin. When no one answered, he rushed for the practice room door.

Randy raced behind him and they both rushed into the rehearsal space. Empty, save for Bronin's bass and amp which were both still powered up. The quiet hum from the amplifier added a spooky undertone to the whole scene that made Randy's skin vibrate with fear. Carl bolted from the room and ran down to the other end of the hallway, yelling out Bronin's name.

Randy stood staring at the lonely bass guitar, rubbing a hand over his sweat-dampened face. As soon as he realized how badly he was perspiring, Will's story sprang to the front of his mind. He quickly sidestepped out of the rehearsal space before the door had a chance to slam shut.

Smoke quietly began to curl around Randy's feet. The hallway felt like an oven and sweat dripped into his eyes. As he dabbed at his face with his shirtsleeve Randy could hear a soft whimpering coming from down the hall, near the door to the alleyway. He fanned the smoke away as it climbed up towards his face and he squinted at the end of the hall. He could barely make out a lone shape huddled in the corner.

"Hello? Nathaniel, is that you?"

As he neared the end of the hallway, Randy could now hear the distinct sobbing and hitching gasps of a crying child. He waved his arms wildly to try and clear the black smoke that had now engulfed him. Somewhere behind him, he could hear Carl calling his name. But he couldn't give up his search for Nathaniel.

Suddenly two pale arms reached up to him from the dark corner. The boy's quiet whisper floated up to Randy's ears. The lonely pleading in Nathaniel's voice was deafening.

"Help me. I don't want to be here all by myself. Please stay with me."

Nathaniel grabbed Randy's hands and pulled. Despite the cold fear lodged in his throat, Randy could only drop down to the floor as the boy guided him. As he pushed himself up against the brick wall, he could feel the boy sidle up against him, still clutching Randy's hands in his own small grasp. The boy's blonde hair was dirty with soot from the fire and black smudges colored Nathaniel's cheeks.

"Randy! Randy!"

Carl was standing near the practice room door when he saw Randy hunker down in the smoke-filled corner. He could just make out the shape of a small child sitting next to him, clinging to Randy as if he could save him from the fire. He had to get Randy away from Nathaniel before it was too late.

He ran down the hall, waving his arms and screaming Randy's name. He looked at Carl and held up a hand to warn him off. He wrapped his arm protectively around the boy. As Carl got closer to them, Randy could feel Nathaniel tense beside him. Randy shouted to Carl.

"Carl! Stop where you are. Don't come any closer."

Confused, Carl stopped in the middle of the hallway just as the ceiling caved in front of him. He jumped back a few steps and waved away the dust from the debris. Coughing, he tried to call to Randy.

"Randy, what...?"

"Carl, please. Just leave. It's okay."

"But..."

"Carl! Get out! Now!"

Carl gagged as more black smoke rolled around him. The more he tried to wave it away the thicker it appeared. Angry and scared, he did the only thing he could. He backed away and headed for the exit at the opposite end of the corridor. Randy watched him disappear into the blackness then relaxed, knowing Carl would be safe.

Randy cried as he rocked the boy back and forth in his arms. In order to end the cycle of hauntings, Randy realized he couldn't leave him alone here anymore. He had to give Nathaniel what he most desperately needed. At least no one else would get hurt now.

Suddenly all the smoke whooshed away as if a strong wind blew through the corridor. Randy looked down at the boy and tried to hide his fear. Nathaniel lipless mouth stretched open as he grinned. His blackened skin was pulled taught over his tiny skull. It had split along his cheek when he smiled. Viscous crimson blood oozed along his jaw slowly dripping off his chin and onto Randy's jeans.

Randy grimaced and smoothed down the few remaining tufts of hair sticking up on the boy's head. Even though Nathaniel's eyes burned out years ago, Randy could still see the soulful expression hidden in the empty sockets - one of longing and sadness.

"Don't worry. I'll stay with you. You'll never be alone again."

Nathaniel giggled with the innocence of a child not charred by death's fiery hand and wrapped his skeletal arms tightly around Randy's waist. The light of the living world faded and slowly the corridor disappeared. As tears slipped down Randy's cheeks, he tried to console the boy with a gentle squeeze. Nathaniel breathed a sigh of release and contentment. And as darkness enveloped them, Randy breathed with him.

Her Descent

By Peggy Christie

She descends.
She walks down the wooden steps
Cracked and worn from age
Leading away from her hell.
She steps gently on the sloped hill
The grass lush and green from the summer rains
Slippery in the morning dew.
She makes her way across the sand
Still cold from the moonless night
Powdery softness tickles her bare feet.
She steps into the foaming surf
Its icy touch is nothing
Compared to the coldness of her heart.
She swims out to the clanging buoy
Tossed gently upon graceful swells
The bell singing for the circling gulls.
She grasps the slippery metal
Staring into the depths of the surrounding sea
Too tempting in its promise of darkened peace.
She takes Death's hand in her own
Briny arms enfold her
The pursuit for rest is finished.
She descends.

A Crowning Repast

By W. S. Cwik

From the crest of the hill Debbie and Les gawked down at the green on white sign:

Welcome to Climax, Michigan

"You've finally reached Climax," Les said. With the Saturn's door open, he pushed, starting the car rolling downhill, and jumped behind the steering wheel.

Debbie watched the welcome sign approach. "Very funny. If you'd stopped for gas back on the highway, we wouldn't be coasting into town."

"Don't blame me. This side trip was your bright idea. You're the one who doesn't want to buy a house close to my brother, afraid we'd be babysitting all the time."

Debbie gritted her teeth and bit back the urge to yell. "So this is my fault? And why were we at the Kellogg museum in Battle Creek? To check the place out for your no-neck nephews, right?"

Les grabbed the steering wheel with both hands, gritted his teeth, and sighed. "You're right. Listen, honey, I don't want to argue. This is our first trip in the three years since our wedding, so let's make the most of it."

The car rolled to a stop. "All right Les, put those muscles to it; I'll steer. We'll find a gas station before it gets dark and maybe a cozy B&B. Who knows, you may get into my good graces yet."

Les leaned his back on the trunk, dug his heels on the tarmac, and pushed. Branches of huge elms arched into a cathedral canopy over the street lined with white clapboard houses like small mausoleums. As the silver Saturn rolled along, Les sensed they were being watched - a curtain swayed in a window, a door closed.

After four blocks Debbie steered the car into a parking space along a small park at the center of town. A bandstand, surrounded by asters, rosebushes, and zinnias, stood in the middle of the grassy area. But no children played, no dogs barked, no cars, no people - only an eerie stillness blanketed the area.

Wiping the perspiration on the sleeve of his forearm, Les shouted, "Not one gas station. I don't believe it."

"This place is charming."

"Charming... charming? Stranded in a town where people won't lift a finger to help a stranger, and my wife thinks it's charming."

"Calm down, you're going to blow a gasket."

Debbie climbed the stairs of the gazebo-like stage. "I love it here. An ideal place to raise a family, don't you think?"

Les banged his fist on the car hood. "I'm sweaty and hungry. Let's get moving."

Debbie twirled on the stage to an inner music. "I love the serenity, the... oh, look, there's a cafe on the other side of the square. We can get a bite to eat, call for help and find a place to stay."

They walked arm in arm across the park. In mock derision, Les said, "What a brilliant idea, she says. Let's go to Climax, she says. It'll be a wonderful experience, she says. I could've been at the motel in Kalamazoo soaking in the hot tub with a long neck. But no, I'm walking around a friggin' deserted town."

A red neon sign, 'Zenith Cafe', hung in the window. A bell over the cafe door tinkled as they entered. Behind them, five shadows, lengthened by the setting sun, plodded down the street.

The walls of the diner were covered with posters of old monster movies - *Dracula, Frankenstein, The Wolfman*. Old church pews lined some of the tables instead of chairs. An old hand-crank cash register sat on the checkout counter.

"Hi, welcome to the Zenith," a raspy voice greeted the couple. "I'm June." A middle aged woman, her auburn hair tied in a tight bun at the back of her head and covered with a snood, walked through the doorway that led to the kitchen. A cigarette dangled from the corner of her mouth, and wisps of smoke swirled around her face. She wiped her hands on a greasy apron tied around her waist.

"Hi," grunted Les.

"Hello, I'm Debbie. That's my husband, Les."

June removed two laminated menus from the counter, wiped them on her apron and led the couple to a table. "Where you headed?"

We're on our way to Kalamazoo and had to stop when we saw the sign to Climax."

"Give me a hamburger, grilled onions and a cold Bud."

"Sorry, Les. No liquor license. Our regulars aren't much for drinking."

"Terrific. Where's the phone? We have to get AAA to bring gas for the car."

"Nobody'll come out here this time of day."

"I don't believe this. We've got to get out of here."

"Les, cool it. Where's the closest B&B, June?"

"We don't get many tourists passing through. The Pine Lodge Inn's eight miles up County Road C."

"For Chrissake. No gas, no beer, no room. What're we going to do now?"

"We'll sleep in the car tonight. I'm not walking eight miles. Just chill out."

Debbie walked around the diner looking at the 40's and 50's memorabilia. "June, where's the realtor's office?"

June stuck her head through the opening from the kitchen. "Down on Second and Vine streets. But they won't be open until tomorrow morning."

"But it's only seven o'clock," Les said.

"Starts getting dark early this time of year and people don't like wandering around in the dark."

On the far wall monster dolls lined a shelf. Plastic heads bobbed in agreement as Debbie touched them. On the counter a cast metal bird with a pointed beak pivoted down to spear a toothpick.

Movement in the front window caught her eye. The 'Zenith' sign cast a crimson hue on two cadaverous faces, gaunt, unblinking eyes, arms hanging limply. Like ducks in a shooting gallery, they sauntered back and forth.

Debbie screamed as Les yelled. "What's that?"

"Our first seating," June's voice bellowed from the kitchen.

Les crept to the window. From every direction decaying bodies homed in on the restaurant. "This is out of the *Night of the Living Dead*."

Debbie gawked at the assembly. "They... they look like..."

"Zombies?" June interjected. "They are."

"You've got to be kidding?" Les said.

"No, they come here every night."

The bell on the door jingled. As the creatures filed in, Debbie and Les clung to each other. Cowering at the back wall of the cafe, they watched the catatonic patrons sit at the tables. A festering arm brushed Debbie's shoulder, precipitating a shriek from her.

"Don't worry. They won't hurt you," croaked June as she returned from the kitchen with a large bowl of salad.

"What're you talking about? They're going to rip us apart."

"No, they won't. They're vegans."

"What!" they cried in unison.

"They're vegetarians."

"Vegetarian zombies? You're crazy! " Les shouted.

Their eyeballs popping, Les and Debbie watched the grunting zombies gnash heaps of lettuce, tomatoes and celery. An occasional appendage, arm or leg, fell to the floor, only to be retrieved by a corpse from the next table and returned to its owner.

50

Avoiding contact with the diners, Debbie and Les weaved their way between the tables.

"Can I get you something to eat? I'm afraid I only have salads."

"No, thanks," Debbie said. "I don't have much of an appetite."

One by one the zombies left with an acknowledging nod to the quivering pair.

June removed her apron, folded it and placed it under the counter.

"That was one surreal scene," Les said. He pressed close to the window, his nose leaving a smudge on the glass. In the distance from both directions, more of the undead waddled toward the 'Zenith'. "Your second seating is on the way," he said.

June walked to the rear exit. "Yes, I know. By the way, they're the meat eaters."

Half way out the door, she yelled, "Like I said we don't get many tourists through here."

Les and Debbie turned in unison as the bell on the entrance jangled the call to dinner.

ERIE TALES

TALES OF TERROR

PRESENTED BY CLAMP

Slaughter of the Doves

By Mary Makrias

I walked out into the quiet night. It's funny how simple things will sometimes take you back to your childhood. Silly things that through some neurological magic bring back memories, even memories you would rather forget. The trigger could be something as familiar as a fragrance, a song on the radio, or a dog that happens to have characteristics of a loving pet. For me, tonight, it was the sound of metal on metal; brakes from a car that should have found its rest in a junkyard long ago. It reminded me of a very specific night in my youth and a particular puke green sedan. A memory that I thought I had purged.

Well, we can't choose what we remember. Even though this happened twenty years ago, it was as clear and tangible as if I were living it now. I was a teenager again and life was simple, safe. I still didn't understand. Truth be told, it was the night I lost my innocence. That night what I lost would haunt me for the rest of my life. It was the belief that for the most part people were generally good at heart. It was the belief that I was safe, that nothing really bad would ever to happen to me. I was wrong.

In my mind, I relived a day that I really wished never happened, a day that I have spent many years trying to erase. No matter what I do, I can't seem to get rid of it. It won't leave me alone. My newest shrink told me to try journaling. She said that if I write it down I can examine it from different angles until I see that just like the boogey man, there is nothing that happened back then that can hurt me now. I'm not sure I believe her, but at this point, I'm ready to try just about anything.

It was dark, or at least it should have been. It was one of those early fall nights in Michigan. The sky was so clear that the stars were like a million diamonds sparkling against black velvet. I know it probably had something to do with suburbia and the lack of city lights competing with the universe or something all scientific that I would never understand even if I wanted to. The truth is we were too young to care. Cindy and I didn't care about the "whys" of anything. We were young, barely seventeen and still in high school.

We were juniors and it was prom night. Most everyone else was at the dance, but we decided it would be more fun to hang out. We were at a school playground. I don't even remember the name of the school; probably because it was one I never attended. I do remember the general area in great detail. The playground was on a corner lot at the intersection of Hatchery Road and Crescent Lake Road. Like most playgrounds it was connected to an elementary school. Unlike most playgrounds, however, it was a stones throw away from a cemetery.

Cindy and I were charter members of a group of unsatisfied teenagers. Unfortunately, we also fell into the category of those who walk the edge, stay in the shadows, and try things they shouldn't to expand their consciousness. We were reading Carlos Castaneda. His mind altering experiences fascinated us, so we experimented. That night we were flying high on LSD. The thing about a hallucinogenic is that you're never really sure what is real and what is your imagination. I've often wondered if would have made a difference if we had been clear-headed.

There we were, gliding back and forth on the swings, leaning back as far as we could go and watching those beautiful glittering, shimmering stars. We felt pity for those who would never experience the world the way we could see it that night.

"Amy, isn't it weird?"

"What's that Cindy?"

"The way there are no cars around."

I sat up and looked around. Then we started laughing. The fact that there were no cars traveling the adjacent roads seemed absolutely hilarious. Once we started laughing, we couldn't stop.

"No, seriously," she said while wiping the tears from her eyes, "it looks like the same three cars keep going around and around. They are like mice in a maze."

So, we watched. As strange as it sounds, she was right. A white van, red truck and puke green car, kept showing up at the light. We didn't know if we were stuck in a time loop or if someone was just having fun at our expense. After seeing them hit that flashing red light for the third time, it didn't seem funny anymore. Funny how fear will sober a person up.

"Cindy," I said, "it is the same three cars." About that time, they pulled into the circular drive of the school like three blind mice. "Maybe we should move on." I knew it was the same three vehicles because the puke green car had a very distinct, metal on metal sound whenever the brakes were applied. It sounded like: do-do-do-do, if you run the "dos" together and keep the same tone. I didn't trust my eyes; the darkness can play tricks on your vision. My ears were something else. I couldn't mistake that sound. It grated on my nerves and made the hairs on the back of my neck stand up.

As high as we were, we understood we were in danger, so we kept low and to the shadows. However, our curiosity pulled us toward the circular drive and the source of our fear. By some stroke of luck, no one saw us approach. Now here is where things get hazy, everything happened so fast. The driver of the puke green car got out and walked over to the van. The driver of the van met him at the back door. The guy in the red truck got out and pulled a large bundle out of the back of his truck. It was long and bulky and he had a difficult time carrying it. Whatever it was, we had the impression that it was significant. We knew there was something wrapped in the carpet because we could see bulges and bumps that didn't seem to belong. We dismissed it as a hallucination; after all it couldn't be anything bad. This was Waterford. Nothing really bad could happen here.

Cindy's sharp intake of breath broke the silence of the night. We were perhaps one hundred feet from the circular drive and we were seen. There was that moment of stillness, that moment when time stops. Across the parking lot, our eyes locked with theirs. Might have been the drugs, but it sure seemed real. Then, all at once, mayhem broke out. Time went faster to regain what was lost.

"Hey!" One of the guys yelled.

Without really knowing why, we bolted like frightened kittens. From over my shoulder I heard a muffled, frantic voice cry out, "Get 'em!" After that, it was just the sound of my heart. We ran as fast as we could, not really caring where we ended up. When we finally stopped, we saw that we were at the outskirts of the cemetery. We had enough sense to stay away from roads, to stay away from easily accessible areas. We ran until we collapsed. Then we lay on the ground and looked up at the sky. The stars no longer looked like diamonds, they now looked like eyes and all eyes were turned on us. Once we caught our breath, we started laughing again. That's what you do when you're scared silly. Maybe this type of situation is what inspired that phrase in the first place. I guess it doesn't really matter.

Once the laughter died, we forgot all about what happened and went on with our evening. Probably a good thing, since we really didn't know what we saw. It was just a series of shadows.

Brushing the dirt off, we decided to walk again. Of course we had no destination in mind, it didn't matter. We walked up Crescent Lake Road until it hit the M-59 highway. Then, in what was probably the only smart thing we did that night, decided not to cross any major thoroughfares. Instead we turned right and headed toward Airport Road. It was the same stretch we had traveled almost every Friday night since we could drive, yet I don't think we had ever walked it before. I know now that we would never walk it again.

Nothing much out of the ordinary occurred until we came up to the donut shop. We looked at the cop cars in the lot and smiled. We didn't smile because they were police. We didn't smile because we felt safe. We smiled because we thought we were cool, we were convinced that flying under the radar was a good thing.

We walked along the shoulder of the highway, so close to the edge that the breeze from passing cars whipped our hair. We noticed the cars only after they passed us. It didn't register when a red truck passed us by. It didn't faze us when it slowed down and the van behind it almost rear-ended it. What threw us was the sound, do-do-do-do. Too fast for us to react, the white van was right behind the puke green sedan. The side doors slid open and hand reached out and grabbed Cindy. I screamed and held on to her other arm. Every nerve in my body was at attention. Instinctively I knew that I couldn't let go. Thankfully they weren't going too fast or she would have been ripped apart. Instead, by some providential grace, two police officers came out of the donut shop, saw what was happening and started running toward us.

The guys in the van let go of Cindy and we sat on the side of the highway just holding on to each other. The police officer asked us about what happened and we lied. It didn't matter that we really were up to no harm. At that time in our lives, we thought the police were just out to get us. They provided no true service to society; they just harassed kids like us.

"Well, you see," Cindy was explaining, "it was just some kids from school trying to scare us." It sounded reasonable to me, so, for once, I kept my mouth shut.

"You girls need to be careful. You shouldn't be out so late or walking so close to the road. Now go find your friends and go home before we take you in for breaking curfew." I guess they were cutting us a break. Looking back I guess it really would have been better if they had arrested us.

I remember walking up to the Elias Brothers Big Boy restaurant trying to fool them. It must have worked because they got in their car and drove off before we even made it through the door. We shifted direction and went back to walking around. About this time we were beginning to sober up. We came to realize that it was the same three vehicles we had seen from the playground. We started to attempt to reason it out. Why would they be chasing us and who were they anyway?

After turning right onto Airport Road, we walked about a half mile when I noticed my shoelace was untied. I knelt down to tie it and caught the airport lights just right. It looked like a magical city, a land of faeries and sprites, of magic and dreams. I stared into the lights for a little while. Cindy followed my line of site and joined me on the ground. It didn't make much sense or even apply to this tale except that I thought it was cool. In a land like that, nothing bad could happen. In a land like that, anything was possible and everything was good. Lost in our separate daydreams, we were brought back to reality by the same sound: do-do-do-do.

We took off running again and managed to cut through a yard or two that led us right to Tubbs Road. There was nothing special about Tubbs Road, nothing particularly sinister or creepy. It was just a dirt road that didn't have street lights and came out by a cemetery. Most of the houses were set back a ways from the road and there were a lot of trees, but it could have been any other street in any number of towns. There was nothing outside of the urban legends that kids like to tell each other about dark creepy roads to make us nervous. There was nothing to give us shivers, at least not before this night.

Cindy had bleached blond hair that was almost white. On most people it would have looked cheap, on her it was beautiful. She was wearing a silver, metallic jacket and yellow slacks. I had on dark jeans, a black jacket and my dark hair rounded out the contrast between us. Cindy was all light and I was all dark. We stayed close to the houses and what little light we could find. I would hide in the shadows and she would find shelter against light cars or houses. We weren't able to get away from the terrible trio. They kept patrolling up and down the street, the do-do-do-do announcing when they were close and slowing down.

It was one-o'clock in the morning and we were sane enough to realize that, on this street, people wouldn't take too kindly to two teenagers banging on their door. Besides, what if the legends we had grown up with about this street were true? What if there were crazies out there with shotguns waiting to molest or slice and dice two young girls? Our nerves were strung so tightly we were ready to snap. Simple fear was the only thing keeping us moving. Perhaps it was the only thing keeping us alive.

It went that way for a couple of hours. We felt like we were in a horror story and we were making all of the stupid mistakes the actors always make in the really cheesy movies. It was real to me and real to Cindy and that was enough.

I guess we had been walking along Tubbs Road for what seemed like an hour. How long it actually was, I can't say. When you are that afraid, time loses definition and meaning. It is no longer about the ticking clocks and passing hours. You begin to measure time in events. We finally passed the library and hit the pavement. That wonderful part of the road that looked like it was part of modern civilization. Blacktop roads, street lights, and homes with porch lights and "Kid Safe" stickers in the windows identifying them as places of refuge, havens for the lost or frightened child. Best of all, we were almost to Cindy's house and safety.

In the chill air, we put our arms around each other and walked that last mile until we hit Crescent Lake Road again. We had walked the entire block. We were convinced that as we approached the familiar sites we would be safe. With Tubbs Road behind us, surely the danger was gone as well. We even began to explore the possibility that we had imagined it all. We had just made the first street light when we heard it again, do-do-do-do. We looked at each other and ran for the first house we saw. That puke green sedan stopped. The driver didn't get out of the vehicle. He just sat there and watched us. From our perspective he was totally unconcerned with anything, simply intent on watching us. This time the door we were pounding on opened. We started rambling on and on about what we had been through. We thought we were saved. The man who opened the door looked tired but surely he wouldn't hurt us.

He very calmly reached behind the door and pulled out a 12-guage shotgun. He pointed it in our direction and fired. A scatter of projectiles flew between our heads and fell short of the puke green sedan. I didn't realize how loud a gun could be. I didn't realize the sulfur smell would travel with a bullet. I didn't realize that grief could turn a mind unstable. Now I knew it. I recognized the name on the door. My mind connected the name with the black grief wreath and the article I had read a few days past about the little girl who had been kidnapped and murdered. That was the first time death hit home for me. That was when I knew that I was mortal.

I looked at Mr. Parson's eyes and there wasn't anyone home. It was just vacant space. He looked at Cindy and me and started talking as if we were his deceased daughter and her friend. We were creeped out and inched our way backward down the driveway. Make no sudden moves, stay calm. That is what they tell you do isn't it? We weren't sure what was worse, the psycho in the puke green sedan or the man whose sanity was slipping with grief. The decision was made for us. Psycho dude in the sedan took off with the shot.

We ran that last mile. We went across Crescent Lake Road and through the field adjacent to the church. It was a shortcut we often used to get to Cindy's house. In times of intense fear, we tend to stick to the familiar. The familiar seems safe. The familiar can be deceiving. Mid-way through the field, we heard an engine. Since it wasn't attached to that do-do-do-do sound, we thought we were saved. We breathed a sigh of relief then ran toward the sound. We were waving our arms and shouting so much that we must have appeared insane; at least we would have if anyone had been around to see us. Suddenly, right in front of us was a red truck.

We'd had all we could take. We simply collapsed, blacked out. When we came to, the truck was gone, the field was silent and we were alive. We made our way out of the field and into Cindy's subdivision. After a few short turns we were walking up her driveway. About a block away we saw the sedan and heard the metal on metal grinding brakes sound. We were home. We were safe. We went inside and went to sleep.

The next morning it all seemed like a bad dream. Surely our minds must have been creating the whole thing. Nothing like that could happen in Waterford. It was easier to believe that our minds went wacko than to think the last twelve hours had really played out the way we remembered them. I went home and spent the rest of the weekend in my room trying to make sense out of that night. What had we seen? Did it really happen?

Sunday morning I picked up the newspaper and saw the headlines. Some freak accident caused a house to go up in flames. The family was asleep when it happened. There were no survivors. I looked at the photograph and screamed. It was Cindy's house. Still in my pajamas, I ran to the lake. I didn't stop screaming for a long time. Eventually I calmed down and went home. Sitting on my front porch, I looked at the picture again. It was definitely Cindy's house. That meant she was dead. My best friend, Cindy, and her whole family were dead. Out of the corner of my eye I saw something in the photograph that scared the hell out of me. The photographer had caught just the front end of a puke green sedan that looked awful familiar. Psycho dude had followed us to her home. He knew where she lived. He'd killed her. But why?

I tried to make sense of it, to fill in the blanks, but I couldn't. I thought about calling the police, but the whole thing seemed too unbelievable even to me and I was there. I tried to think about what we might have seen or what they thought we had seen. But I kept coming up with nothing. About a month later I was walking home from a friend's house. Life would never be the same for me. It was no longer simple. My mind was trying to make a connection. It was really odd, but there was something tickling my memories, something important that I wouldn't look at. As I approached the turn off to my house, I noticed the dead doves. They were all over the place. I looked up trying to make sense out of the dead birds. What could have killed them? Another headline flashed across my mind the way memories sometimes will. It read: "Slaughtered Doves and Foul Play Go Hand in Hand in Quiet Waterford." I heard the metal on metal sound that haunted my dreams, looked up and saw the puke green sedan.

   He had found me too.

The Neighborhood Diner

By W. S. Cwik

Five billion years ago a cloud of dust and gas — remnants of the Big Bang — began to condense. The collapsing cloud spun ever more quickly around its center, forming a sun. Centrifugal force and gravity attracted more dust grains and gases coalescing into masses that orbited the sun. Asteroids collided with these masses like balls on a pinball machine and developed into a solar system.

One billion years later amino acids from cosmic dust particles and comets of frozen water rained down on the planets. Only the third and fourth planets of this sun provided an environment suitable for the growth of amino acids and organic compounds. During the next one and a half billion years, plant and animal cells proliferated in the oxygen-rich atmosphere of the third planet, but harsher conditions of the fourth only sustained the growth of pathogens in the soil and rock. A cataclysmic collision with an asteroid dislodged a huge portion of the fourth planet, hurtling fragments into orbit around the sun. The heat generated from the impact seared the surface of the dislodged piece, sealing the pathogens within. But the planet was moved further from the sun resulting in a loss of its atmosphere. The pathogens leached into the vacuum of space, cleansing the planet.

Millions of years later the dislodged asteroid collided with another asteroid, showering the third planet with meteoroids. One large segment struck in the northern hemisphere and was buried deep below the surface near a large body of water, creating five great lakes. Small grain size particles peppered the surface, releasing the pathogens into the food supply of the dinosaurs which eventually led to the extinction of these creatures.

***

"Two over easy, hash browns fried with onions and green peppers, wheat toast with peanut butter," Dina yelled through the open partition separating the dining counter from the kitchen.

A head, shod in a white paper hat, poked through the opening. Jake yelled in a hoarse voice, "I ran outta peppers, Marv."

"One of these days, I'm gonna buy this joint and turn it into a restaurant," Marv said.

The bell over the door jangled and a short, gray-haired man entered the diner whistling. He sat next to Marv at the counter, folded the Tribune in half-lengthwise, then in half again, and propped it up on the counter.

Without raising his face from the racing gazette, Marv said in a slow drawl, "Morning, Howie."

"Hi ya, Marv; here's two bucks; gimme three and nine in the double today; that's my age, you know."

"You tell me that every morning but six and seven would be closer."

Howie propped his elbows on the counter and supported his head in his hands with his middle finger extended. "Gimme a cup of mud, darlin', with a couple of scrambled and tell that cantankerous old coot to hold the taters. It says here in the Trib the CTA will be drilling for the subway all summer."

Dina placed the order on the clip of the metal carousel.

"We ain't gonna have any dishes left in this place what with walls rattling all the time," Dina said. "Jake, did you hear the news? More java, Marv?"

Jake appeared in the doorway to the kitchen in a white t-shirt pulled tight around a stomach that hung over the strings of a greased-stained apron. He sat at the counter next to Howie. ""Get me a cup a joe," he called to Dina. "Lemme see that paper. What with the buses shaking this place and now

64

all this drilling, it's amazing this joint hasn't collapsed on my head." He removed the pack of Luckies from his rolled up sleeve, tamped one out, and lit it.

Marv coughed, "If the smell of bacon grease don't getcha, those coffin nails sure will."

Jake rubbed his ear with an extended middle finger.

"You guys trying to tell me I'm number one," Marv said.

A muffled explosion shook the dishes and cups like a vibrator run amok. The three men held the edge of the counter and watched little concentric ripples form on the surface of the coffee.

"That's the worst one yet; ain't felt nothin' like it. We're in for a long summer," Howie said.

Dina yelled. "Look at the front wall!"

They watched, eyes wide-open and mouths agape, a crack propagate from the floor to the ceiling.

"For chrissake, I'm gonna call Big Willy," Jake said and walked back to the kitchen.

"That good-for-nothing alderman ain't gonna help," Marv said, burying his face back into the racing form.

Dina topped off the coffee cups on the counter, while Jake went to the phone. She went into the kitchen. "Oh, my God!" she called out. "This place is gonna break like a egg shell."

The three men raced to the kitchen doorway and saw a crack in the back wall like the one in front.

"Been comin' to this joint for twenty-five years; time to look for a new eatin' establishment; don't want a ceiling crashin' atop me while I eat," Howie prattled.

Marv sauntered back to the counter and his racing form, as Jake hurried to the phone. "Godammit, Willy, my place is falling down from all that blasting for the subway," Jake shouted into the receiver. "...I know the city'll fix the place up...I'm losing customers everyday...if that drilling doesn't stop I won't have a restaurant to fix up...okay, okay." He slammed the receiver onto the cradle.

***

The cracks in the walls of Jake's Café generated slowly downwards finding weak boundary lines in the rock formations. With every foot of movement the speed of propagation increased until it reached a meteoroid five miles below the surface. The surrounding strata shifted and creaked. The surface of the alien rock, unmoved for billions of years, split open. A virus, with origins on the fourth planet from the sun, leached into the opening formed by the crack and began a tortuous path upward...upward toward the small diner on a corner on the northwest side of Chicago.

***

Dina locked the front door and turned the closed sign around. She cleared the dirty dishes from the last booth and brought them to the kitchen sink.

"Everybody gone?" Jake asked, as he rinsed off the dishes.

"Yeah," Dina said grabbing a broom.

"Did ya lock the door?"

"Of course." She swept the floor.

"The crack in the front wall is pretty bad. Whatdid Big Willy say?"

"That good-for-nothing SOB told me to wait until all the drilling's over. He's gonna get the city to fix the place. Say, Dina, does it smell like something's coming out from the crack?"

Dina propped the broom against the counter and walked to the front wall. She knelt down and sniffed around near the floor where the crack was widest. "I don't smell a thing," she said. "Maybe your cookin's finally gettin' to you."

"None of your smartass remarks. Come on, let's go. Five in the morning rolls around too fast." At the back door he looked at the cracked wall in the kitchen, sniffed the air, shrugged and turned out the lights.

***

The virus from the meteoroid spread faster up the crevice, mixing with vapors to form an acrid mist that emanated into the diner. The virus diffused through every small, surface opening. A quiescent microorganism that survived four billion years permeated the counter, booths, tables, the refrigerator and into the food.

***

At 5:00 AM Jake thrust open the back door to the kitchen, his usual morning practice. He flipped the light switch on the wall. The fluorescent lights blinked on with a hum filling the kitchen in a garish glow. He hung his black leather jacket and black Stetson in a grey metal locker. On his way to the dining area, he dragged his finger over the stainless steel sink. A grayish-phosphorescent residue coated the tip of his finger; he sniffed at it and touched his finger to his tongue. A hint of sulfur spread through his mouth. At the front door, he twisted the lock, turned the open sign outward and flipped the light switch. The neon script sign, Jake's, in the window glowed fiery red against the pre-dawn darkness.

Back in the kitchen, he opened the locker, took a clean white apron and tied it in front of his stomach. He removed a pack of Luckies from the shelf, popped one from the pack, lit it and rolled the pack in the sleeve of his 'T' shirt.

The front door opened. Without looking into the dining room, Jake said, "Morning, Dina. You want your usual?"

Taking off her coat, Dina came into the kitchen. "Hi ya, Jake. You can scramble me a couple with a side."

Jake grabbed four eggs and six slices of bacon from the fridge. "Gees, even these egg shells feel like they're coated with something. Dina, grab a rag and wipe off the counter and all the tables, while I fix breakfast. All that drilling must'a filled the place with dust or something."

She swiped her hand over the counter top. "Yekk. You're right."

Jake brought two plates to the counter, as Dina finished her clean-up. They sat alongside each other and ate their meal.

"This is gonna be a long summer," Jake said between bites.

"For sure." Dina said. "Do these eggs taste strange to you?"

"Probably all the crap in the air from the drilling. Willy better get those downtown politicians to shake their sorry asses to fix up this place."

"I gotta go to the 'john'. My stomach's botherin' me," Dina said.

Jake put the dirty dishes in the sink, took a raw hamburger patty from the fridge and scarfed it down. The bathroom door swung open. Dina walked to the kitchen—eyes blood red, drool seeping from the corner of her mouth.

Jake asked in a slow, hoarse voice, "How... ya... feel?"

"Okay...but...I could use...something...to eat," Dina replied in a similar voice.

They emptied the fridge of all the raw meats—steaks, ground beef, chops were everywhere. Like two feral animals at a feeding frenzy, they gnawed and chewed the meat. "Good," Jake grunted, gnashing and ripping at the chunks of flesh. With blood soaked hands Dina grabbed at the last shreds of beef in Jake's hand. He grabbed her wrist. She wrenched her hand free before he could bite it.

The bell over the front door jangled.

"Spring better get here fast; I'm freezin'; where is everybody?" Howie said, walking to the counter.

Dina skirted the booths and sidled slowly to the front door. Her eyes fixed on Howie.

Howie turned toward her, "What's the matter; you look like hell; did ya kill the fatted calf in the kitchen."

Jake crept toward him.

Howie turned as Jake pounced on him, knocking him to the floor in the middle of the diner.

"What the hell you doing..it's me.. you gone crazy?" Howie screamed. Dina leapt into the foray. She bit Howie's face as Jake tore at his arms. Howie shrieked as they ravaged his body.

Outside the diner, Marv was about to open the door but stopped. His mouth gaped, his stomach roiled at the perverse feeding scene inside. Other passers-by peered in. As they watched with noses pressed tight against the front window like pigs waiting for a meal, a mist seeped from the wall of the diner. The haze condensed. A sulfurous residue coated their shoes… their legs and arms… their faces…

EERIE TALES

ZOMBIE CHRONICLES

Fear Cage

By Justin Holley

She had no idea any more how long she had been hiding in the attic. Two days, a week? She had slept so much that she just wasn't sure. The stash of chips and Diet Dr. Pepper, a secret fetish of hers—one that she had been glad for in the last days—was gone now. Soon she would need to venture back downstairs. For a while after the recent events, she had heard swishing from downstairs and so had not dared unlock the attic trap door.

In reality, silence had reigned for almost seventy-two hours.

She had hoped that the strange message that had sent her into hiding would have also told her when it was okay to come out.

It didn't. Either that or it still wasn't safe.

She wondered what had happened to the policemen, she hadn't heard them call to her.

The FM radio that she kept along with her snacks for entertainment, had told her little, but confirmed that the strange happenings had spread beyond the confines of Bemidji, Minnesota—something about it spreading rapidly. What it was, she had no idea. The already weak batteries had gone out just as the announcer was getting to the heart of it.

She knew the announcer, small town and all. She also knew that he was prone to exaggeration, so better to refrain from drawing conclusions without all the facts.

The sounds of traffic outside had been heavy for a short while, odd for northern Minnesota. But now it had stopped all together. She had thought she heard the sounds of a crash, but the insulated walls of her attic didn't allow her to hear more. There wasn't even a window for her to look out of.

She sat, hunched next to the trap door, listening, trying to determine if it was safe to come out of hiding. Again, she heard nothing. For the hundredth time, she then replayed the events of the last week in her mind, hoping that she would remember something that she had forgotten, something that would help her decide what to do.

***

Jacob smacked his cereal as he chewed with his mouth open, milk spilling onto the instruction sheet that he was diligently poring over.

The device that the instructions depicted lay on the table next to the skim milk jug, its red lens cover peering like a giant eye, an eye that never blinked.

Judy, Jacob's irritated wife, sat across the table staring, first at the device that had depleted the couple's savings and then, with an evil eye, at Jacob.

Jacob, oblivious to his wife's raised eyebrow, continued to chomp and smack, his eyes shuffling back and forth as he read the document.

Judy sighed heavily. When this failed to rouse her husband's attention she said brusquely, "You look like you're in a damn trance Jacob. How much did you spend on that stupid thing?" Of course she already knew, and it was about to become a major point of contention.

Jacob looked up from his document. He saw the look of disgust in his wife's eyes, but dismissed it. "Oh, not much really. I got a great deal." He went back to his reading.

She had had enough and Judy slammed her hand on the table causing the sugar bowl to jump and spill some of its contents. "You call spending more than what both of our cars are worth, on a gadget, a good deal?"

Jacob stared at her for a moment. Then, "Well, honey, I had to have it. It's the only way to scientifically prove, once and for all, that we have ghosts in the basement!"

She only stared at Jacob for a long while.

Then Jacob stammered, "I… I needed this. You can buy something too, I promise."

Judy nodded, a slow deliberate gesture. She said slowly, "There… is… no money… left… to… spend… darling."

The word *darling* had come out a bit too sharp for Jacob. "Do you want to get rid of the ghosts or not?"

Judy shook her head in frustration. "I have never seen a ghost in this damn house Jacob, nor shall I ever! You are the only one convinced that we have a ghost in the damn basement, and you have never even seen it!"

"Yes, but I can feel it Judy. I know it's there!"

"What about all the other stupid gadgets that you have purchased… what about them? What are they, EMF detector, digital voice recorder, digital thermometer? What exactly have they told you Jacob? Have they told you that we have a ghost in the basement?"

Jacob lowered his eyes and stared at something in his cereal bowl. "Not yet, but the EMF detector, it measures electromagnetic energy that ghosts need to manifest…"

"I know what an EMF detector is, Jacob. You talk about the damn thing every damn day!"

"Okay, okay, but we have a fear cage situation in the basement, just in front of the washer and dryer. We have EMF spikes higher than my device can even measure, prime situation for an entity to manifest. Prime!"

Judy let out her breath. "Jacob, the electrician said we have bad wiring, that's all. No ghosts, no paranormal activity, just bad wiring. With the cash you spent on this new toy of yours, we could have fixed the damn wiring!"

Jacob waved his arms. "That's just it Judy. I don't want it fixed. Ghosts aren't causing the high EMF spikes, but the high amount of energy is like a beacon. It'll help the dead communicate with us."

Judy whistled. "Oh man, you have dropped right off the radar pal. You have gone plain nuts. Since we don't have any ghosts, you want to call some in like a freakish game of some kind."

Jacob nodded. "We have a major fear cage situation here and I plan to take advantage of it!"

This worried Judy. "That's the second time you have mentioned this fear cage. Sounds horrible! What the hell is that? Wait, do I even want to know?"

"Oh, that's an area with high EMF ratings. They call it a fear cage because it can cause feelings of paranoia and fear."

Judy grinned sarcastically. "You mean like the way you're feeling now?"

"Funny, Judy, funny. You wouldn't laugh at the guys from Spirit Warriors. And they look for fear cages all the time."

"You mean that stupid ghost hunting show you watch all the time? Just for the record Jacob, yes. Yes, I would laugh at them too. I'm an equal opportunity laugher."

Jacob rose from the table, indignant. "You won't be laughing when I show you the proof that my new thermal imager is going to capture. You just wait!"

Judy nodded again, a fire blazing in her eyes. "I'm not going to wait much longer Jacob. I want a man not a little boy. I swear…"

"You swear what, Judy? Are you going to leave me?" Jacob didn't wait for her to answer. Picking the thermal imager up off the table, he ran for the basement door and closed it behind him.

Judy heard the deadbolt click and then Jacob's footsteps, as he stomped down into his "fear cage". She whispered to herself, "Yeah Jacob, I just might."

***

Jacob reached the bottom of the wood plank stairs and stood on the cold concrete. He was in his bare feet yet and the cold radiated through the bottoms of them and into the rest of his body. He ignored the sensation and got right to work.

After turning on every light, he walked up to a card table in one of the corners and carefully folded the blue tarp that covered the equipment that was lying there. He ignored his various meters and went right for the four boxes. The four boxes were new also, more gadgetry that Judy knew nothing about.

The four boxes were six inches square with a black screen like a speaker on the front of each.

Jacob placed a folding chair under the large fluorescent lamp in the middle of the room, directly in front of the washer and dryer. He then, in turn, placed each of the four boxes so that they surrounded the chair from different angles. Jacob then plugged each unit in using long extension cords that burdened the already failing wiring. Gathering his equipment, Jacob then sat in the chair, beads of sweat beginning to grow on his forehead, the EMF emitters doing their job. He whispered, "Ha! Judy thought there was a fear cage before. Well, now it is intensified four-hundred times. Put that in your pipe and smoke it, Judy!" Jacob giggled to himself, his insanity burgeoning.

Jacob held his new thermal imaging camera in one hand and rubbed his temple with the other, the pain starting to increase. His head was beginning to pound, his hearing almost gone from the intensity of the energy. Sweat dripped from his nose and chin, saturating his t-shirt and sweat pants. Then he felt pain on the back of his neck and rubbed it with his hand. When he looked at the hand he gasped. It was crimson with blood. He whispered, "I knew high EMF could cause skin irritation. I must really be overdoing it." His breathing became labored. Jacob blinked his eyes rapidly and shook his head so he could concentrate on his readings. "If a ghost doesn't manifest soon, I might die trying."

Clearing the sweat from his stinging eyes, Jacob caught a flicker of motion from the screen of his thermal imager. The movement was from a small orb that floated about with a slow, pulsing cadence. "Hello, who are you now? Hmmm… it's red, a significant heat signature."

Then the orb grew both in size and intensity, until it finally took the shape of a humanoid form.

Jacob quivered with excitement, a grin emerging on his scruffy face, sweat dripping now to the floor, leaving prints like rain drops on the concrete. Making sure the imager was still recording the data, he whispered, "My God, what a sight. What are you?"

Nothing answered him, but still the humanoid image remained. The figure— invisible to the naked eye—stood directly in front of him as if wanting to say something. Then, Jacob remembered his digital voice recorder and turned it on. He said, "Please, speak into this device. It will help us to communicate."

Jacob's hand trembled.

The entity made no sound that Jacob could hear, but after thirty seconds he clicked the recorder off and backed it up to the beginning. He listened carefully.

Static hissed in the background, the byproduct of the electromagnetic energy that saturated the immediate area. Then he heard a faint, seemingly unintelligible, voice through the hiss. Jacob quickly backed the recorder and played it again. What he heard made goose bumps form among the sores that plagued his skin.

The faint voice said, "Why can I see you?"

Jacob took a deep breath and answered, "You can see me because the barrier between our worlds is thin, because of the high EMF readings. I can see you also." Jacob clicked the recorder on again and asked, "Who are you sir? Did you live here while you were alive?"

Nothing answered, all remaining silent save the hum of the high energy emitters and Judy walking across the kitchen floor above.

Jacob again backed up the recording device and played it. Again he heard a voice, "Many... we are..."

"Are what? Many what," Jacob asked

At that moment, several orbs entered the view screen of the thermal imager and grew into apparitions.

"There are many of you..."

Then the imager turned full red, the entities so close that their individual forms could not be distinguished.

"You're so close…I can feel… I, ouch, that hurts!" Jacob screamed as his flesh turned red like a beet, every vein in his neck and head throbbing, his blood pressure rising to dangerous levels.

The EMF levels kept rising.

First, Jacob's eyes began to bleed. He got up off the chair, stumbling, knowing something was wrong. "You're killing me…" He reached for the extension cords to the emitters, but too late. The pressure increased for one agonizing second, his eyes exploding in a fountain of white and crimson into his hands. Jacob dropped to his knees screaming and then flat onto his face, falling silent.

Jacob was dead.

***

Judy, cleaning up the breakfast dishes, thought she heard a faint scream and then a muted thump from the basement. The floor was well insulated from sound and so she couldn't be sure. She yelled, "Jacob, what the hell are you doing down there?"

She got no reply.

Just as she was about to shout again, the power went out. "Oh no Jacob, what have you done now?" she whispered instead. Moments later she thought that she could just make out a swishing noise coming from the basement. She approached the basement door cautiously, not knowing why she was frightened.

But she was.

Judy slowly tried the knob, but the door was still locked. She yelled, "Jacob, what's going on down there? Are you okay?"

There was no answer, just the continuous swishing, faint yet distinct, emanating from the spaces below.

She knew that there was no hope of breaking in the door. It was a sturdy door and she was not a large woman. Judy ran through her options in her mind. Did you call the fire department if there wasn't a fire? Perhaps she should call Bemidji Electric Company — the lights were out after all. In the end she decided to call the police, remembering that they were skillful at both breaking through locked doors and medical emergencies.

Judy dialed the number, her sweaty fingers fumbling with the buttons.

***

James Umbrow pulled up to the curb of the yellow house. At first glance he noticed the rotting 70's style lap siding, moisture obviously destroying the boards from the inside. The structure's shingles looked dangerously close to coming undone and sliding off the roof, many already overhanging the sagging gutters. The cracked windows seemed to wink at him like giant eyes, yellowing and cracked blinds pulled shut behind them. He wondered if the family bothered with maintenance at all. Perhaps they spent their money elsewhere.

Above all that, more than he ever had before, James Umbrow had a bad feeling about this call. He just couldn't quite put his finger on why.

He reluctantly tore his eyes off the withering structure and turned to his partner. "Eddy, central said, the homeowner...um..." He referenced his note pad, "...um...Judy Shepherd, says that her husband went down into the basement after breakfast and locked the door. She heard a possible scream and some other noises and now he doesn't answer, wants us to kick the door in. You have any thoughts?"

Eddy picked the remains of a Danish bagel from his teeth. Then, "Yeah, yeah, I have a thought. What did they have for breakfast?"

This made James laugh. "What? You hopin' for leftovers?"

"The thought had crossed my mind. The call cut our meal period short."

James cuffed Eddy behind the head, playfully. "All day is meal period for you. Let's go see what the hell's what here."

Both men got out of the black and white squad, slamming their doors simultaneously. Black shoes clacking on the broken cement walk, the officers adjusted their gun belts and approached the front door with practiced diligence.

James did the knocking, three short raps. The glass window in the door jiggled, threatening to be loosed from its moorings.

They heard tentative footsteps approach the door. The men exchanged glances and heard the deadbolt turn. Then they heard a voice.

"Yes?"

James cleared his throat. "It's the police ma'am."

The dead bolt clacked as it was opened and the door cracked and then opened wide. "Thanks for coming officers. My husband is in the basement and won't answer. And the door is locked."

James nodded. "No problem. We'll get the door open for you; find out what's going on down there. I'm sure he's fine. Probably just can't hear you knocking or something."

Judy knew deep down that the officer was placating her. "Thank you, come in, please. My name is Judy."

James and Eddy shook her hand and introduced themselves.

After pleasantries, Judy walked them over to the basement door. "Jacob and I had a bit of an argument before he went down. He…" Judy hesitated.

The officers exchanged glances.

"…He thinks we have ghosts down there." Judy shrugged an apology.

James smiled. "Its okay ma'am, we've heard stranger; believe me." Judy knew she was being placated again.

James tried the door knob. It was locked as Judy had indicated. He then yelled, "Sir, can you hear me? Do you need help?"

Silence, then they all heard the swishing noise.

Eddy said, "Sounds like someone walking down there. Excuse me, let me try. With your permission, ma'am?"

Judy understood that the man wanted permission to break the door frame. "Oh absolutely, do what you need to."

Eddy pushed his shoulder into the door. It didn't budge. Slightly embarrassed, Eddie said, "Let me try again." He banged the door harder this time, fragments of wood ripping off the jamb.

The door creaked open.

They were met with nothing but silence and darkness.

James shined his flashlight into the inky blackness. It seemed that the darkness ate the light, like the light had no effect at all. He thought it must be an illusion. "Sir, can you hear me? We're the police and are here to help."

A palpable silence seemed to slither up the stairs and envelope the three. Judy shivered.

James gulped, having no real idea why he was feeling so anxious.

Eddy must have felt it too because he cleared his throat with an awkward hack.

James took a tentative step downward and said, "Let's go, Eddy, seems as though Jacob may need our help." Directing his attention back down the stairs, he said, "Sir, it's the police. Can you hear me?"

Judy watched the two officers disappear into the darkness one step at a time until they disappeared completely, swallowed by the pitch black. She shuddered again, nervous. She whispered, "I wish I knew what was going on." She waited to hear something, anything, but the silence remained. Even the footsteps of the officers were lost. She decided to turn away from the basement door, as if it just might be the doorway to hell, and finally walked toward the table. She nearly swooned when the salt shaker fell off the counter. With a little scream, Judy turned toward the kitchen counter. Then she watched the salt shaker roll across the kitchen floor until it came to a stop at her feet.

"Oh damn, it scared me, just the salt shaker," she whispered. She could feel her heart beating in her chest.

Then the pepper shaker fell, repeating the same course, coming to rest with a clunk behind the salt.

Judy began to tremble.

Then a whispery voice, seemingly disembodied, broke the unearthly silence.

"Hide."

Judy knew it wasn't the officers. Had she imagined it? No, she had felt it even more than she had heard it. Suddenly she felt the overwhelming urge to do exactly what the voice had instructed her. Still she hesitated.

Then an image flickered in front of her. First just a torso, transparent and wavering like an electrical pulse, appeared, and then a full-bodied apparition grew out of the torso like a mirage.

Judy exclaimed, "Jacob, what the hell?"

"Hide!" The voice hadn't seemed to come from the apparition, but from everywhere at once. Then the apparition disappeared.

Judy didn't hesitate this time and headed for the attic.

***

Judy had no doubt that she had seen Jacob's ghost. But she also knew that meant Jacob had to be dead. What killed him? Did whatever kill Jacob kill the police? She had no idea. Maybe the police weren't even dead, but had just left. Maybe they had called out to her and she hadn't heard them. A wave of guilt suddenly hit her, residual effects. She wished now that she had believed Jacob.

Now it was too late.

The hunger pains rumbled inside her gut—that gut now voicing its displeasure at being starved. She knew that she had to take a chance, at least long enough to rifle through the cupboards for anything edible. The refrigerator was ruled out, the food probably all spoiled by now with no electricity.

Judy slowly unlocked the trap door. Then she eased it open, scared but determined. She saw no signs of immediate danger. Judy traversed her way down the steep stairway. Upon reaching the bottom, she turned the tight corner and made for the wider stairway that led downstairs to the kitchen, to the food she so desperately needed.

She listened, but heard nothing save silence. Judy decided not to call out and began to quietly walk down the stairway, the carpet on the steps muffling her descent.

Almost immediately she heard the swishing noise. Then a figure, shrouded by the shadows at the foot of the stairs, stepped from around a corner and stood at the bottom of the staircase.

Judy screamed.

"Hello Judy. We've been waiting for you."

Judy stopped halfway down, scared. What had the person meant that they had been waiting? "W... who are you?"

"Don't you recognize me Judy?" The figure stepped into the light.

Judy screamed again. "J... Jacob! What happened to you?" She noticed with horror that Jacob had no eyes, yet the empty sockets bored into hers.

Jacob laughed a throaty noise, as if his throat was clogged with mucus. Then, "I'm dead," the figure said.

Judy whimpered. "B... but I saw your ghost. Why is your body still moving?"

The figure laughed again. "Oh come Judy, do you think that your own soul is the only entity which can inhabit your body? How naïve of you."

"What? Y... you mean?"

"Yes Judy. Jacob is long gone, vacated the premises. This vessel is mine now. Soon there shall be vessels for us all! May we use yours?" The creature laughed again, this time blood spilled from its mouth.

Judy recoiled in terror and started back up the steps as she spoke. "What are you?"

The creature hissed, "Something that has waited eons to be released! Now it is our time!"

"Did you kill the police?"

The creature sneered, "You are just not getting it Judy! If you are referring to the two men who came into the basement, then yes. We killed them and they have long since joined the battle."

"What battle?"

"The battle for your world of course. You should be proud that it all started right here in little Bemidji, Minnesota. By now, two-thirds of your national guard have been defeated. And every time one of you dies, one of our kind lives. And so it goes until we inhabit every living thing. Won't you join the fun? I promise I'll make it painless."

Judy screamed and ran for the attic.

The voice behind her began to taunt. "Go ahead and run Judy. Hide! When you die of starvation, we'll get your body too!"

Hook

By Robert J. Christie

They say that your life flashes before your eyes in the moment before your death. Well, I found out they are almost right.
Because I spent "story time" playing cops and robbers when I was in school, I don't know shit about telling a story. So I guess, since I have the time, I will just do what makes sense and think this through from the beginning.

The beginning, for my purposes, is two decades before I was born. Lots of stuff went down in the 60s. If you want to know about peace, love, and groovy music, I ain't your man. What's important about the 60s is that Kennedy had a hard on to put Americans in space. More specifically, he wanted an American on the moon. When you are a popular president, you get what you want. So every geek whiz kid, and German rocket scientist that came to the US after Germany's big mistake number two, went to work on manned space flight.

In 1963, the board of the National Academy of Sciences created the Special Subcommittee on Space Science. You see, every once in a while, the eggheads have a good idea. It's like this - the geeks were worried about alien life. Not like in Aliens or Predator though. What they were thinking about was the possibility of a dangerous virus or bacteria coming to Earth on a recovered spacecraft. It was the Subcommittee's job to come up with a set of rules for NASA to ensure that anything shot up into space didn't come back down with a dangerous viral or bacterial passenger.

The Subcommittee on Space Science created some simple rules making it clear that the space administration needed to take every precaution to protect health and agriculture. Like any good bureaucracy, though, NASA was not about to let a good idea rain on their parade. NASA made its own contribution to the Subcommittee's rulebook. They required oversight of the Subcommittee's precautions to ensure that operational aspects of space missions were not compromised. For you cake-eating civilians, that's diplo-speak that allowed employees to ignore the rules if it helped to get our rockets in space post-haste.

Mr. Murphy, whose law is now famous, must have been laughing his ass off. Some paper pushing staff puke puts his two cents into a safety rulebook and forty years later the world almost comes to an end. Just like I learned in Basic School, it's the little things that kill you. But my thoughts are getting a little jumbled up. This is not about me, not yet.

So all through the 1960s and early 70s we were shooting things into space, people included. Some of those people even landed on the moon. It was commonly believed that the heat from re-entry into the Earth's atmosphere would kill off any harmful bugs clinging to a spacecraft; therefore no special precautions were taken on that front. Since it wasn't healthy for the people inside the spacecraft to reach two thousand degrees, NASA had to find a way to be sure they were free of any misbehaving microbes. True to the letter of the Subcommittee's directives, NASA made sure the first men who walked on the moon were sent directly to isolation for medical observation. Not wanting to impede operational aspects of the lunar mission, however, this isolation was cut short so the astronaut heroes could do a promotional tour and talk to *Life* magazine.

History lesson over. Here's the shit only a few of us know. NASA began the Ascent missions to Mars immediately following the success of the Polar Lander expedition. Ascent was designed to collect samples of soil, rock, and ice from the surface of Mars and return them to Earth.

It was a simple concept.

A rover was sent down to the surface of Mars to collect a specific type of material. That material was placed in a container that was then shot into orbit. The container then linked up with a satellite and made the long trip back to Earth. Like I said, a simple idea but the technology to make it happen was cutting edge stuff.

The NASA people got their poop in a group and made the technology work. There were twelve Ascent missions. When the last mission was completed, nine containers of material were collected and returned to Earth. Amazing, right? I mean, we can collect Martian dirt, but we can't get an order for drive thru tacos right. Here I go getting distracted again. It's so hard to keep my thoughts straight.

Portions of the samples from Ascent were delivered, in secret, to military installations all across the United States. As for the Subcommittee's directives on safety, well, who were they to impede the operations of the U.S. military? Especially when it came to the possible weaponization of space rocks.

When I finished my second tour as a combat infantryman in Iraq, I was assigned to Installation Management Command (IMCOM). The 'lead from the back' commander of IMCOM detailed me to force protection at Selfridge AGB in Michigan. As it turns out, those air farce forces needed some serious defending. Unfortunately, it wasn't the kind of protection that could be provided by an M16 and harsh language. You see, some of that Martian dirt made it to Michigan.

What the hell those bio-weenies from USAMRIID, The United States Army Medical Research Institute for Infectious Diseases, were doing with those Martian samples is above my pay grade. Why it needed to be done in Michigan is also something they felt this E5 grunt did not need to know. However, I did find out what effects those samples had on people. That Martian dirt made dead people a lot less dead than they should have been.

Everything started in the lab. Some of the USAMRIID staff got sick. The illness came on as suddenly as a kick to the gut and it had those guys falling over gagging almost as fast. That was the bad news. The worse news was that the infection spread like a brush fire in high wind. The USAMRIID doctors were still confidant that they were in control of the situation. That all changed when the condition of the infected went from sick to dead in less than a day. Not twenty-four hours from the onset of the infection, the call went out for more USAMRIID specialists and the lab building was placed on lock down. My unit was called in to secure the quarantine zone.

A lot happened in a short period after the quarantine was established. If there is one thing this army can do it's mobilize resources and set up temporary structures. Soldiers, scientists, doctors, nurses, and support staff came in from everywhere.

In a way, things were easy because we were on an air base with plenty of runways for bringing in people and supplies. The first plane to arrive after the establishment of the quarantine brought us the chief of USAMRIID, General Tom Axelton. He was a natural leader with an easygoing nature. Since I took lead on force protections role in enforcing the quarantine, it wasn't long before the General and I were on a first name basis. He called me Jim and I called him General.

In addition to the runways, the base had plenty of open space for us to use. The USAMRIID specialists wasted no time in using some of that space to set up a field bio-containment research facility. Once the research equipment was operational, the eneral sent men in space suits in and out of the quarantine zone to do whatever was needed. Still, those people going in did not bring one person out of the building, living or dead.

The USAMRIID specialists weren't so bad when you got to know them and I shared a cup of coffee and a joke with more than a few. Like soldiers who have been in combat, most of them were fairly tight lipped about what was going on in that building. Still, it only took a few days of working around that lab and quarantine building for us to learn a thing or two. They called it Hook. The scientists said it was because the organism looked like a barbed fishing hook when seen under the microscope. Many of the grunts said the name fit because of what Hook did to your body.

Many of the lab workers were struggling because they were not used to the conditions of working in the field. I spent an hour helping one of them, Pete, get settled in to his temporary housing. I saw Pete only a few hours later leaving the field research tent. He had seen what Hook did. Although he didn't say that much, I could tell whatever was going on in there scared the shit out of him.

Later that night the General called a meeting. He felt it was important for us to know what we were up against. The symptoms started like the flu. First came the puking, then fever, the shivers, and serious joint pain. That pain spiraled down into agony as the connective tissue in the joints shrank. The victim would start to twist as Hook bent his spine and neck. The hook also pulled its victims' elbows in to the body and the arms up and in towards the chest. This gave the impression that the infected were hugging themselves in pain. The surface of the patient's tongue would slide off. Many victims choked horribly on it as it slid down their throats. After that bit of unpleasantness things really got bad as the victim bled freely from the eyes, ears, mouth, and privates.

We knew the situation had gone completely SNAFU when the men in space suits were going in but stopped coming out. From what I put together by listening in on the radio, somehow one got infected, then three, then five, all within a few minutes of each other.

Infection was a death sentence but it seemed that Hook changed all the rules. It killed you fast, and then it brought you back. That was the secret those scientists were keeping from us. Once the teams inside the quarantine zone became infected, the secret got out through frantic calls on our radios.

Some really smart guys were telling us that dead people were getting up and moving around. The USAMRIID team told us that the men inside had become infected and were delusional. The doctors outside felt it was time to send more doctors in. The General decided that my team should suit up and go in with them. Great idea.

The inside of the building was a nightmare. There were horribly sick people everywhere. Then there were the dead ones. I've seen plenty of dead men in my two combat tours. It's never pretty but all those corpses had one thing in common: they stayed where they fell. This was a whole new ballgame.

The dead shuffled through the hallways aimlessly, their bent and twisted bodies spreading blood, and Hook, everywhere. Their blood red eyes were vacant, unseeing, but if they got close to you they would stop and lean in as if asking for help.

It was more than a little disturbing.

Contact with the "walkers" could mean a torn suit and certain contamination with Hook. I knew I had to keep my men focused. I have to admit to being terrified but a warrior can take that fear, channel it, and turn it into positive energy. I ordered my men to focus on protecting their suits. Adding to the difficulty was that it seemed the whole building was made of broken glass and splinters.

As we picked our way through the chaos, we held little hope of finding anyone who had not been infected. We feared that we would soon be among them. A couple of us discovered damage to our suits. We quickly slapped sticky tape to plug any breach and it seemed none of us had been cut.

We worked our way from floor to floor keeping the walkers away from the USAMRIID team. It was slow going because we had to avoid the clambering for help from the sick as well. Then in a locked lab on the third floor we found what the USAMRIID team had been looking for.

His name was Daniel Crippen. He was a USAMRIID biologist, and he wasn't sick. Random chance had acted in his favor. Only a few days before the outbreak, David had been bitten by one of the many raccoons living on the base. The raccoon was never captured so David was undergoing treatment for rabies as a precaution. Crippen was a smart guy.

Figuring out that something in his rabies treatment was protecting him from Hook was not a huge leap of deduction.

Free from the fear of infection, David worked hand in hand with the labs outside the building to isolate a treatment. He had found an answer at the same time all hell was breaking loose with the infected USAMRIID team. Now it was clear why the General sent us in. We had to make sure the treatment was tested and, if it worked, made it out of the building.

He called it RC2 and it was soon clear that it worked. Crippen asked us to round up some of the walkers. We carefully went into the hall and brought back two for him. We found that if you got them to lean towards you and you moved slowly ahead, they would follow. Crippen prepared RC2 shots for the walkers and plunged the needle home.

They fell on the spot, instantly behaving like the corpses they were.

We repeated the test several more times on other walkers and each time they fell. I even gave a few of them the shot myself. I would swear to you that they felt the needle before they fell.

The USAMRIID guys decided that given the circumstances, it would be acceptable to administer a non FDA approved drug to the dying in the hallways. Unfortunately, RC2 did not reverse the effects Hook had on the living. On the plus side, they did not get up for round two after they died.

The question was: Would RC2 protect the uninfected? As the only healthy non-USAMRIID pukes in the building, we got volunteered as guinea pigs.

Orders are orders.

We all rolled up our sleeves and Crippen began injecting us with RC2. Just as he bent in to give me my shot, I vomited. It was red with blood. Turns out, a small splinter had punctured my suit and allowed Hook to set up shop in my lungs. I would soon join those hopeless souls in the halls waiting for my turn to die. It was reassuring to me in my final hours of agony that at least there would be an end.

Fucking science.

Those USAMRIID doctors were so confident in their cure they didn't cremate any of the corpses. They just dug a giant hole and pushed the bodies in. But RC2 is a lie. Hook killed my body but not my mind. I lay here, my body dead, buried and slowly rotting, and my mind still lives. I feel every maggot as they burrow into me and eat my flesh. I can feel my guts rot and turn to liquid.

They say that your life flashes before your eyes in the moment before your death. That's not true. You see, Hook has given me eternity to remember.

On The Island

By Michael Cieslak

Sept 7, 2009
11:30 p.m.

I should really be getting some sleep.
It is my last evening indoors, the last night I will sleep on a bed for a week. Naturally, I am wide awake. Everything has been checked and re-checked. I can't think of anything that I forgot to pack. I will even be taking this journal and a pen along.

All right, I will admit it, I was not very jazzed about writing down my feelings, but Dr. Ross thinks it will be a good way for me to "address the experienced emotions, rather than burying or belittling them." If nothing else, I will have something to read on the boat ride back.

I miss Janice.

I have been doing a pretty good job of not thinking about her lately. This could be repression or it could be me moving on. I know what Ross would call it.

She didn't really pop into my mind until after I crossed the bridge. It is only natural to think about her. Our last real vacation was the trip up here. In fact, I expect to dwell on the divorce because of that fact, but I am not about to let the possibility of thinking about Jan deter me from doing anything.

Especially not something I have planned on doing for the last five years.

That's enough thinking about her for now. Why dwell on the past when I have tomorrow to look forward to? The television only gets one station, and that is showing the news.

Some kind of industrial accident somewhere. At least I won't be tempted to stay up and watch reruns. I need to get some sleep. I have a big day ahead of me, the start of a big week.

Tomorrow I take on The Island.

Sept 8, 2009
11:00 a.m.

I am sitting on the Isle Royale Queen IV, just a little behind schedule. My journey almost ended before it began. The harbor was enveloped in dense fog. For a while it looked as if they were going to cancel the trip out, which would have been devastating.

This late in the season, there are not many people heading out to the island. In fact, there were only five other people waiting on the dock with me, two couples and another loner. We huddled in the mist sharing stories.

The first couple is young; they are big nature buffs, back-country hikers who have been to all of the major national and state parks. Their equipment was high-end, but worn in. I felt very outclassed and out of shape standing with them.

The other loner is a nature photographer. He is going to kayak around the island. I hope he is skilled. I can't imagine fighting a storm on Lake Superior in a tiny plastic canoe. This is his fourth or fifth trip here. He said he has taken a number of good moose pictures, but has yet to see a wolf.

The other couple, an older couple, is planning on spending the night at the resort. Tomorrow they take the ferry tour around the island, then return to the mainland. They seemed very excited. I did not have the heart to tell them that the "resort" is a cinderblock building which more closely resembles the dormitory of a rural college. I know because Jan and I stayed in one of the rooms when we came. We did not camp, but did a lot of hiking. The hiking took its toll. I remember sitting in an old, uncomfortable chair with Ziploc bags full of ice on my knees. That was when I vowed to come back when I turned 40. Since then I have had a couple of years to whip myself into shape. Things should go a lot more smoothly this time.

That was a good trip. Jan and I hardly fought at all. At least, that is the way I remember it. Maybe nostalgia is coloring my memories.

Sept 8, 2009
6:30 p.m.

A very productive day.

The crossing was relatively smooth. After we landed, I headed straight to the Park Office. There were no problems with my reservations. My backcountry pass was all ready to go. I filled out all of the required forms then mapped out my proposed route. It is good to know that the Rangers will know where to look if I break my leg.

After that I set out for Rock Harbor campground. I was prepared to have to hike all the way out to Three Mile Campground just to get away from everyone, but I was in luck. This early in the day, few people were there. Most were packing up and heading to the docks for the return trip to the mainland. As the day progressed, a few more people arrived, but I had the area mostly to myself.

This included a welcome lack of mosquitoes. My last trip here had been in the height of the bug season. Between the mosquitoes and the horse flies, it was a nightmare. The blood from the bites never did wash out of Jan's outfit.

Well, time to boil some water and cook my dinner. I think Pad Thai tonight. I am curious to see what freeze dried Thai food tastes like.

Sept 8, 2009
11:18 p.m.

There is a radio playing just loud enough to keep waking me up. At least, I assume it is a radio. It sounds like an audio book or something. Every once and a while I catch an outburst of talking. I think it was a gunshot that woke me originally. For a moment I thought I was back in that little East Side apartment that Jan and I had when we first started dating.

Yes, it is definitely an audio book. I swear someone just said something about a corpse rising. Ridiculous. I suppose this is what I get for not hiking further in on my first night. Honestly, don't most people come here to get away from all of the lunacy? I suppose that I could say something, but…

Silence. Lovely silence. Well, not silence, but a definite lack of human sounds. It will be nice to close my eyes and fall asleep to the sounds of the trees around me.

Sept 9, 2009
12:05 p.m.

I struck camp early to make sure that I was back at Rock Harbor in time for the ferry. I slept okay, once the noise dropped off.

I must admit, I could have packed up quieter, but I took perverse pleasure in the fact that my noise was interrupting the radio owner's sleep. Jan always said I was passive aggressive.

The boat ride to the far side of the island was uneventful, but full of beautiful views. It is a shame that there are no trails which follow the southern shore all the way back. Still, it is nice to know that the trails I have chosen are usually less populated, even in the summer. Now that the boat has gone, I suspect that I will not see anyone for most of the rest of the week.

Enough stalling. Time to eat a power bar and hit the trails.

Sept 9, 2009
6:47 p.m.

I am glad that I chose the counter clockwise route. The trek up and over the western end of the Greenstone Ridge was tougher than I expected. It is nice to know that I will be going downhill when I head back to Windigo.

The trail was quite nice and there was a wide variety of scenery. I started out at the bay then made that hellacious climb. Yes, I am definitely still a little out of shape. Of course, I am also toting a full pack, including food and water. Shortly after I cleared the ridge, I headed into forest. I think that I saw some bark scrapings--moose?

The weirdest part of the trek was towards the end. I was hiking below the old beach lines which, according to the guide book, were caused by glaciers. It really did seem like I was hiking below the water line, very disconcerting.

It was also a little disorienting. Feldtman Lake should have been just around every bed--I was walking near beaches, after all. It was an illusion. The lake itself was still more than an hour away. I was very grateful when I reached the campsite and could stop for a while.

The campsite itself is nice. A few fire rings, a pit toilet, and some nice level ground. As expected, I have it all to myself. I set up the tent then walked the small spur down to the big lake. According to the book, this is Rainbow Cove.

I don't see any rainbows, but as I write this I am watching a beautiful sunset over Lake Superior. I have taken a few pictures with the little camera I brought. Now I wish I had packed the good camera.

I am going to give myself a few more minutes to watch the sky change colors, then I had better head back. You always forget how truly dark the night is when you are away from all of the light pollution of the city. I would hate to twist an ankle in the dark. That would end my trip really quick.

Random Thought: The ranger at the Windigo station said something odd. As I was preparing to head out he asked if I was glad to be on the island. I said of course, I had been looking forward to it for years, ever since the last time I left. I was all prepared to tell him about my big quest in celebration of my 40th birthday, but I never got a chance.

"No, I mean away from the outbreak," he said. He pointed at the little television on the counter. It looked like CNN or Fox News, one of those stations with the permanent crawl along the bottom of the screen.

The subtitles were saying something about the numbers of infected while the picture showed rioting in some random city.

How sad. Given the chance to be out here, surrounded by the beauty of nature, and he chose to watch television. I guess nobody really appreciates what they have right in front of them.

That sounds like a lead in to some morose thoughts about failed relationships. Time to get back to the tent.

Sept 10, 2009
1:48 p.m.

Just a brief entry to jot down the incidents of this morning.

The day started off as a nice peaceful morning with birds singing in the trees overhead. Then I looked at my watch. It was almost nine in the morning! I had slept in, in fact overslept. This is the first time that this has happened in years. Even on the weekends I tend to wake up at five, certainly no later than six or six-thirty.

Breakfast was a rushed affair, eaten while striking camp. I made for the trail as soon as possible, desperate to make up for lost time. Unfortunately this meant rushing past the scenery. This was difficult to do as much of the trail has been uphill so far.

I did stop for a moment or two at the top of a knoll with a spectacular view of Feldtman Lake. I am glad that I did. As I was rummaging around for a power bar, I glanced down at the water. There, at the edge, was a moose! I managed to take a few pictures, but the telephoto on the small camera leaves a lot to be desired. You can definitely tell what it is in the picture, but the details are lacking.

I am currently sitting at Lookout Tower. It seems like I can see the whole island from up here, or at least the western half of it. I have taken a number of pictures that I hope will make good screen savers. It would be nice to be able to remember my time here alone when back in the cubicle farm.

Now is not the time to think about that. I am going to enjoy a few more minutes of solitude while finishing my lunch, then it is back to the trail.

It is so nice to be away from everyone.

Sept 10, 2009
5:18 p.m.

I made excellent time after leaving Lookout Tower. The remainder of the hike was either downhill or relatively level. A large portion of if towards the end was an empty grass plain with nothing to trip up a lone hiker's feet.

I think that the bushes I passed right before the fields were thimbleberries. I am by no means an expert on local flora, but they looked like thimbleberries. The monks at that monastery that sells jellies and jams showed them to us. That was excellent jelly. Of course, Jan hated it. To hell with her. She can eat all of the Smucker's Grape she wants.

Speaking of eating, I should set up camp and get some food in my system. Tonight I'll go for the dehydrated lasagna. I think that I liked that last time.

Note: Buying food for this trip was a pain. While there are a lot of companies that make lightweight, dehydrated food for hikers, most seem to think that no one hikes alone. The vast majority of the meals which were in stock at my local outfitter were "Meals for 2." Since I have to tote everything I don't finish off the island with the rest of my garbage, this is a real pain. I had to special order most of my dinners online.

What do other people do? Do they save the remains and have it for breakfast the next day? Ugh. The cook in the bag meals are a breeze to make -- just add boiling water. I have been eating right out of the bags instead of using the collapsible bowl I brought. While they are easy to prepare, this makes them very difficult to store.

At least I don't have to worry about the smell attracting bears. None live on the island. I wonder if wolves like lasagna.

Later: Ready to turn in. Remember to inquire about that monastery when you get back to the mainland. Were they near Eagle Harbor? Do they still have any of that thimbleberry jelly?

Sept 11, 2009
7:15 p.m.

What a very strange day. It started out great but has been clouded over by...

Well, let's ignore that for now and focus on the positive things. Today's hike was spectacular. While it is less than five miles from where I camped last night at Siskiwit Bay to where I pitched my tent today at the Island Mine campground, I took most of the day to cross between the two. Instead of shlepping quickly down the trail, I took the time to enjoy the scenery.

Unlike yesterday, I started off early enough that the undergrowth was still wet with dew. Rather than soak my pant legs, I opted to walk along the shore of Siskiwit Bay. There, in the sand, was a trail of paw prints. At first I wrote it off. I can't count the number of times I have come across the twin tracks of a dog and its owner while walking in the morning. In the months that I took to prepare for this outing I must have come across hundreds.

These, however, were a little different. For one thing, there were no human footprints next to them. However, the paw prints were close to the water line, so I assumed that the incoming tide had washed away the signs left by the dog's owner. Indeed, the water was starting to erase the prints left by the big dog.

Then it hit me. No pets are allowed on the island; something about passing disease on to the wildlife.

So if these were not the prints of a big dog, they had to have been left by a wolf!

I would love to say that I quietly and patiently tracked the prints to their owner, then crept closer, ever so slowly, and approached until I was within camera range.

That would be a lie.

In fact, once I realized that I was following the path of a wolf, a strange terror took hold of me. Rationally, I knew that the chances of seeing a wolf, despite the secure

population which lives on the island, were slim to none. But isn't that what they said about seeing moose? I had already seen one of them. What would a wolf do if I came across it? Probably run. I knew this, but fear still gripped my heart. I headed back up to the trail proper, wet undergrowth or no. I paused only long enough to take a few shaky pictures of the paw prints.

Now I wish I had had the courage to follow the tracks, at least for a little while.

Dr. Ross said this should be a "no regrets" trip. Besides, I saw plenty of other interesting (and photograph worthy!) things on the trail.

The first thing that I passed was the remains of a stone building. According to a small sign nearby, this is where the mining company had stored their explosives. A little further up the trail was one of the mines. I did not explore too much, as the guide book noted that there are still drop-offs waiting to catch unwary travelers.

The most spectacular part of the day which ended up being photographed the most, as the subtle change in trees. Just past the mine was a stream or tributary of some river. I will have to look it up later. Up to this point I had been following a smooth path which was probably one of the old mining roads, now taken over by vegetation.

The trees were mainly of the evergreen variety, probably spruce and fir. I gauge this only by the Christmas trees I have purchased in the past. There were also a number of those paper bark trees that I used to strip to make little canoes when I was a kid.

On the other side of the stream, the trees suddenly changed. The deep greens of the evergreens were replaced by a riot of bright reds, yellows, and oranges. As I wrote before, I am no expert on vegetation, but even I know a sugar maple when I see one. I think the others were some kind of oaks.

I am so glad that I delayed coming here until the fall. While the differences between the forests would have been noticeable in the summer, the abrupt and unexpected blast of color was amazing.

In the midst of all of this color was the Island Mine campground. I could spend the night here or head back to Windigo another 6 miles down the trail. While sitting in my apartment looking at maps I could not decide which to choose. Standing in the middle of the beautiful fall colors, there was no choice to make.

I almost wish now that I had continued on. Then I would not have met Stan and Cindy.

Even with my side trips, I made it to the Island Mine Campground with plenty of daylight left. I set up my tent then collected and purified some water. I was finding the dehydrated dinners difficult enough to swallow; I didn't need to add Giardia to my problems. The last thing I needed was a diarrhea inducing parasite.

After resting for about a half an hour, I decided to head up Sugar Mountain. I had not seen anyone for a few days now so I left my pack in the tent. There was no one around to steal it. My food was sealed in a "bear-proof" container, so nothing should have been able to smell it either. I got out my camera and headed up the trail.

The route was steep in places and soon I could feel my legs burning with exertion. I was glad I had left my pack behind. Unfortunately, I will have to retrace my steps tomorrow since this is the route I will be taking. Of course, I am going to have to do it with all of my equipment. I have to remember to make sure I stretch out well before starting off.

I made it to the top without incident. All around me was the beauty of nature. I set the camera for "panorama" and started clicking away. I had taken maybe a half dozen pictures when I heard voices. They were coming from the eastern portion of the Greenstone Ridge trail, which leads to Mount Desor. They were still far enough away to be indistinct, but they were getting closer. While I could not make out the words, I thought I could detect a note of panic in their tones.

Soon the voices, one low and one high, were close enough that I could make out at least one word out of every three. They were arguing about something; it sounded like which trail to take. The lower voice, which I assumed was male, wanted to keep "going forward." There was a distinct note of panic in his insistences. The other, higher, probably female, voice seemed to want to go back.

I was torn between slinking off back to my campsite and waiting where I stood. The Good Samaritan side wanted to stay and offer to help the couple find their way. I had one of my maps in my back pocket. The more selfish part wanted to slink back to my campsite and hope they did not come anywhere near it. The last thing I wanted to do was become embroiled in a lovers' quarrel.

I was still standing where the two trails met when my decision was made for me. The air was rent with a horrible scream.

The male hiker had spotted me and screamed.

A few embarrassing minutes later, introductions had been made and I discovered why they were arguing. I will not try to recount the conversation verbatim, but the gist of it was that Stan and Cindy had been hiking for a few days. They had started at one end of the Greenback Ridge trail and were moving west to Windigo where they had made an appointment for the ferry to bring them back to Rock Harbor.

They were both avid outdoors-people. It was apparent from their gear that they spared no expense when it came to gadgets. They each had a high end GPS unit attached to their bags. The bags themselves were ultra-light and expensive looking, as was their clothing. I had no doubt that their tent would be able to withstand gale force winds but only weighed a few ounces.

Not that I was jealous or anything.

Among the gizmos which they had brought with them was an emergency radio. It was the kind which monitored the weather and national emergency stations and alarmed if anything was announced. They said when it went off they had expected to hear about a storm brewing on the lake. To their surprise, they heard the same thing repeated every five minutes.

"All citizens are advised to seek shelter immediately. Emergency shelters have been established at fire stations, foul weather shelters, and some schools. Tune into your local news broadcast for further details. If you are unable to reach a shelter, remain indoors with the doors and windows securely locked. Do not allow anyone in until given the All Clear by local authorities.

"The National Guard has been mobilized in some urban areas to assist with crowd control and disease containment. The CDC is currently researching the disease, but at this time they do not have a treatment. They have established quarantine areas in the worst hot zones. These quarantines are being enforced by the police and the National Guard. Anyone attempting to violate a quarantine area by either entering or leaving is subject to immediate arrest.

"Do not attempt to treat anyone showing signs of the disease. Avoid contaminated individuals at all costs, regardless of their age or relation to you. If you come in contact with an infected individual, report to the authorities immediately. Do not attempt to restrain infected individuals. Authorities have been sent to all areas of the outbreak to care for the infected.

"The infected display a number of symptoms including poor motor control, lack of higher cognitive function, slurred speech, and a grayish green pallor. Physicians assume that there is some form of nerve damage by the vector which causes infected individuals to appear impervious to pain. If you see anyone displaying any of these symptoms, or behaving erratically, err on the side of caution and inform your local authorities."

At least, that is what Stan said the broadcast said. I doubted that he could remember all of the announcement verbatim, even if he did listen to three repetitions of it. Of course, they could not get a signal on their radio for me to hear.

Their argument stemmed from their inability to decide what to do next. One of them, I am not really sure who was on which side, wanted to head back to Rock Harbor. There would be people there. This was also the port which has the most activity, so it was more likely to have someone with recent news. The other person wanted to press on to the Ranger Station at Windigo.

After more bickering amongst themselves, they turned to me for my opinion.

I told them that both sounded like good ideas and each had their merits. However, if they really wanted information, Windigo was their best bet. They could make it easily from where they stood.

I neglected to tell them that I was headed there myself tomorrow. Nor did I say that I was camped a short walk away. I assume that they saw that I did not have a pack and surmised that I was already set up for the night near the Ranger Station. They did not ask, and I did not divulge.

It was incredibly selfish of me, but I did not want to give up my last night of peace and quiet. Odds are they will still be in Windigo when I get there. The ferry is not due until the afternoon. We will have all morning to discuss the news of the larger world when I get there.

I admit, I am a little curious, but I am going to do my best to put it out of my head for now.

I wonder if Jan is alright.

PS. The sunset was brilliant. I think the batteries in my camera are just about dead.

Sept 12, 2009
08:45 a.m.

The sunrise was even more brilliant today than the sunset was last night, even if I am on the wrong side of the island for sunrises. This may be because this is likely my last moment of solitude. I prefer to think that it is due to the low clouds hanging overhead. The sun tinted their edges a brilliant pink while their centers remained gray.

If I remember my grade school meteorology correctly, the color of this morning's sky indicates that sailors should take warning. I assume this goes for people on an island in the middle of a lake large enough to be called a landlocked sea as well.

Although it was nice to have the time alone, I do not like the look of those clouds. I think it is probably a good thing that I am leaving today.

Time to pack everything up and head on up the trail.

Sept 12, 2009?
8:20 p.m.

Karma is a bitch.

I dragged my heels today, not wanting to spend the whole day in Windigo with Cindy and Stan. The hike itself was not bad, mostly downhill. Like the rest of the Greenridge trail, there are some areas where the trail is marked by rock cairns, some of which are easy to miss. I took it slow and managed not to miss any this time. When I was here with Jan we missed one of these turn offs and our hike ended up three times longer than we had intended.

I saw Stan and Cindy again, but not at Windigo. As before, they were bickering and I heard them coming up the trail near the Washington Creek Campground, less than a mile away from the Ranger Station.

Once again, I felt the urge to hide. This time I gave in to that urge. "There is no one there!" Stan whined.

"Maybe the Ranger was sick."

"Even if he was sick, he would have come. Especially with all of the noise that we were making. There was no one there and there is always someone there on days when boats are due to arrive."

"Okay, fine." Cindy sounded exasperated. I could understand why. Stan's voice was starting to grate on my nerves.

"So what makes you think that there is going to be anyone at Rock Harbor? Maybe
they all left. Maybe the boats aren't coming."

"Maybe they are waiting there for us with cake and ice cream. Either way, we won't know until we get there, so there is no use worrying about it now, is there?"

Stan's reply was unintelligible.

"Is there?" Cindy asked again.

"No, dear," Stan replied, utter defeat in his voice.

I waited off of the trail until I was sure that I would not be seen. Then I crept out. I watched my back trail for signs of the couple's return. Finally, I headed off the way they had come.

The trail was mostly downhill from here. I resisted the urge to jog down the trail. Although part of me wanted to reach the station and confirm the ferry's arrival, another part of me did not want to see the end to my solitude.

Perhaps Dr. Ross was right. Perhaps I just needed some time to reacquaint myself with myself in order to feel at ease without Jan. Perhaps all of the time alone in the woods had scrambled my brains. Psychobabble nonsense.

Of course, one has to be careful of what one wishes for. I was mourning the impending loss of solitude. I needn't have worried. I would have plenty of opportunities for more self-reflection.

The ranger station was abandoned. It was also ransacked.

Someone, I assume Stan and/or Cindy, had emptied the display case of most of the consumables and that whoever had done so was not acting in any official capacity. The cabinets were not simply open, they were smashed. Jagged pieces of glass twinkled on the shelves which had held chocolate bars, packages of trail mix, and energy drinks.

The chalk board behind the desk announced the weather forecast, sunrise and sunset, and tide times for the 10th. No one had updated it in at least two days.

This worried me.

As Stan had said, someone was always there when a boat was due to arrive. At least, there was supposed to be someone there. I had a few hours to wait before the boat was due, so I went back out onto the low wooden porch and sat.

The longer I waited, the more anxious I got. Finally, knowing that the ferry was not due to arrive for hours, I walked down to the dock. From there I had a commanding view of Lake Superior and the sky overhead. The water was an ominous dark gray. The waves looked cold and menacing. The sky did not offer much in the way of hope. It, too, was gray, the gunmetal clouds hanging low.

Soon, it began to rain.

I had managed to go the whole trip without getting too wet, so it was inevitable that it should begin to pour while I was out of the wilderness and waiting for the ferry. The rain was cold and insistent. Soon I was soaked, despite my poncho. I toyed with the idea of heading back to the ranger station. Surely the boat captain would come ashore to look for his passenger.

But maybe not.

I waited on the dock.

I waited in the rain.

I waited until the ferry was hours overdue and the sun had sunk below the horizon. There was no spectacular sunset this evening. There was only a brief flare of orange where the clouds met the sea, then a more complete darkness.

The ferry had not come.

Had I gotten the days wrong? Was I early by a day? I could not have misjudged my time on the trail that by that much. Or was I late? Had I spent too much time on the trail and missed the ferry? Again, not possible.

No, I was certain of it. If nothing else, I had this journal to prove my internal calendar.

So I was at the dock at the right time on the right day, but the ferry was not there. If the mistake was not mine, it must have been the boat captain's.

So where did that leave me?

Sitting in the dark, in the rain, on the dock.

The Windigo campsite was not far off. It would be less than a half a mile, but it would mean hiking in the dark. It would also mean setting up in the dark and the rain. There was probably a shelter there. These were generally a sloped roof over a pallet with a screen door.

I opted instead to head back to the ranger station. Technically there was no camping at the station. I would be happy to get kicked out. That would mean that someone had shown up. Perhaps a ranger or other park official would have more of an idea of what was going on.

I looked around for a phone, or a radio of some kind. There was something in the back that looked like a CB, but it didn't work. I am going to grab something to eat, then try to find that little TV that the ranger was watching when I got here days ago.

Sept 12, 2009
10:15 p.m.

There is nothing here of any use. I cannot find anything with which to contact the outside world, or even the other ranger station. The TV is useless. I think the storm, and it is a storm now, is messing with the signal. All I get is "Looking for signal" no matter what station I put it on.

I am going to try and get some sleep. Maybe things will look better in the morning. At least I have someplace dry.

Sept 13, 2009
12:00 noon

The rain has let up a little today. It is vacillating between a fine mist and a steady drenching. I spent the morning sitting out on the docks, looking for the ferry. I have left my gear at the ranger station along with a note stating where I am.

I had to wait an extra day for the boat so the captain can damn well wait a few minutes for me to run up and grab my stuff.

Sept 13, 2009
8:48 p.m.

No ferry, no rangers, no signs of anyone but me. My longed-for solitude has become something of a curse. I don't know if I should stay here and wait for someone to come pick me up or head back to the other side of the island. Maybe Stan and Cindy were right.

I am too tired to decide now. I will think about it in the morning.

Sept 14, 2009
5:17 a.m.

Slept poorly. Storms were very loud. I alternated between trying to sleep, my head buried in my sleeping bag, and trying to get reception on the little television. I did manage to get in part of a news broadcast. I was able to watch about five minutes of a panel discussion between a doctor, someone in military uniform, and someone in a suit who was so smarmy that he must have been a politician. Unfortunately, I caught the end of the broadcast. Any actual discussion had ended long before I got the signal. All I was able to witness was discordant yelling. No information, other than something bad has happened somewhere and everyone is too busy blaming everyone else to actually do anything about it.

Perhaps it is a good thing that I am stuck here on the island. At least I am relatively safe from any contagions spread by inter-human contact.

Of course, the problem with staying here is that I am quickly running out of supplies. The gas canister for my little stove is almost empty. Not that it matters. I ate the last of the dehydrated meals last night for dinner. I have a few power bars and a handful of energy boost gel packs left. The bars make a decent, if small, meal. The gels are really just carbs in a foil package. They are good for a quick burst of energy, but will not sustain me long.

If only there was something left here at the station. I checked the back rooms last night. Nothing in the storeroom either. Stan and Cindy cleaned the place out completely.

I definitely cannot stay here. There should be stores of food at Rock Harbor, but even the hotel may be low on supplies this late in the season. I wonder if there are any people who live on the island year round.

The big decision now is how to get there, via the Minong Ridge Trail or the Greenstone. Fortunately, they left me some maps and guidebooks.

Sept 14, 2009
12:35 p.m.

The hot shower I took before leaving Windigo was refreshing, but I would trade a week's worth of warm water for a good breakfast.

Both Minong and Greenstone should take anywhere from three to five days to hike.

Minong runs along the north shore, so I would have a better chance of spotting passing boats. It is also the more difficult of the two. Greenstone should be a faster hike, so I opted for it.

Unfortunately, the first leg is mostly uphill. There is a lot of up and down and my thighs are burning. I have only stopped for a little while to catch my breath. If I want to make it to a campsite by dark, I will have to press on soon.

I can see the Canadian shoreline from here. It does not look as if anything horrible has happened. If everything is falling to pieces like the news seems to indicate (and what Stan said), then wouldn't I be able to tell?

Maybe not from this far away.

Maybe not at all.

Sept 14, 2009
9:55 p.m.

I am not sure exactly where I am. I know that I am on the far side of Mount Desor, but beyond that, I have no idea. Trying to push it was a mistake.

I started off the day climbing Sugar Mountain. I could have taken the side trail to the Island Mine campground, but I thought I could push forward and reach South Lake Desor.

The combination of all of the steep climbing and the lack of food has slowed me down immensely. The sun is now completely down. My flashlight beam is getting weaker. I should have grabbed batteries back at the ranger station.

The campground is near the lake, but I have not hit the lake yet. I am afraid to keep pushing forward for fear of losing the trail. It makes more sense to stop here for the night and start up again in the morning.

This is a breach of the contract that I signed stating that I would only camp in "designated areas." Of course, I also had a contract with the ferryman to pick me up. I know it is childish, but they broke their word first.

Besides, if everything is as bad as it seems, I guess sleeping on the trail is fairly small pickings.

There are two pieces of good news. One, at least it stopped raining. And two, I found another one of those bushes with the thimbleberries. Sounds like dinner to me.

Sept 15, 2009

4:55 a.m.

There is enough sun to write by, so there is enough sun to walk by. If I start now I should be able to bypass South Desor for the next campground down the trail.

A quick stop for a breakfast of berries and I am off.

Sept 15, 2009
1:28 p.m.

Those were not thimbleberries.

Sept 16, 2009
4:45 p.m.

Whatever those berries were, I should not have eaten them. Two days of hiking lost. I was forced to stop at South Desor after all. There I spent the better part of the last two days too sick to move. I still feel weak as water. I do not know if it is what I ate or what I have not eaten.

Regardless, I have to get moving soon. I am not going to get any stronger waiting around here. If only Stan and Cindy had left a little something. I could have been at Rock Harbor by now. I would not have had to eat those damn berries and been so sick.

Sept 17, 2009
9:58 a.m.

I have reached the lookout tower which marks the halfway point between the last campground and the next. Normally I would rest here and have a bite to eat. There are no bites to be had and my stomach is still sore from being ill. I am just pausing for a moment to catch my breath, then I will press on.

Sept 17, 2009

2:01 p.m

Hatchet Lake Campground. I should stop here, but there is still plenty of daylight left. I feel energized for some reason. Continuing on, despite common sense which tells me to stop.

Sept 17, 2009
11:47 p.m.

Definitely should have stopped at Hatchet Lake.

Sept 18, 2009
07:28 a.m.

Another cold, hungry morning. I managed to get much farther than I have ever done before, doubt that I will be able to do it again, but I am strangely surprised at my abilities. I pushed further than I would have thought possible.

Dr. Ross was right, I have learned a lot about myself on this trip.

I traversed two mountains yesterday. Normally one would have taxed me. I am so hungry and tired.

Last night I camped at Chickenbone West.

I know that there is another campground a little further down the trail. I know that I can make it at least that far.

Last night I thought I heard something as I was setting up camp. There is no way that I could have heard what I thought I did, especially if they are at the next camping site.

I could have sworn that I heard the arguing of that abhorrent couple of food thieves. I will find out soon enough.

***

What have I done?

I swear I did not mean to,

I would never. It was an accident.

I was just so mad and he kept lying and the wood was right there.

Date and Time Unknown

Although I shudder to write this, I feel that it is in my best interest to record the horrible things that have transpired since my last entry. Perhaps the writing of it will give me clarity.

The sounds that I had heard that night were indeed Stan and Cindy. They had been camping at Chickenbone East for a few days. They were prevented from getting any further, despite their two day lead, because of Stan's injury. He fell or slipped or something, I did not quite follow the story. The result was a leg which was swollen and dark. The skin was mottled and foul smelling.

I did not like the look of that leg.

I had not planned to confront them. I had not planned to do anything at all. When I reached their campsite, Cindy came running towards me. She asked for a first-aid kit, then for food.

Something happened to me then.

I began screaming at them, accusing them of stealing all of the food from the ranger station. I asked why they didn't leave anything for me, why they didn't have anything left for themselves, and what had happened to all of the stores.

They denied taking anything. They said that the ranger station had been ransacked when they got there. Cindy said that was why they did not stay there.

I did not believe them.

I demanded that they share with me whatever they had taken from the station. I do not know what happened next, or in what order.

I remember Stan's whining denials and threatening him with a piece of the firewood that they had collected.

Cindy was very quiet while Stan and I argued. I remember Cindy screaming.

The next thing I can recall clearly is looking down at the bloodied chunk of wood I held in my hand. The first thing that went through my head as I stared at the clumps of hair and tissue which dotted its length was that this was fresh wood. It was strong and sturdy. Firewood was supposed to be limited to what hikers found, "down and dead."

Someone had been breaking the rules.

Stan was lying there, practically in the fire ring. His features were unrecognizable from the shoulders up. His head and face were a pulpy mess of red and gray with little bits of hair and exposed bone.

Cindy was nowhere to be found.

All of the frustration, all of the anger, which had been welling up inside me, rushed out in a horrible, murderous flood. It was not just the ferry and the hunger. It was Janice and the loneliness and everything else which had gone wrong in the last eighteen months. It all spilled over and I killed Stan.

I killed Stan.

And I was so hungry.

It would have been a crime to let all of that good meat go to waste. I ate what I could. I left the purplish, injured limb alone.

I did not like the look of that leg.

Later, night.

I do not know how long I have been here. Has it been one day or many? Has it been a week?

Stan is gone, at least the edible portion of him. But Cindy is still out there somewhere.

I thought I heard her rustling around in the bushes last night. I ran out after her, whether to assault or apologize I do not know.

I tore down the path towards the sound. I almost ran headlong into the dark shape which stood there, half on the trail, half off.

I would not have believed it if I had not seen it myself. Of course, I did not have my camera.

A pair of yellow eyes gleamed at me out of the darkness. The dark, dog-like-but-not, shape could have only been one thing.

The wolf did not attack, nor did it run away. It stared at me coolly, appraisingly, measuring me. Then, as if it recognized something in me, it turned and calmly walked away.

I will look for Cindy in the morning. If I find her, I will stay here for a few more days. If I do not, I will assume that she has followed her original plan and headed off to the east and Rock Harbor. It will be difficult going for her without food or supplies, but she will be traveling light. Perhaps she will make it, perhaps not.

I might meet up with her on the trail and find her, tired, weak, injured like Stan.

Rock Harbor is definitely the correct destination. There will be more supplies, maybe food. And if not...at least there will be more people.

Feed

By Peggy Christie

To feed.
To feed removes all pain.
To be without pain is to be free.
To be free is to live.

My empty veins need blood.
My naked bones need flesh.

I do not live to feed.
I feed to live.
Again.

Find a Need and Fill It

By Peggy Christie

"**M**om! Dad! Got another one!" CJ called out to his parents.

"Just throw it in the freezer with the rest," his father answered.

While CJ dragged the fresh catch to the basement freezer, his father continued to butcher the butt roasts from yesterday's hunting. He'd gotten a few steaks as well but not as many as he'd hoped. Some days the hunt brought great results, and sometimes just stringy bits of flesh. With the way the world was now, it wasn't all that surprising but that didn't make it any less frustrating.

For the past eighteen months, the sun had been throwing beams of radiation at the earth. No one could explain why or if it would ever stop. Even the most learned scientists of the world couldn't predict the strength or location of each incident. The levels changed every time and they never occurred at regular intervals. But wherever the radiation landed, the people…changed.

The dead began to walk. The living died from radiation poisoning, then walked. Not all were affected. Those who had died before embalming became common practice did not reanimate. The same was true for anyone who had been melted in acid, burned by fire, or in any way had their muscle tissues destroyed. Seemed reanimation required more than brain and bone. It needed flesh.

Once the reanimation began it spun out of control. Those who had escaped the sun's damage didn't always escape the walking dead. Their bites and scratches passed on the infection, for lack of a better word. Within hours of contamination, the once living victim died and joined the ranks of the undead. It was like that old shampoo commercial. 'I told two friends, and then they told two friends. And so on and so on and so on…' The dead multiplied out of control while the living dwindled away.

Now Karrie, her husband, Carl, and their son, CJ, were all that remained of Clawson, Michigan. Granted it wasn't that big of a town to begin with but eight thousand was better than three. They weren't the only living left in the world, though. At least, Karrie believed they weren't. She hoped they weren't. She prayed.

Karrie stepped up behind Carl and wrapped her arms around his waist. She gave him a quick squeeze and kiss on the shoulder.

"What're you thinking about?" she asked.

"You know, the usual. The Superbowl, taxes, what's happening on 'The O.C.'" She slapped him on his behind and he snapped his fingers.

"Oh, right. Those things don't exist anymore. I forgot."

"Uh huh. Where's CJ?"

"Downstairs," Carl jerked his thumb over his shoulder. "He brought in a catch for the freezer."

"Another one? Wow, those traps you set are really working, huh?"

"Well, men are the hunters, you know. And women are the gatherers. Why don't you go make yourself useful and gather me a sandwich?"

"If you weren't the only living man within a hundred mile radius, I'd so leave your ass here and hook up with Jensen Ackles."

"Well, if you weren't the only woman, I'd hook up with uh, with uh, crap. What's the name of that actress from-?"

"Sarah Michelle Gellar?"

"No, no. She was in that comic book movie."

"X-Men?" Karrie offered.

"No, the other one."

"The Hulk?"

"No. The Four Fabulous ones…" Carl rapped his knuckles against his forehead. "Jessica Alba?"

"Yes! Thank you. Damn, that was going to keep me up all night if I couldn't think of her name."

"Ha! She'd never allow it. I'm going to see if CJ needs help."

"Okay, hon. Wait. What do you mean she'd never allow it?"

Karrie laughed as she headed downstairs where she found CJ struggling with the freezer. The kid was tough for his age but he was still only eight.

"Hey, peanut. Need some help?"

"Yeah, Mom. Thanks."

Karrie lifted the heavy lid of the chest freezer and propped it open with the built in locking latch. She bent down and hefted the carcass into her arms. Dumping it into the freezer, she blew out a heavy breath.

"Whew! That was a heavy one. How on earth did you get it down here by yourself?"

CJ flexed his biceps and grinned. He ran upstairs, yelling to his Dad about popsicles. Smiling, Karrie bent down to clean up the trapping equipment. She coiled up two lengths of rope and hung them on a hook by the freezer. One of the wooden stakes used to anchor the rope to the counterweight in the trap had splintered. She tossed it into a box reserved for firewood and made a mental note to talk to Carl about fashioning another one. The blue plastic tarp lay open in the corner. Pools of blood filled the creases and folds. She'd deal with that once it dried.

CJ's hunting knife lay on the floor in a puddle of viscous blood. She grimaced as she grabbed some rubber gloves and a rag to clean it up. It was then she noticed several small dark red spots on the basement floor. Beyond those were a few splats and short lines.

Karrie threw the gloves down and stormed upstairs.

"Young man! How many times have your father and I told you not to drip blood all over the house?"

Just as she reached the kitchen, a loud crack echoed outside. She stared at Carl, the shock on his face seemed to match her thoughts: someone was shooting out there. Someone alive. Though the dead reacquired their mobility this past year and a half, they did not regain their higher mental capacities or intricate motor skills. CJ ran to the front window and peeked through a gap in the boards covering the glass.

"It's Mr. Daniels. He's up on his roof!"

"Robert?" Carl asked.

"He's still alive?"

"We haven't seen him since last Christmas. Where has he been?" Karrie wondered.

Carl ran to the hallway. "I'll ask him."

"We're coming with you!" Karrie shouted behind him.

He pulled down the retractable ladder and Karrie and CJ followed Carl into the attic. From there Karrie started up one of the three generators they had on hand to power whatever they needed in the house. Carl accessed the speaker system he'd wired up six months ago. He could broadcast and receive radio signals, as well as announce to the neighborhood the color, texture, and frequency of his bowel movements, if he so desired. He used it religiously for a month as he tried to find survivors. But when no one responded, he shut it down and never touched it again.

Until now.

"Rob? Rob! Is that you?"

Carl turned on the surveillance cameras and monitors that he set up along with the broadcast radio. They could all see Rob on the third screen from the left. Carl flipped another switch to turn on the microphone system so they could hear what was going on outside. Rob didn't say anything as he spun around, as if trying to figure out where Carl's voice was coming from.

"Rob, it's Carl. Across the street, man."

Rob turned his attention on Carl's home. Understanding seemed to finally dawn on him and he waved in the general direction of the security cameras. Karrie smiled, happy to know their neighbor, and friend, was still alive.

She caught movement from the corner of her eye and turned to the far monitor on the right. A lone zombie shuffled its way down the street. As Karrie recognized the details of its fireman's uniform she heard another loud crack. The back of the zombie's head exploded and it fell. She looked back at the third monitor and saw Rob eject the spent cartridge from his rifle and then reload it.

She and Carl scanned the remaining monitors but saw no other zombies. More would be sure to show up as they were attracted to loud noises. Carl clicked on the loudspeaker.

"Rob! Hold up. I'm coming over."

Rob made a thumbs-up gesture and headed back inside his house. Within minutes, the two men stood in the street, shaking hands. Karrie and CJ listened to them from inside the attic.

"Rob, it's been months. We thought you were dead. Where've you been?"

"I locked myself inside," Rob jerked his head toward his house. "I had enough provisions to last me a while and I thought this would all blow over by the time I ran out. But I guess my calculations were a bit off, huh?"

"What do you have left?"

"Not much," Rob replied. "A sleeve of Saltines, half a jar of peanut butter, a few bottles of water. I figured I'd just start shooting until I had one bullet left. Then-" his voice trailed off.

"Why didn't you just come to us?"

Rob shrugged. "Honestly, I didn't know anyone was still here. Those that survived got the hell out of town. There's no radio or TV anymore. My house is soundproofed and locked up tighter than a Scotsman's coin purse. I never heard anything or anyone. When I realized I was going to starve, I got on the roof. If I saw zombies shuffling around that meant it was still hell out here and I'd take out as many as I could."

"What if you didn't see any?" Carl asked.

"Well, I guess I'd start walking and see how far I'd get on a handful of peanut butter cracker sandwiches."

Carl raised an eyebrow at him. Rob smiled.

"Okay. Maybe I'd bust into a couple homes, raid a few panty drawers, and then walk outta town."

"Rob, we have plenty to eat." Carl slapped him on the back and directed him over to his house. "Please come over. Karrie will be glad to know you're all right."

"Thanks, Carl."

Karrie and CJ made their way down to the living room and watched the two men from the front window. CJ darted off towards the front door but she stopped him.

"CJ, you stay here."

"But Mom," CJ whined.

"We don't know if it's completely clear yet. Wait. Here."

The boy pushed his glasses up on his nose and folded his arms in what had become his trademark posture of frustration. But he stayed inside while Karrie walked out the front door to greet her neighbor.

"Rob, it's so good to see you."

She threw her arms around him and gave him a big bear hug. He pulled away, flushing pink in embarrassment.

"Karrie, I told you before. Not in front of your husband."

She laughed and directed him to the front door. As he entered, CJ ran up to him. Rob held up his hand.

"CJ! High five."

The boy jumped up and slapped Rob's hand. He offered his own in return and Rob swiped it. CJ grabbed Rob's arm and pulled him over to the couch.

"Rob! Where have you been? What happened to Roscoe and Dozer? Wanna see my hunting knife? Where's Annie? Have you killed any zombies? Wanna see my room?"

Before he could even consider answering the first question, let alone the following dozen, Karrie shushed the boy.

"CJ. Give Rob a break. He just got here. We need to feed him first, okay?"

CJ slumped against the cushions, defeated. Rob hooked his arm around the boy's neck and whispered in his ear.

"Hey, while your Mom cooks dinner, you can show me your room. Cool?"

"All right!" CJ shouted.

The boy jumped up and dragged Rob by the hand.

"Roast is okay for dinner, isn't it?" Karrie called to them as they walked down the hall.

Rob pulled up short. He turned to stare at her.

"You…you've got a roast? How? All the stores, all the farms are empty, closed, or gone."

"Oh, there's still good hunting around here. As a matter of fact," Karrie jutted her chin at her son. "CJ just brought in a catch this morning. Carl's got traps all over the neighborhood."

Rob allowed CJ to pull him further down the hall but his face was still pinched in disbelief. Karrie could hear CJ prattling on and on about his hunting adventures but Rob only responded with muffled grunts. She laughed and began to prepare dinner.

***

Three hours later, Rob sat back on the sofa and patted his full belly.

"Karrie, I haven't had that good of a meal since Annie was alive. I think I'm going to burst."

"The secret is how you cook it. You've got to cook low and slow to get the roast fork tender."

"How much do you guys have?"

"We've got a freezer full. You're welcome to come over whenever you want. We can even give you some to take home. We also grow our own veggies in the back so you can have some of those, too. CJ?"

The boy jumped up from the couch and grabbed Rob's hand. "C'mon, Rob. I'll show you where the freezer is."

Karrie followed CJ as he led Rob downstairs and into the back corner of the basement. He thunked his hand on top of the freezer.

"Here it is. I have a little trouble getting it open sometimes…"

"I'll help you, big guy."

Rob heaved the lid of the freezer up and locked it in place. He stared down at its contents as Karrie pointed out each item.

"As you can see, we've got several torsos, eight legs, ten arms, a few odds and ends. When we section a body like a side of beef, it's much easier to stack and store."

CJ grabbed a plastic bag filled with fingers and toes and turned toward Karrie.

"Mom, can I have a popsicle?"

"Sure, peanut. Take the whole bag upstairs so everyone can have some, okay?"

Karrie stared at CJ's back as he skipped upstairs. She turned to Rob. He seemed dazed.

"Rob, are you all right?"

He nodded without speaking. Karrie patted him on the shoulder. "C'mon. Let's head back up."

Karrie jogged up the stairs. She smiled at CJ and Carl as they each popped a finger in their mouths.

"Hey, save some for us!"

As Rob stepped up into the living room, he pulled a .45 Kimber custom automatic from a holster at the small of his back. He raised it and pointed it at the three of them.

Karrie, Carl, and CJ stopped eating the frozen 'treats' as he entered and stared at the weapon Rob pointed at them. Carl raised his hands.

"Whoa there, Rob. What's going on?"

"How could you?" Rob shouted. "How could you kill people and eat them? Survival? Because, let me tell you, that is not surviving. That's murder!"

"It's not murder if they're already dead."

Rob blinked. "What?"

"We didn't kill any living people, Rob," Karrie spoke as she stood. "Those bodies in the freezer are zombies."

"You mean we ate," Rob paused to swallow. "Zombie roast for dinner?"

"Uh huh," Karrie nodded. "It's only fair, don't you think? They eat us so we should return the favor."

"But--"

"Look, Rob," Carl said. "I know it sounds odd and a little immoral. But when the animal food source depleted a few months ago, we thought it was the end for us. We even had a final plan, you know?"

Rob looked over at Karrie as she wrapped her arms around CJ. He looked down at the gun in his hand and tucked it back into the holster as if ashamed for pointing it at them.

Carl continued. "One day I went out to check one of the traps I'd laid a while ago, just one last hope there'd be an animal in it. What I found was, to say the least, unexpected."

"A zombie?" Rob asked.

"Yep. It was a simple snare trap. A rabbit probably could have wiggled its way out. But you know zombies. They can't pick their noses let alone slip a loop of rope off their feet. Well, I couldn't very well let it live but after I killed it, I had a flash. Sure it was a little rotten, kinda gamey. And a person. But maybe it could sustain us a little while, maybe until I could think up something better. So I brought it home and after a short screaming match with Karrie," he nodded in her direction. "We ended up eating the best meal we'd had in months."

"But the infection," Rob started.

Karrie shrugged. "We worried about that, too. We're not sure why we haven't changed. Maybe freezing the flesh, and cooking it, kills whatever causes the reanimation."

Rob sank onto the sofa, seemingly incredulous of their story. CJ broke free from Karrie's embrace and sat on the couch next to him. He put a hand on the man's shoulder as if to console him.

"It's okay, Rob," CJ said. "We all thought it was really gross at first, too. But at least they're not people anymore. And we get to keep living. It's a win-win for everybody."

Rob nodded but his face seemed to darken with dismay. "This hell is never going to end, is it?"

CJ tugged at his sleeve. "Would it make you feel better to play some catch in the backyard?"

Karrie stared at her son. The boy's eyes were bright with what appeared to be the pure hopefulness of youth. Rob laughed and ruffled the kid's hair.

"Is it safe?"

"Oh, yeah. You should see the wall my folks built. Nothing is gettin' in here. It's like the great big wall of China!"

After spending the afternoon and evening together, Karrie and Carl waved to Rob as he returned home. She felt a new sense of hope lighten her heart. She prayed it would carry them all long enough to see an end to this undead plague.

Several months later, Rob accompanied Carl and CJ on their weekly trap check. He'd been helping them with their catches ever since he had reconnected with them. It was amazing to him how easy it was to trap the zombies. And if by some stroke of luck one managed to escape, they were easy to hunt down.

Carl pointed to the left of the trail they walked.

"I've got a trap in there. Will you go with CJ to check it while I head up the path a little further?"

"Sure thing," Rob replied. "C'mon, CJ. Last one there's a rotten zombie."

Rob pretended to trip so CJ could sprint ahead. He bolted forward, yelling back at Rob about being lame and old. As Rob straightened, he watched CJ turn to face him. The boy pointed and laughed as he walked backwards towards the trap. When CJ started jumping up and down, claiming first place in the world of coolness, Rob saw a hulking rotten zombie shuffle up behind the boy. Most of its flesh was sliding off in chunks of green slime and he could smell its fetid stench from here.

"CJ! Get out of there!" Rob yelled out.

CJ turned then ran into the zombie. He bounced back and fell to the ground. Screaming, CJ fumbled for his hunting

130

knife. Rob lurched forward, pulling his own knife from an ankle sheath. He couldn't risk using his gun and accidentally shooting the boy.

He ran towards CJ, holding his knife high. He thought he heard someone crash through the bushes behind him but didn't have time to worry if it was another roaming zombie or just Carl. When Rob reached CJ, he leaped forward and plunged the knife into the zombie's shoulder. CJ used that time to scuttle away to safety. From the corner of his eye Rob saw Carl scoop up his son just as Rob and the zombie fell together to the ground.

The zombie growled and clamped its teeth onto Rob's neck. He howled in pain but managed to push the creature off him. As it lay on its back, Rob pulled out a gun from his leg holster. He raised it just as the zombie sat up. Pressing it to the creature's temple, Rob pulled the trigger.

With the zombie now part of the laying dead, Rob shrugged off his jacket and pressed it against the wound at his neck. Rivulets of blood ran down the front of his blue shirt, staining it with lines of purple. No matter how much pressure he applied against the bite, he couldn't stop the bleeding. He looked at Carl and Rob's heart filled with regret. But he also felt his muscles relax with a calm acceptance.

"Is CJ okay?"

Carl nodded and hugged the boy close. "I'm so sorry, Rob."

"It's all right. I'm not scared. I'll finally get to be with Annie again."

Rob coughed into his hand. He pulled it away and squinted at the bright glistening blood. He wiped it on his pants and motioned to his friend.

"Carl, I need to tell you something."

He coughed again and Carl kept his distance until he finished. Once Rob quieted down, Carl told CJ to stay put. He walked over to Rob and knelt beside him.

"What is it?"

"It's a request, actually. Something I want you to do. Something I need you to do."

Later that evening, Karrie, Carl, and CJ conducted a small funeral. CJ wrote Rob's and Annie's names on a small plaque and hung it in the backyard. The three of them held a barbeque in their friends' memories. As Carl watched the sunset, Karrie turned to watch CJ as he ran out into the yard carrying a plastic bag, filled with ten fingers and ten toes, marked 'Mr. Daniels'. She smiled as he approached.

"Mom, can I have a robsicle?"

"Of course, peanut."

Beyond Dead

By Mary Makrias

Everything changed in the twinkling of an eye. I went to bed a twenty-five-year-old vegetarian with a bit of latent telekinetic abilities and woke up dead. Okay, so it doesn't make sense, but it is true, nonetheless. I never really understood telekinesis. Of course I knew about it from college studies, but I didn't truly believe until I died. There were a lot of things I didn't believe in when I was alive, a lot of things I didn't even know about.

I guess it's not really fair to start in the middle of the story. I'll tell you everything I can, though I have to warn you, it's not pretty. Some of it is simply conjecture since I don't really know what happened. All I can tell you is what I know, what I experienced and what I remember. Whether or not you believe is entirely up to you. So, as I said, I woke up dead. It took me a while to figure it out. My alarm went off and the snooze button wasn't working. I couldn't activate the snooze function, which meant I wouldn't have my extra ten minutes. So, I got out of bed, went into the bathroom and tried to turn on the light. My fingers slid through the light switch. Perplexed, I tried it again only to experience the same results. That's when I figured something was wrong. I walked out of the bathroom and back to the bed. I surmised that I was still asleep, maybe even sleepwalking. Then I saw my body still in bed and thought I had to be dreaming. It's hard to explain how creepy it was looking at my body. I lay down in an attempt to reconnect my consciousness to my body and it worked, well, sort of. I mean, I could feel the sheet against my flesh, but I couldn't control anything. All I felt was this intense craving, a craving for human flesh.

Suddenly, my eyes popped open and I stood up. Step by step in an almost mechanical rhythm, I was walking. My stupid body didn't even stop to put on make up or wash my face! My physical appearance meant a lot to me and it took work to look this good. I was five-foot seven-inches tall, with long blond hair and a body that most women would kill for. I didn't even mind the Barbie nickname I had since high school. After all, she was a knock out for a doll. Plus, Barbie gets perks. That's how I ended up on this yacht, the SS 4-Ever Young, for a weekend getaway on Lake Superior.

I was from the Michigan Upper Peninsula, or the UP as it is referred to by the locals. There were two reasons you lived in the UP - either you were born there or you had a lot of money and craved seclusion with beautiful surroundings. I was born there. Robert, our host for the weekend, fell into the second group. He was there doing research, trying to find a cure for aging or something. Frankly, there wasn't a lot to do in our small town, so when the opportunity to go on a weekend sail came up, I jumped at the chance. I should have stayed home.

My body walked through the door and out of my stateroom. I literally ran into Troy, the first mate. He had only been married about two years and his wife was expecting their first child. She was due to deliver in three weeks. My body didn't care. He was alive and I smelled his blood. I heard his pulse running through his veins. It called to me. I no longer had control. I grabbed his head and bit at the soft flesh of his throat. I crunched into his Adam's apple. Blood gushed out as I saw myself rip out his flesh and dine on him. Eww. I screamed from inside my body, "Stop it! You're a vegetarian! You don't eat meat!" My body wasn't listening. It was just eating. Troy wasn't a big man, but he had muscles, lots of muscles, yummy muscles. Overpowering him took strength. Where it came from I have no idea. Barbie isn't known as being strong, but I sure was.

Blood was smeared all over my face, my throat, even my favorite pajamas! This was so not fun. I didn't like being in my body anymore. It was functioning strictly by instinct now and was drawn forward by the sweet smell of blood. I didn't like being dead. Something was really wrong. My consciousness, my spirit left the carcass that I once thought was me. Where was the White Light? Where was the peace? There was nothing I could do but try to stop this madness. I followed my body. When I was separated from it, I didn't feel the blood hunger; didn't have to fight for sanity. Still, watching yourself go on a killing rampage wasn't nice.

There were four crewmen, Robert, our host and captain, Steve, Owen, Mya, and me. Steve, Owen, Mya and I all knew each other from school. We had grown up together. Steve's claim to fame was that he excelled in athletics and was ever so easy on the eyes. I think the term "eye candy" must have originated with him. No one should be so good looking, except of course Barbie and me. Owen was smart. Everyone knew that one day he would change the world. His specialty was math - ugh - but he could apply it to so many things. Mya was musical. When she sang everyone around her stopped to listen. She could play just about any instrument she chose. At first glance, Owen and Mya were like math and music, they just don't seem to go together. But music is math in a raw form. For Owen and Mya, it worked.

I got up on deck and saw Mya and Owen huddled under a lifeboat. Steve was gorging himself on one of the crewmen. That left one other crewman and Robert. Where was Robert? I hovered above Mya and Owen. To avoid drawing attention to themselves, they were whispering. Is it eavesdropping if you are dead? I don't think so, and even if it is, I didn't care.

"What is going on?" Mya asked.

"I don't know," Owen replied. "But it has to be connected to Robert's research. Last night before dinner I saw him adding something to the red wine, the wine that Sarah and Steve drank. At the time, I wasn't sure what I was seeing. He has been so hospitable; I didn't have any reason to think he was up to anything sinister, and he didn't hesitate. Plus, they were looking a little green; I chalked it up to a little seasickness."

"Where is Sarah?"

"I wish I knew." Owen got a faraway look in his eyes as he stared off into nothing. "I'm right here!" I screamed, but they couldn't hear me. Frustrated, I slammed my ethereal hand into the side of the lifeboat. To my surprise, it made a noise. Mya and Owen jumped so they must have heard it too! I thought back to everything I had ever seen or heard that might explain how this could happen. That's when I remembered telekinesis. I thought back to those few times when things moved for no apparent reason. It didn't happen frequently, but it always scared me. Not this time. Now I put it all together, the college courses, the horror movies, the bizarre events. I had telekinetic abilities. The skill was virtually untapped when I was alive, which is why I referred to my abilities as latent. The telekinesis was hidden, but it was still there. Somehow, it was stronger now, easier to tap into. I may be dead, but I could still move things! How cool was that?

The first mate came up the stairs and he looked as dead as me. He wasn't Troy anymore. He had that same mechanical, empty shell on a quest for flesh attitude that my body had when I awoke. If I had a stomach, I'd throw up. Now the crewman that Steve was eating - did I just say that? - joined the band of murderers in search of food. They were heading right toward Mya and Owen. They must have heard the sound of my fist slamming into the side of the lifeboat too.

"Get out! Run, hide, do something!" I screamed. "Please don't make me watch you get eaten! Doesn't anyone remember that I can't stand blood - it's why I became a vegetarian for goodness sake!" But they couldn't hear me. Where was Robert? Why wasn't he doing anything? Mya and Owen ran down below deck toward the galley. The zombies and I followed them. Owen found the gun that Robert predictably kept in the cookie jar and started shooting.

"Yeah!" I cheered. "Kill these flesh eaters, Owen." The first one, Troy, took a bullet right in the chest. It knocked him down, but then he got right back up. Bullets don't kill zombies. I guess I didn't really know a lot about the undead. Then again, I never expected to meet one let alone be one. Mya grabbed a sword that was mounted on the wall and swung at Steve, tears flowing down her face. She loved Steve when he was alive. Not romantically, but it was love nonetheless. Now that he was dead and trying to eat her, she must have been second guessing her emotions. Funny how seeing someone with flesh caught between his teeth and blood smeared across his face will change how you feel about him. Just before her sword connected with his throat to sever his head, she hesitated. Steve grabbed her arm and started eating, a vacant look on his face. Mya screamed. I screamed. Owen shot. Steve fell down dead again and Mya didn't hesitate this time when she cut off his head.

I couldn't watch anymore. People were dying and then eating each other. It just didn't work for me. I went in search of Robert. Surely he must be doing something. I found his quarters and went through the closed door. Being able to walk through doors was pretty cool. I told you being Barbie gave me perks! Then again, it probably had nothing to do with being pretty and more to do with being dead. Once inside Robert's quarters, I looked around. He had monitors everywhere and a laptop computer. Robert was sitting at a desk and typing away.

Robert was a good looking man with sandy blond hair and blue eyes. I looked around his room and saw all of the pill bottles. He was on a lot of medication. There were two pictures on the nightstand. In one, he and his wife were on a rock climbing expedition. In the other she was in a hospital bed. She was not aging well. I decided I didn't have time to look at the family photos and focused again on Robert. There were papers spread out on the bed, they seemed to be about a disease called Progeria. The disease causes rapid aging in children, who age about eight times faster than normal. I scanned the pages and realized the woman in the hospital bed that I thought was his wife was actually his daughter. That must be so hard on a parent - watching a child die slowly from a disease he didn't understand and couldn't stop. As fascinating as it was, I had no time to read. My friends were being slaughtered.

The keyboard tapping behind me brought me back to the stateroom. I realized that he must have been more focused on what he was typing and not paying attention to the monitors that gave him a bird's eye view of the massacre that was going on. Peeking over his shoulder, I read what he was writing:

"Captain's log, July 18.

"The experiment was unsuccessful. Subjects S & S altered genetically. Not dead, but not alive either. The crew is falling. In addition to myself, one crewman and subjects M & O remain untouched by the virus. It seems to spread by saliva or ingesting the blood of an infected person. Modifications to the virus required. I have isolated myself in the steel-lined stateroom. The antivirus given to subjects M & O untested. However, it is only a matter of time before they are infected and results can be documented. Antivirus created as a safeguard, in the event of negative reactions or side effects. I thought I had all possible contingencies covered. I did not foresee this scenario."

That pig! We were test subjects, nothing more than lab rats. What was he trying to do? Surely he knew this was illegal, which meant he just didn't care. He must have been searching for a cure for Progeria. Though I could understand his motive, and his need for speed, this was wrong. You can't experiment on people like this! There are laws and the laws need to be obeyed. He needed to pay for this heinous violation. I put my phantom fingers over the keyboard and focused. Then I began to type. I only hoped it would work. I typed: "You will die for this," over and over again. To my surprise, the words I typed popped up on the screen in front of me. This is when I figured out another aspect of the telekinesis thing. I could use electronics! Robert looked at the screen and turned white. I was freaking him out. This was good. Take that, dude! My view shifted to one of the monitors and I saw Owen and Mya surrounded by zombies, my body included. Though, if it worked, the serum might stop them from becoming zombies, it couldn't stop them from being food. I don't think you recovered from being eaten.

These were my friends. I had to do something. I went to the galley area and looked around. There was a kerosene lamp on the counter. It took me a couple of tries, but I managed to knock it over. Lighting it was harder. I could hear the attack going on behind me. Mya and Owen were in trouble, big trouble. Cutting off a head wasn't easy, even if it was the head of a zombie. I found a lighter and lit the kerosene. The fire spread. Mya and Owen ran up to the deck and toward the lifeboat. The zombies were slower, much slower. Zombies don't run. Owen figured out how to work the lifeboat controls, they got in and lowered themselves to safety.

With my friends taken care of, the only thing left to see to was Robert. The fire would take care of him and, unfortunately, all evidence of his heinous acts as well. For all of his planning, he didn't prepare for fire. Obviously, most of the boat was made of wood but there was still the steel-lined stateroom, and steel sinks. As the rest of the boat went up in flames, I had no doubt he would go down too. He must have noticed the shortcoming in his plan because he was now on deck yelling at Owen and Mya to come back for him. I hoped they wouldn't, but feared they might. They didn't know he had caused this.

As much as I enjoyed watching Robert as he began to realize the severity of his predicament, I deserted him and went in search of my body. I didn't have to look far. It was walking toward Robert along with the other zombies. Finding the sword Mya had dropped earlier, I focused my attention on one task. I had no idea if it would work, but I had to try. Using all of my concentration, I managed to lift the sword telekinetically and swing. My head fell and rolled toward the fire as my body collapsed. Barbie was no more. Robert would be eaten and then burned. I didn't think Owen and Mya would risk coming back for any thing or any one. Robert was oblivious to the walking dead reaching out for him.

Out of the corner of my eye I saw the White Light. I wasn't quite ready for it yet. I went back to Robert's quarters and typed my story, the story you are now reading. Only one thing left to do, upload my story to the internet. I hope that someone will see it and rescue Mya and Owen. Once I hit enter, my work here will be done. Then, I'm going to go to the Light. I hope that wherever I end up, they don't eat meat and they don't bleed. Who would have ever thought that Barbie would save civilization as we know it? Go figure.

Brains

By Michael Cieslak

The frontal lobe, the temporal lobe, and the parietal lobe are all part of what physical structure?"

"Brains."

"Very good. Can anyone tell me what an EEG takes pictures of?"

"Brains."

"Correct. Neurons and glial cells are found where in the human body?"

"Brains."

"Excellent. What is the largest organ in the human body?"

"Brains."

Mr. Feldstein shook his head.

"No, I am sorry. The correct answer is skin."

Feldstein looked out over the class. Their milk white eyes stared back at him. Their grayish flesh was beginning to putrefy. Some areas, especially around the restraints, were decaying to a black liquid. That might become a problem.

The smell was definitely a problem. He sprayed the air around his desk with a liberal dose of disinfectant.

Yes, the smell and the rot were problems. Of course, he could not get too close to them, either. Tommy Comstock had tried to take a bite out of him just the other morning. He always had been a trouble maker.

Still, three out of four answers correct. His students were better as zombies than they had ever been when they were still alive.

Now if he could only get them to raise their hands.

.75"

ERIE TALES
ZOMBIE CHRONICLES

Made In

By MontiLee Stormer

*T*HE *DAWN BREAKS so fast. I need more time.*
Rena ran her hand across the wind chimes, smiling
at the random thought. She browsed in the head
shop that doubled as a trader of world market goods designed
to make the average consumer care for two minutes about
indigent Balinese women suffering from dysentery while they
hand-painted wooden beaded curtains for room dividers. She
thought again, I need more time and stopped cold. She
checked her watch. She was forgetting something. Something
pressing and important.

One o'clock. Plenty of time to look around, maybe sample
some exotic chips and salsa on the other side of the store.
There was a pungent smell like tortillas and seasoned rice
overlaying the scent of wood and pillar candles and she
figured there must be freebies to munch on. As soon as she
made a decision on some chimes, she would wander over to
grab a bite, and there was one more errand she needed to run.
She'd meant to make a list before she'd left the house. There
was always something Rena was forgetting.

She gave a sigh, inward and heavy. Everything looked so
familiar she figured she'd been through this store twice,
holding these same wooden wind chimes. The wind chimes
she considered purchasing were missing a bell on the end, or
what would probably be a clapper and one of the – arms,
chimney things whatever– was broken into jagged point. The
string holding it all together looked flimsy and there was a
film of dust or grime covering it from top to bottom that
brought an unconscious grimace to her face, but she was
falling in love with it nonetheless. She would see if perhaps

there was a discount for broken or damaged merchandise but no matter what it was going home with her.

A loaf of bread, a container of milk, and a stick of butter. Rena was all about the random thoughts this morning. She remembered that from her days of watching Sesame Street as a child. All about the random. Her mind was refusing to focus this afternoon and it was getting later by the moment.

Okay, she needed to concentrate on the task at hand. Grab the chimes and do the thing she knew she needed to do before she got distracted by the chimes and the smells. Somewhere in the store a child was crying, a muffled, mournful sound as if troubled by baby fears in sleep. The chimes in her hands tinkled as she walked through the store and the child quieted. If she came across the mother, she might convince her to buy a set, if there was a set that wasn't broken, that was.

The dawn breaks so fast.

Now three-thirty. Her decision, or lack of, would end up being her downfall, she just knew it. That she could stand in one spot trying to make up mind about things like groceries or tires was a mystery to most people, but it was just the way her mind worked: all random thoughts and indecision.

Her stomach rumbled slightly and she really needed to drag herself to the front. The chimes in her hands were bamboo, or what looked like bamboo, could have been particleboard for all she knew. The tag on it said Made in Indonesia and the bamboo was smooth and weathered. Rena held it up and listened to the hollow noises the sticks made when they gently rattled together. The rocking chair nearby was nice too and when she sat down, it was comfortable, the rails conforming to her back like they were made for her.

The bowl on the counter was painted red and green and felt polished to within an inch of its life. It caught the light in weird refractions and looked bigger on the inside, expansive.

There was no real decision to make. Rena hadn't let go of the chimes since she walked in, practically drawn to them. If she would just make her way to the cashier, she could leave.

Five o'clock, and the baby began to cry. Rena shook her hand and the chimes made hollow tones. The baby quieted. There was always a baby nearby. Babies in headshops and second-hand stores were as common as the smell of fried rice these days. The store was cramped and it gave the illusion of being much smaller than it actually was. The fabrics were colorful and stiff and more than a little worn. The knickknacks were chipped, most items seemed broken or missing pieces, and there was a smell underneath the tortillas and rice like bloated wood and wet carpet. End tables were patched with brown tape; a bed frame was missing a knob. The more she looked around, the more the little store was losing its charm. Even the air felt second hand and used.

And smelled. It smelled like meat and blood, so very faint beneath the pervasive scent of fried rice and strong coffee. Little icy fangs of fear began to gnaw at the edges of her shopping euphoria. She knew that smell and she needed to get out.

She stood before the automatic doors and waited for them to slide open. Nothing. She ran her hands in front of the electric eye, slightly pushing on the doors, but there was no give. They wouldn't open. Someone turned out the lights and the store became the dark night just before the dawn, the last possible moments for evening tide to do its worst. "Hello," she called out. The baby began to cry again. She heard a woman's mother's voice calming the child in Spanish, tinny, soothing tones from something electronic and close.

She followed the tinny sound and more hurried voices in Spanish to a point not far from the doors that refused to open. Her preferred language in high school was French, but these words she seemed to already know.

¿Usted tiene la cámara fotográfica?
Do you have the camera?

On the table with a tag that said Made in New Brunswick was an Intercom and she picked it up, pressing the buttons, all of them. "Hello – who's there please? We're trapped. Can you send someone to open the door? There's a baby with me."

Now real alarm in the answering voices "Hurry," she said again, her voice dropping to the whisper of desperate resignation. "Please, the dawn." Thoughts in the back of her mind began to break the surface of her conscious like rays of light through a dirty window. It was too late. She'd missed her chance.

Five forty-seven by her watch. She wasn't going to make it.

Above her a light went on, not the fluorescents or recessed lighting of boho stores and second hand treasure attics. It was dim and gray and bare, a simple overhead light missing the decorative cover. Rena felt despair. In the growing light from the window, she could see not the automatic doors of a store, but a bedroom door barely cracked to allow a hand to slip through to flip the bare, dirty switch. All around her were sticks of broken-down second hand furniture, an end table, a rocking chair, a crib. The baby inside looked up at her and cooed, his pudgy arms reaching up to her. His fingers - she was sure the baby was a he as sure as she knew she'd blown another night, another chance to escape - brushed the bottom of the windchimes above his crib and she shivered.

The dawn took on a more golden hue, solidifying, canceling out the impersonal incandescent above. She brushed her fingers through the chimes and they gave a hollow clacking. The baby cooed again. The forgetting was over because the dawn always brought the truth. These chimes weren't made in Indonesia but Indiana where the man took her body, cut it into pieces with saws and lathes, and made things with the parts. Brown Wicker, not New Brunswick, was the name of the second hand shop that received the delivery of furniture with no return address: – the rocking chair from her ribs and femurs, the bowl from her skull, the painted lampshade of stretched skin. It must have been a deal for this family, as they'd purchased every single piece. An entire bedroom set made from her bones. 100% Authentic Rena. What they weren't counting on was that the unmentioned extended warranty came with the former owner of those bones, lingering, fawning over the merchandise, all because she couldn't remember to simply walk out. She needed to learn to trust her initial instinct, even now in this strange limbo of ethereal reality like she should have trusted the warning bells in her head when she'd met the man with the sharp knives who smelled like meat and blood and madness.

The bedroom door opened fully and mother and father stood in the opening, digital camera held by one, a drug store point and shoot by the other. Above the door a small round camera as if for a laptop or computer was mounted, pointed towards the crib. Watching. Probably for whatever rattled the chimes and disturbed the baby.

She knew the look of concerned parents when she saw it, as she knew the baby was a he, as she knew she was - what – bound, tethered to this furniture. There was a flash of light followed by two more, and they stood with wide eyes, seeing her stand over their baby but almost not, the dawn's light getting stronger and her form growing dimmer and less corporeal. Staring at her. *The dawn breaks so fast,* she said with words that sounded like the breeze through chimes of bone connected by intricately braided strands of her hair. I need more time. She spoke to them in tones only the baby could hear and he giggled.

She could leave this place if she could remember, if only she'd stop lingering over the merchandise.

EERIE TALES

Saturday Evening Ghost

EDITED BY:

BOB STRAUSS

Reflections

By Mary Makrias

JENNY'S TWENTY-FIRST birthday was bittersweet. Her friends wanted to give her a party, and though she enjoyed parties, she didn't much feel like celebrating. She looked at herself in the mirror and saw Julie, her twin sister, looking back at her. Eleven years ago to the day, Julie drowned.

Jenny and Julie had been playing with their Barbie Dolls in the back yard of their suburban Detroit home. Their house on the lake was beautiful. The twins were trying really hard to stay clean. It was their tenth birthday and their mother was baking a cake. Jenny and Julie loved the cakes their mother made them. Many of their friends wanted the store-bought cakes, but the twins chose homemade every time. Like most ten-year-olds, they were impatient. They couldn't open their gifts until their father came home and the girls had been sung the Happy Birthday song. It was tradition.

Julie's hat blew off and rode the wind to the edge of the pier. The girls knew better than to play near the water. The house rule was they couldn't go any closer than the swing set unless at least one of their parents was with them. Rules were important to Jenny but Julie was more afraid of getting in trouble for losing her hat. Besides, the twins always wore matching outfits on their birthday. It wouldn't be right if she didn't have her hat, they wouldn't be the same. Jenny yelled for her not to go near the water, but Julie just turned and smiled. The pink ribbon on her hat caught on the post at the end of the pier. Julie didn't hesitate as she ran to retrieve her hat. She didn't think about the rules or the danger. She just wanted to get her hat and then go back to playing with her sister until it was time to eat cake. She didn't make it. A strong wind blew just as her foot hit a slick, wet board. Her momentum was broke and Julie lost her balance. She hit her head on a post and tumbled into the water unconscious. Jenny ran to the house to get her mother, but she was too late. By the time they got to the dock, all that remained of her sister's presence was a pink ribbon floating on the wind.

Growing up near the water, the girls could swim practically before they could walk, but skill isn't always enough. Even experienced swimmers can have accidents. All the time spent in the water hadn't helped Julie. The doctors said she didn't have a chance. Jenny knew better. *It was my fault. If I had only run to the edge of the dock instead of going inside to get Mommy, I could have saved her,* she thought.

"You could have, but you didn't," snarled her reflection.

"That's not fair, Jules! I ran in the house and grabbed Mom. If I had been bigger or stronger, I would have made her go to the water, I would have made her listen. She just wouldn't get off the phone, wouldn't pay attention to me. Besides, I was only ten."

"Still, I'm the one who's dead."

Jenny remembered what her doctor told her to do when she heard Julie's voice. She spoke back to her reflection, "You're not here Jules; you're dead! You're not real; you're a hallucination, a piece of undigested food." She closed her eyes and counted to ten. When she opened them, it was her own reflection looked back at her from the mirror. Julie was gone for now. Jenny had a party to prepare for; after all, she was the guest of honor.

Jenny knew that Julie could always find her through the mirrors. She never knew when her sister would make an appearance. But it was curious how Julie's reflection seemed to age along with Jenny. It might have been because they were twins; it might have just been a quirk of the spirit. Jenny liked to think her sister was living through her.

The party was a simple gathering of close friends. Mary and Matthew, Theresa and Andy, Jimi, Becky and Lori would all be there. These were the friends that had survived the best and worst life had tossed them and managed to come out closer every time. They had been together since high school, knew the dirty little secrets and loved each other anyway. God willing, these were the friends she would have for the rest of her life. *Maybe tonight won't be that bad,* she thought. They were going to go to Greek Town in Detroit for dinner and maybe a play. Perhaps they would do a bit of gambling at the Greektown Casino if they felt lucky. She only played the penny and quarter slots, but Jimi was a Black Jack guru and Lori ruled on Roulette. Truth was, she didn't know what the plan for tonight included.

Trying to get into a good mood, Jenny tuned her radio to a classic rock station; Cheap Trick's *"I Want You To Want Me"* was playing in the background. She remembered how much fun she and her sister had rockin' out to the oldies with their mother. Julie was more outgoing often using their mother's wooden spoon as a microphone, whereas Jenny was introverted and often felt invisible. Still, those were good times. The music helped lift Jenny's mood while she dressed for the evening. The knock at the door startled her.

"Jenny! C'mon birthday girl, time to celebrate," said Theresa.

Jenny took one final look in the mirror. She always felt Julie was prettier. They were identical twins, but Jenny couldn't see her own beauty. When she saw herself in the mirror, her long auburn hair looked like straw, whereas she remembered Julie's as being soft and silky. She focused on things that others didn't see, such as the dark circles under her eyes, or nonexistent enlarged pores and acne scars. Even though she wouldn't see it, Jenny was very pretty, every bit as attractive as she imagined Julie would be; she just refused to accept it about herself. Always quick to see the beauty and goodness in others, she was blind to it in herself.

"Happy birthday Jules," she whispered into the mirror. "I miss you." She didn't notice that, as she turned to answer the door, her reflection didn't imitate her actions but instead hesitated.

Julie's face lingered just long enough to say, "Happy birthday Jen," before vanishing.

"Hey Girl! Are you ready to par-tay?" Theresa's exuberance was radiating.

"You bet," replied Jenny, a little half-heartedly.

"Liar. But that's okay. I know this is a hard day for you, only do me a favor and please try to be open to being young, being legal and being with friends. You're the last of us to turn twenty-one, this is a big day!"

"I'll give it my best," Jenny said. She put on her infamous fake smile and grabbed her purse as they walked out the door.

Mary and Matthew were in his SUV waiting for them. Jenny and Theresa climbed into the back seat. "Where's Andy?" Jenny inquired.

"He's going to meet us there along with the rest of the gang. I wanted to make the grand entrance with the guest of honor."

"Of course you did," Jenny smiled. "Couldn't have me make my entrance alone now could we?" Theresa and Andy had been together since Prom. Mary and Matthew met more recently, but it seemed to be going well for them. Jenny was happy that at least everyone wouldn't be paired up. Jimi, Lori and Becky would also be unescorted tonight. Ever so briefly she entertained the thought that perhaps tonight, in the company of her friends, it wouldn't hurt her heart so much to be without a date. Perhaps she wouldn't feel left out because, as usual, she didn't have a boyfriend. Perhaps she wouldn't miss Julie quite so much; right, and perhaps pigs would fly.

"Let's get this show on the road!" Matthew declared as they began the long road trip into Detroit. The traffic on I-75 was pretty light and they made good time. It was just after eight o'clock when they pulled into the public parking lot. Matthew paid the attendant and the foursome got out of the SUV and walked to the Parthenon.

Inside, the ambiance was exactly what you would expect in a Grecian restaurant, complete with the shouts of "Opa!" ringing through the air and the Ouzo flowing all around. They were shown to their table. Andy, Lori and Becky were already there. The friends stood and applauded as the birthday girl entered. As they neared the table, Andy got up and kissed Theresa on the cheek and then held the chair out for her. Jenny turned a little green with envy wondering if she would ever know what it felt like to be so in love. After the waiter checked their IDs, he quickly brought shots of Ouzo to kick off the evening. Some people don't care for the licorice-flavored liquor, but it packed quite a punch and she had always wanted to try it. Jenny requested two additional shots, one for Jimi and one for Julie. Julie's would remain untouched, she was the invisible guest. No one at the table besides Jenny ever knew Julie, but they knew about her and they knew what a void her death had left in Jenny's life. They also ordered Saganaki--a salty fried cheese that is laced with alcohol and set on fire immediately before serving--to nibble on while they waited for Jimi. So good, yet so bad. Today wasn't a day to worry about that. After all, everyone knows that calories don't count when it's your birthday.

Jimi arrived about the same time as the drinks. He snuck up on Jenny from behind, put his hands over her eyes and whispered "Guess Who?" as he kissed her on the top of the head.

Sheepishly, she smiled and thought, *What am I, 12?* He started to take the seat next to Jenny, thought better of it and moved to the next one. Julie always sat next to Jenny on their birthday, always. Jenny thought about how lucky she was to have such good friends. She was very thankful they put up with her craziness. *True friends somehow manage to love you warts and all,* she thought and the thought made her smile.

They ordered dinner. Jenny chose the Fisherman's Greek Salad, a traditional Greek salad topped with crab and shrimp. They were all having a good time. Becky had the waiter bring out the cake she brought with her. After the wait staff and friends made Jenny feel like a complete idiot by singing and smashing plates, she opened presents. One final "Opa!" and they were off to the casino. Jenny turned around to make sure they weren't leaving anything behind, glanced at Julie's drink and gasped. Julie's drink was gone. The glass was still there, but it was turned upside down. There wasn't any liquid surrounding it. She grabbed the back of her chair to steady herself. Jimi was quickly by her side. With two fingers, he ever so lightly pushed the strand of hair out of her face. Then he moved his fingers under her chin and lifted her face to look into her eyes.

"Are you okay?" he asked.

"Sure, I'm fine. Must have been the Ouzo," she replied. "Jimi, did you drink Julie's shot?"

"No, why?"

"Someone drank it. It's gone."

"Don't be silly, Jenny. It must have got knocked over and someone stood it up, just upside down."

"Yeah, sure. You're probably right."

"I ask again, are you okay?"

"Absolutely" she stated with more conviction than she felt. "Let's go win some money!"

"That's the spirit," he said as he guided her to the door.

***

The casino was beautiful, full of glitz and glamour. It was part of the allure. It was also the way they got you inside and spending your money. Once inside, Jenny made her way to the ladies' room while the rest of the group scattered to their preferred gaming areas. When she looked into the mirror to check her make-up, her sister was looking back at her.

"Jenny," Julie began, "I miss you so much. Wouldn't it be nice if we could be together again, just once, like old times? This mirror thing is fun, but it simply isn't the same. I can't touch you."

Jenny looked around and, once she was certain she was alone, responded. "Julie, you know I wish you were still here with me. It's like I'm going through life as half a person.

"I can't come back, but if you died, we could be together forever. That wouldn't be so bad, would it?"

"I don't want to die, Jules, but I don't really want to live either. Not like this. I think I'm going crazy."

At that precise moment, a woman walked in on her. She had big hair, all poofed out in the kind of style that was popular back in the eighties. Her clothing was full of sparkle, a lot of sequins and rhinestones. Too many layers of makeup completed the trashy look.

"Honey," she said, "everyone goes crazy here. How much did you lose?"

Jenny was startled at being caught unawares but recovered quickly. "I haven't lost anything yet," she answered.

"Then child, you haven't even begun to enjoy the evening! It isn't fun unless you lose everything or take home a jackpot!"

Jenny couldn't get out of the restroom and away from that woman fast enough. There was something creepy about her, the way she moved so silently, surprising her during one of her private moments then practically vanishing just as quickly. She brushed off the goose pimples, gathered her belongings and left, hoping to leave the bad feelings behind as well. Just outside the door, she ran into Jimi.

"Hey girl, fancy meeting you here," he chimed.

"Jimi! I am so happy to see you." In fact, she was so happy to see him that it gave her pause. For the first time in a long time, she looked at her dear friend, really looked at him. Jimi, who began spelling his name after his idol, Jimi Hendrix, had long, straight blond hair and a slender build. His baby blue eyes were penetrating, giving the impression he was looking right into your soul. His nose was perfect and his dimples were disarming. He was very good looking. *Why haven't I ever noticed how attractive he is?* She wondered momentarily and then took another look at her friend.

"Come on Darlin' let me introduce you to my good friend, "Double Diamond," he said as he guided her to the slot machines. "You like the quarters, right?"

"Right," she smiled.

"Well, today we play the dollar slots!"

They played the machines together, sitting side by side. When they had both dropped down to their last twenty-five dollars, they looked at each other and made a pact. "When it's gone, we quit, not before."

Money doesn't last long on the slot machines. Perhaps Jenny had won a little more often, or maybe she just didn't play as quickly, but she had ten dollars left on her voucher when Jimi was down to his last three. That meant he had one more pull playing all the credits or three smaller pulls. He pulled the lever and they watched as the double diamond fell into the first slot. A few more turns around the cylinder and the second double diamond landed on the pay line. They held their breath and waited. The third double diamond landed and the bells and whistles went wild. It was the sweetest sound Jenny had ever heard. Jimi put his arms around her and pulled her close. Whether it was the liquor, or the excitement of the evening she couldn't say, but she kissed him on the lips. He responded. As the slot machine registered his winnings, their mouths opened and the kiss deepened. It felt so right.

"I think this is going to be a birthday to remember," Jenny whispered between kisses.

"Less talk, more tongue," Jimi replied.

When the machine finally went silent, Jimi had won nearly $25,000 in the progressive jackpot. Jenny squealed in delight as the couple embraced again. The casino floor manager came over, got his social security number (they were required to report larger winnings), and gave him his winnings. The casino had a photographer take his picture as a memento. Jenny saw the eighties fall back woman standing off to the side nodding her head with a knowing smile on her lips. *Creepy*, Jenny thought.

Jimi and Jenny went to find the others and share the good news. They gathered in the bar and had a celebratory drink before deciding to call it a night. As they were leaving, still pumped up from the night's good fortune, Jimi offered to give her a ride home. Since Theresa and Andy were riding together, it made perfect sense. That way, Mary and Matthew could go home without making a detour to drop her off.

Jimi was so full of adrenaline, he couldn't settle down. "Let's go grab a bite to eat before we head out, Jenny."

"I'm still full from dinner," she said. "But, I'll go with if you want to get something."

"Great, 'cause I could use something greasy to help sober me up before we drive home," he admitted.

"Sounds like a date."

"Sounds exactly like a date. I hope there are more in our future," he teased as he put his arm around her. "Besides, I still have another gift for you."

"You've done more than enough. Just being here was enough."

"Yeah, but you see, not all gifts can be returned."

In the car, Jimi gave her a dozen long-stemmed red roses surrounded by white carnations. "I bought these for you on the way over, but I wasn't sure you would accept them. Fact is I was afraid you wouldn't."

"Jimi, they're beautiful, thank you." Jenny hoped she sounded happy, but would settle for sincere. She didn't like flowers. They reminded her of Julie's funeral.

"Jenny, I have wanted to kiss you like that for a long time, but I was afraid that it would ruin our friendship. I've had this fear that if we ever kissed like that, it would end in disaster."

"Now you're just being silly. Something happened tonight, something wonderful."

They drove off to find a greasy spoon. The restaurant was a dive in a strip center, but there were a lot of cars in the parking lot and it looked busy. Busy parking lots at hole-in-the-wall diners were usually a good indication that the food would be good.

Jenny made another quick stop at the ladies room. Once certain she was alone, she looked into the mirror hoping to find her sister's reflection. She was not disappointed. Julie stared back at her and she didn't look happy.

"Jules!" Jenny exclaimed. "Something wonderful has happened."

"Hello Jenny," Julie replied flatly. "How can you just stand there and be all happy with me dead?"

"Why can't you be happy for me?"

"Sometimes I know things; sometimes I catch a glimpse of what might be."

"You sound so weird tonight."

"Sometimes you don't listen."

"What are you talking about?"

"We could be together Jenny."

"I'm finally liking my life and thought you would be happy for me. But you're not, you're just selfish. My world doesn't always have to revolve around you!" Jenny replied as she turned and left.

Jimi ordered fried eggs, bacon, hash brown potatoes, toast and coffee. Jenny had water and decaffeinated coffee. Jimi raved about how good everything was, but then it was understandable since tonight he was the big winner. Tonight he won at Double Diamond and he won the girl who had stolen his heart the first time they met. They talked and laughed and got to know each other in a different way. Both of them thinking how nice it would be if they could be a couple. At the same time, they were each afraid that if it didn't work out they could lose a good friend. By the time Jimi paid the check, they had decided to throw caution to the wind. On the way out of the restaurant, Jenny bumped into the eighties throw back woman from the casino.

As she turned to thank Jimi while he held the restaurant door open for her, Jenny saw Julie. This time she didn't seem ethereal, but rather she appeared solid, flesh and bone. "Jules!" she cried out.

The girl turned around and said "be careful." The air shimmered and things changed.

Suddenly, Jenny wondered how she could ever have been so wrong. Since the time Julie started appearing in mirrors, she had aged right along with Jenny. This woman didn't resemble what Julie would look like in the least. This woman had at least forty pounds and ten years on Jenny, even the color of her hair was wrong. But Jenny had been so certain.

"Jenny, are you alright? What's wrong?" Jimi asked.

"Nothing, I just thought I saw Julie."

"That's impossible, Julie's dead."

"I know," she said. She stopped herself before telling Jimi that Julie had been visiting her in mirrors for years. Maybe it is just because I miss her so much, especially on our birthday."

Jimi closed her door and walked around to his side of the Camaro. Alone in the car, Jenny looked into the side mirror and saw Julie. "Don't be afraid, Jenny. You're not alone in this. Someday we will be together again, forever." For fear of looking like a complete crazy person, Jenny didn't respond.

The red Ford 350 came out of nowhere. In what seemed like a split second, there was a head-on collision; metal hit metal at sixty miles per hour. The force of the impact released the air bags and sent the front of the car to the back. Glass shattered, tires skidded and time stopped. Jimi's Camaro looked like an accordion. The night became silent. The driver of the truck wore a red baseball cap and a plaid flannel shirt. Jenny saw him get out of his truck and look back at the site of the collision, at the pile of metal that had once been his truck, at his dead body; and then he began to walk away. Almost as an afterthought, he turned, met her eyes and said that he was sorry. He was smiling. She blinked and he faded into the shimmering night. It could have been the blood in her eyes, but she thought that she had actually seen his spirit walk into the next life. She turned her head to see if Jimi was hurt. There was so much blood and his head was in an unnatural position. His eyes were open, but empty. Those beautiful eyes that could see her soul were now vacant. He was dead. Now another birthday was tainted by death. Jenny felt cursed. Then she thought she saw Jimi move, but he didn't. What she saw was his spirit leaving his body. She watched him walk toward a shimmering light in the distance. Just like that, he was gone.

She heard the fire before she felt the heat. It crackled as it devoured the leaves on the road, gaining strength before igniting the fuel that was released upon impact. The fuel tank was ruptured. She was going to burn to death. She pleaded for help, but none came. She reached for her cell phone, but was restricted by the mangled car. The dash pinned her legs and the door held her arms in place. She was in so much pain. She searched for something to look at, something to take her mind off the surrounding horror. Her eyes found the bouquet of flowers Jimi had given her but the white carnations were now covered with drops of blood as red as the roses. Then came the darkness.

The darkness was nice. It was peaceful and there was no pain. From some distant place she heard the sirens. Jenny turned and looked at the Camaro. She saw her broken body, contorted and twisted. She saw the fire and her own dead eyes looking back at her. For a brief moment, she wondered if she was dead, then she knew. There was no other explanation.

She saw a brilliant white light and Julie was walking toward her. She looked back at her body again and saw the rescue workers put the fire out and the paramedics pull her from the car. "I got a pulse!" one cried out. Jenny wanted to stay in the silence. She didn't want to survive.

***

When she awoke, she was alone and she was in a hospital. She pressed the call button to summon the nurse. At the nurses' station, Emma was surprised when the call came through. It was always like that when a patient came out of a coma. You don't know when, or even if to expect it. She called for the doctor and hurried to Jenny's room.

"Welcome back," she said with a smile. "You've had a lot of visitors, though this last week, they have called more than visited. You are one lucky young lady."

Jenny tried to talk, but her throat wouldn't cooperate. She used her hands to communicate that she wanted a pen. Emma gave her a pen and a pad of paper she had in the pocket of her uniform. "What happened?" she wrote.

"Oh my, you were in an accident. You've been with us for just about six weeks, don't you know. Now you be still. The doctor will be here in a little bit and he will answer all of your questions." She spoke with the lilt that was more common in Minnesota or Canada than Detroit, but it endeared her to Jenny almost more than the injection for pain she gave her through the I.V. It didn't take long before she was sleeping soundly again. Just before she dozed off, she thought how bizarre it all seemed. She just awoke from a six-week coma only to be drugged back to sleep.

The next time she opened her eyes, the doctor was there. He was explaining to her that she had been badly burned and suffered major injuries. Both of her legs were broken, she had three cracked ribs and suffered a concussion. Repairing her body would require multiple surgeries and there was no guarantee she would ever walk again. As for her appearance, it would take extensive reconstructive surgery to remove the scar tissue and give her back even a semblance of normalcy.

"What about Jimi?" she asked hoping that she was wrong, hoping that he had somehow survived.

"I'm afraid no one else survived the accident," he answered. "You're the lucky one."

Jenny felt the hot tears running down her face, the salt burning her raw skin. She didn't feel lucky. "Mirror?"

"I don't think that is a good idea. At least not yet. You were very badly burned."

"Need to see." Her voice was hoarse, and it hurt tremendously to speak, but she was tired of writing.

The doctor shook his head and walked out of the room. A few moments later, he returned with a small handheld mirror. Keeping it just out of reach, he asked, "Are you sure?"

As a response, Jenny took the mirror but closed her eyes as she mustered up her strength in preparation of what she might see. It wasn't enough. When she saw her reflection, she screamed, in spite of the pain. She had become a monster. There was severe scaring and she could hardly see any trace of the girl she had once been. Doctor Johnson reached for the mirror. "Leave it, please," she begged. Her voice was little more than a whisper.

"No. We need to get you stronger physically before we can make you pretty again. Looking at your reflection won't help you heal." Doctor Johnson left the room with mirror in hand and Jenny stared off into nothing.

Hours passed before she got the courage to assess her surroundings. She needed to see her reflection. Her eyes saw the metal bed tray. She decided to give it a try. Looking into the bed tray, it was Julie she saw. Julie was perfect, free from scars and fully functional. She looked just like she did the night of the accident. The night Jimi died.

"You are messed up, Jen."

"I know."

"You could have died; then we would be together."

"Jules, it isn't my fault that I lived. I would rather be with you, especially now. But what would happen to Mom and Dad? They would be alone."

"Don't you ever think about how hard it has been on them? Every time they see you, the see me and remember. Every time they look at you, they remember the loss of a child. As long as you live, they can't recover."

"No, I don't believe you. The nurse said they came every day, she said that they would be back this evening."

"Think about it, Jenny."

"I don't want to."

"You've been through a lot. Get some rest now."

"I don't want to rest! Why is everyone trying to make me go to sleep?"

"I'll never leave you, Jenny."

"But you're dead."

"Okay, I'm outta here," and just like that Julie was gone and Jenny saw only her own disfigured reflection staring back at her. With what little strength she had, she slammed the compact mirror down and cracked it. Emma must have given it to her, though she couldn't remember when.

After she regained consciousness, Jenny picked up the mirror again. The glass was cracked into eight sections. In each section there was another person's reflection staring back at her. She was seeing ghosts. She realized that from that day forward, when she looked in a mirror, she would never be sure if she would see her reflection or the image of a dead person. She would lose her mind. Jenny let out a frustrated scream.

***

When visiting hours came that evening, her parents were there. Jenny noticed that they had trouble looking at her. She thought about what Julie had said and began to think that her sister was right. She caused her parents pain simply by being alive. It didn't occur to her that perhaps the pain she saw in them had nothing to do with Julie. She couldn't imagine that it was from seeing her so near death. She didn't see the relief in their eyes that she had survived. After they left, the only other visitor she had was someone she didn't really know. It was the creepy eighties woman from the casino. She was even dressed in exactly the same outfit. She had the same big hair, lots of sequins and way too much eye make-up.

"Hello there! My name is Martha."

"What are you doing here?"

"I'm here to help you to the next life."

"Leave me alone. I'm so tired. Besides, I can't go anywhere."

"You must. It is your time."

"What are you talking about?"

"Your sister came to me and told me you wouldn't come. Asked for my help she did, and I am going to give it."

Jenny watched Martha stretch her phantom hand out and slide it into her chest. She felt her heart struggle with the pressure, her chest tighten. Her left arm went numb just before her heart stopped. She heard the beeping of the monitors change into one long piercing note as she flat-lined. She watched her life pass before her eyes and thought about everything that Julie had told her recently. She stopped fighting and gave into the darkness. She was finally dead.

Martha faded into a mist, a knowing smile on her face. "Wait!" Jenny cried, "What do I do now?" But there was one to answer her. Then she saw the white light and Julie walking toward her and knew where she needed to be. The sisters embraced and together they walked into the light. "Jules, where are we going?"

"We're going to the next life and it is wonderful."

"Will I ever see my friends again?"

"The live ones?"

"Yes."

"You can, through the mirrors, if you really want to. Mostly people don't want to come back to what they left behind. There is too much to do, too much to explore and experience over here. Plus if someone on the other side of the mirror catches a glimpse of you it can freak them out. Once people die and cross over like you did, you can see them again. Don't worry Sis, you will see your boyfriend in just a little while," Julie teased, "but I want it to be just us, for now, okay? Let's go play!"

"Okay. I guess I've got a lot to learn."

"Yeah, but you've got a good teacher."

In the mirror, if you had the sight, you could see the spirits of the sisters embrace and fade into the mist hand in hand. They got younger as they skipped away until finally, two ten-year-old little girls turned around and bid farewell to life. They were together again.

The Vessel

By Colleen McEuen

T HE BLIZZARD WREAKED havoc on the small diner in Bay City. As the winter days grew shorter so did my window of opportunity. This was my last chance to seek out that one person for redemption. Finding my way into the warmth of the diner, I smelled the patrons regret. Its salty goodness nestled its way down my throat. The lament they felt tasted sweeter than the day-old pumpkin pie in the display case. My job wasn't an easy task, but it sure was a fun one.

I circled them all until I found just the right appetizer. There was the bedraggled alcoholic at the counter sipping coffee. Though he was sober the distinct taint of whiskey wafted from his dingy coat. Tempting.

The waitress with her black eyeliner smeared over puffy eyes offered to refill his drink. She was sweet and rejected. What was even more tantalizing was her pain. It was recent and clear in her mind. I hovered over her as she made her way to a table full of miscreants. I salivated when I sensed the blood flow between her thighs. This was not Mother Nature's doing.

"So, can I get you all anything else?" She brushed away a stray blonde strand of hair. Then poised a pen over her order pad. Her nametag read 'Bonnie'. She shifted her feet two times while awaiting a response.

"No, just a check please." The young man said. His spiky brown hair withered in the late hour.

"Jeremy," his girlfriend tugged his sleeve, "I want a piece of pie."

Jeremy draped his arm across her shoulders. "You sure?"

165

"Yeah. Besides, I don't want to go out into that storm yet. Maybe after the pie comes it will slow down." She flipped her brown hair and batted her big doe eyes up at him.

"Sure thing, baby." Jeremy turned back to Bonnie. "Can we get one piece of pumpkin pie first?"

"Of course, I'll be right back with your piece." Bonnie twisted her hips, causing the joint to crack, and went to retrieve the dessert. She mumbled under her breath, "When will this night end."

"*Soon my dear. I promise.*" There was a sense of freedom in being able to say whatever I damn well pleased. It wasn't like any of them heard me, unless I wanted them to.

I stayed behind with the lovebirds. Young love was almost as intoxicating as the whiskey on the alcoholic's coat or the blood between Bonnie's legs. There was more to their tale though. Their past spoke to me as if I were there when t heir journey to my dinner party began.

Jeremy stroked her arm. "What do you want to do after this?"

"Could we go back to your place? I really don't want to be home alone." She snuggled into him.

"We can do that. Baby, you shiverin'? It isn't that cold in here."

"I'm not cold. I'm just." She pulled away from him, "I'm just a little scared."

"Elizabeth Adams, what's got you so scared that you shake that hard?"

She stared out away from him, across the table. A glossy expression marred her beautiful face. Our eyes met for an instant. Which was not impossible but improbable. Being nothing more than a spirit has its advantages when eavesdropping on conversations. Nonetheless, she looked right at me.

When she spoke, next her words did not change her expression, only her moved. She was a blank slate, "I've got a funny feeling tonight that I haven't had in awhile. Not since my dad died."

Did my luck change? Had I found what I've been desiring all this time? I leaned across the table. This was my chance, my first contact ripened to perfection. She was open to me. Was Elizabeth the willing vessel that would aid me in my charge? All I needed was that one touch.

"Lizzie," Jeremy turned her away from me. "You don't need to be scared of anything with me here. I've got you. And that was a long time ago. You gotta move on."

She blinked and gave him a half-hearted smile. "You're right. I don't know what I was thinking."

The gateway between us shut. An ache churned my stomach. *"Damn."*

Lights flickered. The bell on the door chimed though no one walked in from the cold. The cook yelled out a string of profanities.

"Sorry about that everybody." Bonnie rounded the corner. "It's just the storm picking up, but we should be okay. I'm heading out back to kick on the generator."

"Miss?" Jeremy called out to her.

"I'll be right back with you pie. It'll be just one minute."

"Thanks, but that isn't what I was going to ask about."

Bonnie shifted her weight to one side, hands on her hips. Her complexion paled. "Yes?"

"Is the cook all right?"

She shifted once again. Her gazes went down and back up. Bonnie's cheeks now had a rosy tint to them. "He's fine. When the power flickered, the burners shut off. Then they flared back up. He got a little toasty, but he's used to that."

"Right. Can't be a fry cook and not be used to getting burned every now and then." His grin didn't reach his eyes.

"Exactly." She gave a light giggle. Then pivoted toward the manager's office.

Within minutes, the hum of the generator as it fired up was heard over the stylings of some random pop song. Bonnie walked in a brisk stride to the counter. She cut a slice of pie. Then served Elizabeth. They exchanged polite words.

Tweets from a bird that popped out of a wall clock reminded me of my limited time. The hour was growing near. I had to make my move now.

I followed Bonnie back to the alcoholic. "Are you sure I can't freshen your drink?"

"I'm fine." He scratched his dirty face. Flakes of skin fell into his cup.

"Bernie, you are in here every night. You sit there staring at the classifieds as if your life depended on it, sippin' on a single cup of coffee until the morning rush. If you want my opinion you need to be home, in bed, so you can get up refreshed."

"Last I checked Bonnie, I didn't ask for your opinion."

"Whatever." She snatched the coffee pot from t he burner. Before he could protest, she poured in the lava hot sludge. "By the way, refills are free."

"Bonnie!"

"Don't give me no lip. You're gonna drink it and be happy with what you've got. Understand." She beamed at him.

"I owe you one."

"You don't owe me a thing." With that, she went back into the kitchen.

One would think that being offered anything for free would have made his day. Instead, his frustration came off him like waves. Though he didn't feel me in physical sense, my presence was felt. As I massaged away the heavy burdens that lay upon him, I whispered. *"You could really use a drink. No one will know. All you need is one little sip to take away the sting."*

His shoulders sighed under my strength. I stabbed a pressure point in his back. Bernie winced. He rubbed his eyes and groaned. "God, I can't. I just can't." Even as he spoke to himself, he reached for the bottle.

He did a once around the room. No one was watching. Bernie poured the amber liquid down his gullet. With a jerk, her twisted the lid back on then thrust the bottle into the pocket hard enough that he could have shoved it through the material. "Three years down the fucking drain. Fuck."

He went back to sipping the coffee as if nothing had happened. His eyes watered. Bernie rubbed his face and brushed the unshed tears aside.

I loved denial. While he wiped away his sorrow, I stepped into him. Every part of me became one with him. All of his memories were mine. I sifted through those hazy regrets from a lifelong addiction to booze. I hungered for the sweet spot. That moment where he lost who he was and how he came to be a cheap suit for an old haunt such as myself.

***

Three years ago, Bernard Langenthal was your average drunk. Tossed out of bars at closing though loved by bartenders from Bay City to Detroit. Back then, he was a car salesman, a thankless job where your customers automatically thought you were out to cheat them. After a hard day's work, Bernie did what Bernie always did. He went to the bar.

"Bernie, sweetie, I've got to close up and you need to get on home. I'm sure that pretty wife of yours is wondering where you are." Sherry, his favorite bartender, said as she escorted him to the door.

"I need ta go home." He slurred. "Do you 'member where I parked my car?"

"Where you always park it. Right next to mine. Walk me out."

They walked, arm in arm, and kept each other from slipping in the snow-covered parking lot. Sherry helped Bernie get into his red pickup truck. "Drive safe, sweetie. I'll see you tomorrow."

"You too." Bernie started his truck. He squinted at the dashboard as he made out the gears. Once he figured out where 'drive' was located, he put the truck into gear and tore out of the parking lot.

"Dang it." He said when he noticed a sign for Midland. He moaned and steered the wheel to make an illegal u-turn. It was then that he saw the headlights coming for him.

The truck fishtailed. Black ice kept his wheels rolling as the brakes locked up. In a moment of clarity, of sudden sobriety, Bernie's truck smashed into Sherry's sedan.

"What have I done?"

The ringing in his ears mingled with the sound of Sherry's blaring horn. He staggered from his truck. "Sherry? Sherry, you okay?"

She was slumped over the steering wheel. Bernie pushed her back against the seat. Blood gushed from a head laceration. She was not breathing.

"Shit." His thoughts raced as he tried to come up with what to do next. Unsure as to what to do he leaned against the car. Through tears of fear, he saw the river that ran beside the highway.

He ran to the river's edge. It was frozen, but not solid. There were plenty of dark patches where the ice was weak. He wiped the adrenaline-inspired perspiration from his upper lip, and knew what he had to do.

***

Bernie finished wiping away his tears and blinked. Sherry stood behind the diner's counter. Her skin has a bluish tint to it. She was bloated ad her tender eyes bulged. She was dressed the same as she had the night Bernie killed her. She slammed her hands on the counter. *"How could you?"*

"Sherry?" He whispered.

She reached over the counter, grabbed the back of his head, and pulled him down onto his steamy coffee mug. The porcelain shattered. Splinters sliced his face. Some got buried in his cheeks. The drink scolded his skin, searing away bits of flesh.

He shrieked. "Help. Oh god."

Bonnie rushed out of the kitchen. When she saw the damage to Bernie's face she said, "On my. Hold on." She ransacked the cupboard under the cash register in search of a first aid kit.

"Did you really think you wouldn't have to pay for what you did to me?" Sherry was inches from his face.

"I'm sorry." He cried.

"You dumped my body in the river, and all you can say is you're sorry. You don't know the meaning of the word because if you did you wouldn't have had that last shot. But you will." Sherry slipped through the counter as if it weren't there. She straddled Bernie's legs. "Eye for an eye." She kissed him.

The steam from the coffee on Bernie's face stopped. The liquid cooled until it froze his skin. The blue tint in Sherry's skin brightened to that of a more normal shade as Bernie's lightened. Under the dirt and the grime, his coloring changed as the hypothermia set in.

"Let me take a look at you." Bonnie said as she came to attend to Bernie's wounds. The first aid kit fell from her hands. Bernie's head dropped backward, lifeless, and frozen.

Unbeknown to anyone in the room, other than myself, Sherry climbed off her murderer. With newfound life in her step she came to my side. *"I couldn't have done this without you."*

"No need to thank me. I'll get my payment."

"Do you really…"

"If you want to know then stick around." I interrupted her.

Sherry stood by my side. Her eagerness radiated off her life a heat wave. Her desire for justice was a charming side dish. The main course lay before me.

I stuck my hand into Bernie's chest. I hungered for his sorrowful soul. It was like mother's milk to me. To my dismay, he was nothing but an empty shell.

The lights flickered. The florescent bulb over the table beside the lovebirds burst. Elizabeth shrieked. She gave into Jeremy's insistent tugs. They ran from the table to the counter in the main hall.

I glared at Sherry. Had she stolen my soul? Was it she I needed to punish? I couldn't finish my mission without feeding. Fulfilling my pledge to the Gatekeeper by aiding vengeful ghosts weakened me. The further back the incident the occurred the harder the memories were to obtain. Thus the more difficult it was to cross ghosts to this side. There was more at stake than petty acts of vengeance.

"What the hell happened?" Jeremy asked Bonnie, who stared at him wide eyed. I asked Sherry the same question.

She shrugged, "Don't look at me. I just killed the bastard. That was it."

Elizabeth stepped away from Jeremy. She inched her way to close to Bernie, closer to me. "What do you think you're doing?"

I jerked my hand from Bernie's empty chest cavity. All I could do was stare at her. This young, naïve woman saw me. She had to have been a clairvoyant of some kind. This newfound knowledge solidified my previous assumption. She was my vessel.

Bonnie walked between us. "I tried to save him. But I was too late."

"Save him from what?" Jeremy asked, "Why the fuck is he blue? Did he just come in from outside? Is the storm that bad?"

Sherry barked out a laugh, "*Are all humans this stupid?*"

"*You were once.*" That got her to shut up.

Elizabeth walked around Bonnie to me. "If you're not human then what are you?"

"Baby, who ya talkin' to?" Jeremy maneuvered to intercept.

"Him." She pointed at me.

"He's dead. We've been through this before. Remember, when you're dad died. You can't talk to dead people."

"Not him." She shoved Jeremy. "Him."

"There's no one else there."

"But,"

"*Boo!*" Sherry jumped at her.

She shrieked.

I backhanded Sherry. She flew into the front door. The glass cracked. Lacking any reason for the door to crack caused all those living in the room to jump. I really hated the living and sometimes the dead pissed me off, too.

"Leave spirit. I'm tired of your games. You achieved what you came for." Lying on the floor, Sherry laughed as she faded across the divide.

"I'm calling the police." Bonnie announced and stormed into the kitchen area. I refused to allow officers in blue to steal my last opportunity. I had strength for one last grab at a soul. Judging the smell of the blood that flowed from her there was a ghost bound to her pain.

Elizabeth cried with her face snuggled into Jeremy's sweater. She mumbled on and on about how impossible this all was. Her sobs quieted. "I want to go home."

"We can't. At least not until the cops get here." Jeremy stroked her back.

Swift as the wind I raced after Bonnie. She ran past the fat cook.

"Hey, what's the problem out there?" He asked.

"Chuck, just give me a minute. I gotta call the cops."

"What?"

She ignored him. I followed her out the back door. The motion sensor light was already on due to the heavy snowfall. The brisk night air hit her hand and fast. She ran her hands up and down her shivering arms. Her breath came out in a fog. After she lit a cigarette there was no telling where the smoke she exhaled ended and her breath began.

Bonnie dug out her cell phone from her back pocket. She trembled as she tried to dial out. On the third attempt, she gave up. She kicked the wall as she flipped the phone close. "I can't do anything right."

She plopped down on the snow mound. Bonnie took another drag from the cigarette. "Come on God, give me a break. I realize he's the one that died, but is all this supposed to be some kind of lesson. Huh, all life is sacred. Is that what you're trying to tell me? You tryin' to prove to me that I made a bad choice? Well, guess what. I already knew that."

Blaming God was always an easy scapegoat. If I had a soul for every time, I heard that one than I supposed I would have completed my mission long ago.

173

Off in the distance church bells rang loud and clear. The reverent sound echoed off the nearby building. Sunrise was fast approaching.

She inhaled again before doubling over. "Fuckin' cramps."

I kneeled in front of her. The pain her body was putting her through generated one lonesome tear. I smeared the salty drop across her cheek. *"You can make it all stop; the pain, the regret, even death itself. Relax."*

She rested back and shut her eyes. I accepted her invitation and merged with her as I had Bernie. Her painful memory was a surface thought, easy to read. Within seconds, I was transported to two weeks ago.

***

"Ms. Kipling, the doctor is ready to see you now." The nurse told her. The technician pushed a wheelchair into the room.

Bonnie lay prone on the examination table dressed in a hospital gown. She sighed and prayed she made the right choice. The technician helped her off the table and into the chair. Her fear must have been written across her face because the nurse said, "Don't worry. This is a quick and painless procedure."

"You're gonna knock me out, right?"

"As you requested." She nodded.

"Good. I don't want any memory of this."

The technician transported Bonnie down a chilly, oxygen-enriched hallway. She yawned long before she reached the operating room. Bonnie tried to put on a brave face when she saw Dr. Tanner waiting for her.

"Good morning Ms. Kipling. How are we going today?"

"As well as can be expected." She shrugged. What was the right answer to that question before this type of procedure?

He nodded with a solemn look in his eyes. Dr. Tanner laid a gentle hand on her shoulder. "Before we go in there I want to ask you one last time if you are sure this is the choice you want to make."

174

"Absolutely." Bonnie confirmed without hesitation. She had spent many sleepless nights pondering over this dilemma. In the end, she had come up with three options. One was obvious, but there was no way she could take care of a baby. She couldn't even take care of herself. The second was to carry the baby to term and give it up for adoption. That plan was snuffed out by her selfish nature. Bonnie knew she would have grown attached to the child in nine months and wouldn't want to give it away. This was the only other choice she was left to pick.

As the icy numbing agent and sleeping gas coursed through her body, she reassured herself that this was the best thing she could do for both the child and herself. No, not a child, she scolded herself. It was an *it*, not a child or a baby. To think any other way was too painful.

An hour later Bonnie woke with a start. She rubbed her abdomen and cried.

***

Bonnie threw her cigarette across the alley. The snowfall slowed. The shadows ate away the light on the ground. A giggle chimed from the darkness.

"Who's there?" Bonnie snapped to her feet. The only response she got was another giggle.

The shadows pooled in the ambiance of the light. It was as if something blocked out the light, but there was nothing in front of the light and nothing above her, only plump clouds. The heart shaped shadow flowed over the snow toward Bonnie.

She backed away from it. With her back to the wall, she attempted to scale the flat surface. The giggle grew louder and more joyful.

I exited her body to enjoy the full effect of the show. I watched with her in astonishment at the creativity of this premature haunt. It bubbled up as if the cells were still formulating what it was meant to become. It spoke to me without words. Since it was unable to communicate, I had to translate.

"No." Her mouth gaped open.

"Yes."

"It can't be."

"You are correct. 'It' cannot be. So what is 'It'?"

"No." She whispered. She shut her eyes and prayed. Then reopened her eyes. She whimpered.

"What is 'It'?"

"It's a baby."

"Whose baby?"

"Mine." She dropped to her knees. Bonnie opened her arms out to the shadowy infant. "I am so sorry baby. Come to mommy."

The infant wobbled a bit, but was a fast learner. The baby took its first step. What was once a baby charged its mother at full speed. The ghost encased its mother in shadow. Then continued on to collide them both against the diner's outer wall. Her skull cracked upon impact.

The child giggled one last time. Then faded through the gate to the other side.

"You are most welcome."

I did not have to search Bonnie's body for her soul. It stood before me. I cocked my head to the side. She was not just a soul, but was now a ghost.

"You right wrongs for ghosts?"

"I facilitate in such matters."

"Then I need your help."

I grew tired of this. I was always the one they came to for aid. I was always the one with the helping hand. Did no one care that I might have needs, too?

"I do not have time to track down the person you hold responsible for your troubles. You made your choice. You got what you deserve." I walked away.

"What if I told you the person I have a problem with is in that diner?"

"Who?"

"Guess."

I rushed upon her with such furious momentum that it made the baby look like a tortoise by comparison. I hauled her into the air by her throat. *"Speak now haunt or I shall hurl you into oblivion myself. Gatekeeper be damned."*

"Jeremy. He was the father." That got my attention. I set her down. *"He refused to help me with the kid."*

"Because of Elizabeth."

"Yeah. He cheated on her with me and when I got pregnant he told me to take care of it."

This worked to my advantage. I would have been a fool if I passed up such an offer as to handle both my vessel and last meal in one shot. I was many things, been called many other things, but a fool I was not.

"Deal." We shook hands. Then together we walked through the wall into the diner. I held Bonnie back in the shadows of a support pillar. We needed to remain undetected by Elizabeth for my plan to work.

She and Jeremy cuddled at their table. It was a disgusting sight. She was half asleep curled in his warmth. Soon it would be my cold touch she felt.

"Ready?" I asked my partner in crime.

"As I'll ever be."

With a flick of my fingers, the lights went out. The white and orange emergency lights went on. The cook cursed in the kitchen. Elizabeth bolted up. Jeremy stood quick as a whip. The bird chime clock tweeted.

"What was that?" Elizabeth asked. She reached for Jeremy.

"Just the clock. Chill. The generator must have blown. I'm going to find Bonnie." Though she pleaded for him to stay at her side, he left Elizabeth all alone.

I whispered into Bonnie's ear, "Don't let him leave the room. I want Elizabeth to hear his crime."

Bonnie circled behind the pillar to cut off Jeremy. Instead of stopping before him, she walked through him. *"Jeremy.'*

He stopped dead in his tracks. A shiver ran through him. A fog of breath escaped between his lips.

"Jeremy, tell her what you did." Bonnie let her words blow across the back of his neck. *"Tell her about me."*

"Bonnie?"

"Did she come back?" Elizabeth crawled out from the booth.

"*Confess.*" Bonnie stepped through him again. Then turned and draped her arms over his shoulders.

"How'd you do that?" Fear muffled Jeremy's speech. It was the sweetest taint of I had tasted in a long time. "We need to get you warmed up."

"*It's amazing the freedom that death brings. You have our child to thank for this by the way. He wanted mommy to pay a price. Frankly, with the way child support is divided up nowadays I figured daddy has to pay up, too.*" She fiddled with the small hairs at the back of his neck. "*But if you confess what you did with me to Elizabeth I think I may actually let you live.*"

Elizabeth walked up to them, tying up the loose end of their haunting love triangle. "Bonnie, you remind me of…" When she stopped, I hoped she had done so to analyze what was before her. She had to figure it out. I wanted her to figure it out. Elizabeth reached out to Bonnie. Her hand went straight through her. "You're a ghost."

"*Brava.*" I clapped my hands once as I stepped out from my hiding place.

"Who the fuck are you?" Jeremy asked over Bonnie's shoulder.

"*I think you have more pressing matters to attend to. I'll just be over here.*" I leaned against the pillar.

Bonnie yanked his attention away from me to her by pulling down his chin. "*Tell her Jeremy.*"

"Tell me what?"

"Uhm, you're dead. I think the present is a bit more important than the past."

"*You think wrong.*" Bonnie punched her fist into his chest. "*Tell her or I squeeze.*"

He screamed. "You're holding my heart."

I held back my laughter. It was quite poetic. I hadn't realized Bonnie was that inventive.

"*I won't ask again.*"

Jeremy's knees buckled. I figured the constricted blood flow to his limbs, particularly his brain, left him with a small window to confess to Elizabeth.

"Stop it. You're killing him." Elizabeth tried to pull Bonnie off Jeremy with no success. She slipped through Bonnie's body as if she were nothing more than a cloud of smoke. Elizabeth fumbled into the wall. "Just tell me what she wants you to say. No secret can be worth your life."

"Fine," he choked out. "I knocked up Bonnie and told her she needed to get an abortion. Satisfied?"

"Not yet." Bonnie applied the last amount of pressure required to crush his heart.

Jeremy's eyes rolled back into his head. He slumped the rest of the way to the floor as Bonnie's hand came free. Much to my surprise, she was not empty handed.

She clenched Jeremy's soul as if she was afraid it would slip away with the slightest of breezes. Finally, a haunt learned how to pay back a promise. *"A deal's a deal."*

"That it is." I took the offered soul. I enveloped him. The process was similar to how I tormented mortals only reversed. He was forced into my essence. I savored the pain he felt for cheating on the woman he loved, the anguish he had for forcing the mother of his child to end the pregnancy, combined with the fear of the last few seconds of his life. The cries of all those before him that I carried within me bellowed into the dining hall, greeting him with their own suffering.

"What are you?" Elizabeth crept along the wall.

"What I am is of no consequence to you." I circled the room as I spoke, *"You see when one does his job right a crack in the world appears. The very fabric of reality splinters and the unusual happens. For some they get the chance to shine brighter than before, prove their worth as it were. Like you, Elizabeth you've proven to be quite more than you first appeared to be. You are a creature of tremendous gifts. However, for beings such as myself, well, the consequences are more tangible. I have a rather gluttonous occupation. And I was famished and exhausted."*

I cut off her means of escape. *"Now I am not hungry any longer. I am full and enriched by every life I have ever touched. There is just one thing I need."*

"What's that?"

"Your light." I slipped into her, not unlike any smitten man, but with my whole body, mind, and soul. Our psyches linked. My memories became her memories. She knew the meaning behind my mission. She accepted me with an open mind, a kind prayer and love.

***

The sun glinted off snow into the front window. Elizabeth woke to a man in a white grease-covered shirt shaking her. "Hey, you okay? With everything that happened last night I was worried you weren't going to wake up."

"I'm fine. You can stop shaking me now."

"Oh, yeah, sorry." He offered her a hand up. "My name's Chuck. Do you have any idea what happened?"

"No." As she stood up the memories came back to her in bits and pieces. "Bonnie and Jeremy are dead."

"Yeah, Bernie too."

"Who's Bernie? Never mind." She rubbed her stomach. She felt nauseous and hungry at the same time.

"Are you going to be okay? The police and paramedics are on the way." Chuck guided Elizabeth to a bench near the front door.

"I'll be fine. It's just that in all the excitement I should have been more careful." She brushed her hair back from her face, leaned back, and closed her eyes. "I'm pregnant."

Chuck took a step back. "Crap, was Jeremy the father?"

"No." She remembered the father of her baby. The mysterious man from her dreams had emerged from shadows and given her the greatest gift of all, his life.

The Stairwell

By Michael Cieslak

I

I WAS SO, so lonely and scared. Perhaps it was selfish of me to have returned, but where else would I go? Where else but this little house on the shore of Lake Huron? This was the only place I had ever known real love. I never meant for anyone to get hurt, at least, not at first.

II

Her screams when she first saw me pierced right through me. Of course, everything goes right through you when you are non-corporeal, but you know what I mean.

I don't know what I expected, but it wasn't screams.

That's a lie. I know exactly what I expected. I thought she would see me and burst into tears of joy. I thought she would rush to me, arms open, only to stop a few steps away. Melancholy would wash over her features. I would tell her that our love would be different now but the sheer fact that I was there was testament to the power of our connection. Even the grave and all that.

Yes, I had a little speech prepared.

So you can see why it was so painful when instead of tears and cries of love I was met with shrieks of terror.

Time. She just needs a little time to adjust to the idea.

III

Apparently not.

The problem isn't a matter of adjusting to the idea of my return. It's that she doesn't even know who I am. As if she has hundreds of other lovers who would defy death to be with her. Maybe she does have someone else. Maybe she has already forgotten about me, moved on, found comfort in the warm arms of someone whose heart still beats.

She did seem rather enraptured by that fool from the cable show. Maybe she was impressed that he had come all the way from Los Angeles to our two stoplight rural Michigan town. Maybe I was just being jealous.

Again, I never meant for anyone to get hurt. Really, what do you expect when you run around in the dark with night vision goggles on rather than turning on the lights?

Who watches these programs anyway? Does anyone really believe two idiots weighed down with flashy equipment being trailed by cameramen weighed down by less equipment?

At first, it was kind of funny. I was leaning against the wall at the end of the upstairs hallway while they were slowly walking up the stairs. The one with the beard was staring intently at the little flashy thing in his hand. The other one maintained a constant monologue for the cameraman trailing behind. Some nonsense about the history of the house, which bore no resemblance to anything, which had ever happened here.

They were three quarters of the way up the stairs, still a good fifteen feet from where I was, when the fool with all of the tools stopped short. I'm sure the well-crafted panic on his face played well in the green not-light of the night vision cam.

"Did you hear that?" Fake fear made his voice rise.

"What was that?" His partner was almost trembling. I smelled Emmy.

"It was the echo of your own big feet," I hollered. Of course they could not hear me.

"It's cold. Yes, we have definitely entered a cold spot."

They were whispering now. but loud enough for the next door neighbors to hear. I approached them in spite of myself. They were both shivering. I don't know if it was supposed to be from the cold or from fear. I was sure the camera was capturing it, either way.

"Spirit of the staircase, we mean you no harm."

They crept a few steps higher.

"We are simply scientists seeking knowledge."

The little gizmo that the bearded guy held started to emit a droning sound, which rose in pitch as he climbed the stairs. Was there something to their crazy equipment after all? He pointed the thingamabob at me and the tone dropped noticeably. He swung it in a wide arc. When it was pointed towards the other end of the hall it started to whistle.

Both men turned their backs to me and addressed the empty hallway.

"If you are there, can you give us some sort of sign?"

I stared at them for a moment. I felt the urge as a little tickle in the back of my mind. It was that same feeling I used to get when I was a child. My grandmother said it was the devil on my shoulder, prodding me on.

I could blame the two goofballs with their flashing lights and beeps and whirls. They were asking for it. Literally, they were asking me to give them a sign. Maybe something in the way they asked compelled me to do what I did. Then that part wouldn't be my fault. Still, it wouldn't explain what happened later.

Whatever the reason, demands of the inquisitive, naughty urges, or just plain meanness on my part, I glided forward until I was just inches from the two of them.

Then I manifested.

I wish I could adequately describe the process. It's not as if I was a wispy nothing in the air one minute and something, if not solid at least opaque the next. It was something I had to concentrate on. There is a squeezing feeling, which I supposed I should not have since I don't have a body anymore. The only comparison I can think of is a little vulgar.

It's kind of like when you have to belch.

When you really need to belch.

You know, when you have that dull pain in the center of your chest and you know that if you focus on it just right you can get rid of it? I bet you do. I bet if I asked you to tell me what you do to get rid of that feeling you wouldn't be able to tell me. Sure, you swallow, but then what? Is there a muscle or three involved? What is it that you tense, or relax, or whatever?

Well, it's like that. I concentrated or focused or whatever it was that I did. I felt the air swirling around me. I mean, I actually *felt* the air. It tingled like static electricity. I felt myself getting heavier. I was, somehow, more than I had been.

It took the two geeks a couple of seconds to notice me. The host guy, the one who talked a lot, noticed first.

"As our regular viewers know, a sudden drop in aggregate temperature, localized to one geographic area, is a common factor in many hauntings. We call this a cold spot..."

He turned his head a bit, caught a glimpse of me, and stopped. For the first time that night, he was silent. His eyes widened. I tried to smile, but by that point I was so ticked off I'm not sure that I managed it. In fact, I'm not really sure what I look like when I try to go solid. The first time I did it was for her and it made her scream. This time the reaction was pretty similar.

Talking Guy, now Not Talking Guy, grabbed Bearded Guy's shoulder. Bearded Guy spun, took one look at me, and screamed like a small child.

I'm not sure what made me do it, but I leaned in and said, "boo."

I don't know if they heard me. I don't know if they even really saw me. I do know that Bearded Guy dropped the little whatsit and ran. It stopped beeping and flashing the second it was out of his hand. It hit the floor with a dull thud.

By that point, they were already halfway down the stairs. I watched them from the landing.

184

I did not follow them. No matter what they may have said later, I did not chase them down the stairs.

I was still at the top of the stairs when the Bearded Guy's foot slipped. He reached out for the railing. His hand went between two of the carved wooden uprights and stayed there as his body continued forward. There was a snapping sound followed by another scream. He slid down the rest of the stairs on his backside. His right arm was bent funny and in the wrong place. It looked like he had a second elbow. The hand swung uselessly from his already swelling wrist.

Talking Guy didn't fare much better. When Bearded Guy slipped, his partner almost crashed into him. To avoid contact he jumped. As the banister snapped Bearded Guy's wrist, Talking Guy leapt over him. He missed him completely. He landed on the stairs with both feet, three steps below his partner. It was just like something out of the movies.

Of course, in the movies he would have kept his feet under him. Instead, he pitched forward and slammed face first into the newel post at the bottom of the stairs, only a few steps from where one of the technician types stood. I could hear the crunch from where I stood. Blood gushed. It did not stop him. Talking Guy picked himself up and kept running, down the hall, out the door, and into the night without so much as a backward glance to see if Bearded Guy or any of the crew was following.

IV

You would think that would have been it, right? I know I did. I had come to the sad conclusion that she was not happy to see me and really did not want me there. If I knew how to leave I would have, but I didn't. So I made up my mind to "live and let live" if that can be said about the dead.

When she came upstairs, I went downstairs. I made sure to stay as far away from her as I could. No "localized temperature changes." No attempts to talk to her. No attempts to touch her.

I watched, but from a distance

I resigned myself to being an unseen, unheard, and ultimately unimportant part of her life.

Every day I felt smaller, less than I had the day before. Maybe if I stopped concentrating on being near her I would just disappear. I told myself that each glimpse of her would be the last. If I could only let go…

But the project wasn't moving along quickly enough for her.

I was upstairs again when the door opened. That back corner of the hallway seemed to be where I ended up when I wasn't concentrating on being somewhere else. It was my default setting I guess.

I heard the outside door open. For a change, I was able to force myself not to steal a glance at her. The door closed. There was the rustle of people moving about, coats being removed and stored in the closet by the door.

People.

Plural.

She was talking to someone. That someone was answering back. His voice was low. Volume low, but also register low.

She had brought another man into our house.

I could not make out much of what they were saying. He seemed to be trying to convince her of something. I heard the plaintive tone of her words, but not the words themselves. I distinctly heard the reply.

"It's for the best. If it is him, don't you want him to be at peace?"

She said something else and he replied.

"No, it's best if you don't watch. Maybe you should wait in the kitchen."

She said something else and he answered. I heard a door open, the coat rustle again, and then another door open and close.

She had left.

Left me alone in the house with a strange man.

I looked over the railing. The man in question was dressed all in black. He was hunched over a bag, his back to me. He pulled what looked like a scarf out of the bag, kissed it, and slipped it over his head.

I knew what he was before he turned around. I had a pretty good idea who he was, too.

The black robed man started up the stairs, bag in one hand, Bible in the other.

Father O'Flanagan.

I turned to leave. I hadn't cared for the man and his heavy-handed, fire and brimstone preaching when I'd been alive. I certainly wasn't going to listen to him now that I wasn't.

I couldn't glide.

For the first time since I had come back to the house, I could not simply glide across the floor. I tried to will myself into the bedroom and failed. I was rooted to the spot.

Father O'Flanagan continued his slow ascent. He was chanting something in Latin. I took a bit of the language back when I was in school. We all had to. What he was saying now made no sense to me. It didn't sound like words at all. It was more of a buzzing sound that wormed its way into my head.

The priest's voice rose. The buzzing sound turned into a skull-splitting shriek. I tried to clap my hands to my ears, but of course, I had no hands, ears, nor skull. A dull ache started in what I thought of as my chest.

O'Flanagan was at the top of the stairs now. He turned his head to the right, to the left, then back to the right. He continued towards me. He could not see me, but he was walking right towards me. The ache at my core had bloomed into a fiery pain.

He could not see me. That was it! Maybe if I could make him see me I could scare him off like the others. I did my best to ignore the pain and the buzz-saw whine and focused on materializing. At first, I could not even remember how I had done it before.

I heard a gasp and knew that I had managed something. Father O'Flanagan stopped his chanting. It was just a moment, but that moment without pain gave me the clarity to focus.

I revealed myself to him. I willed myself to be as frightening as possible.

O'Flanagan dropped the bag. He started chanting again. He held the Bible up before him like a shield. His right hand slipped into his pocket. It came out with a small silver flask.

I wanted to make a wry comment about needing a drink. I wanted to try the "boo" again. The agony in my center prevented me from doing anything coherent. I shrieked. It was the sound of anger and pain wrapped around each other.

I'm pretty sure he heard me.

The top of the flask flipped open. He snapped his wrist and the contents splashed out. They hit me and I felt them. It burned. The new pain broke whatever had been holding me in place. I ran forward. I did not glide or slip, I ran. I was more substantial than I had been since death.

I don't think the good Father was expecting that.

I ran forward and slapped the flask from his hand. It spiraled over the railing and hit the first floor hallway. He shouted something at me. It wasn't Latin or English. I think he was cursing me in his native tongue.

I reached out and grabbed him. I was moving too fast; I was too angry to be amazed by the fact that I could actually touch him. Touch him I did. I grabbed him by the vestments and lifted him over my head. I held him there for a moment. For one brief second he hung there.

Then I pitched him over the railing.

His head and shoulders hit the small table by the stairs, the one we always put the day's mail on. There was a small vase there holding a single flower. The vase shot off and shattered into tiny blue shards. The table splintered under O'Flanagan's weight. He hit the floor among shards of glass and wood. The flower was nowhere to be seen.

The pain stopped. It didn't wane; it simply vanished. I stared down and the unmoving corpse of the priest. I knew he was dead. The mad jumble of limbs and the awkward angle of his neck made that clear.

V

I don't know why I didn't think of this before.

Sometimes the answer won't come on its own. Sometimes you have to be shocked by something so abnormal, so unusual, that the friction of that thought sparks other ideas.

As I stared down at the dead priest, I came to a realization. I would never be what she wanted me to be. I would never be flesh and blood again. I would never be able to wrap my arms around her and hold her. Our love would never be more than a shadow of what it had once been.

I can never again be like her.

Soon she will return home. She will be horrified by what she finds. She may run out of the house. She may even stay away for a while.

Yet she will come back. At some point, she will return to our house. She will climb the stairs to her bedroom.

I can never again be like her.

But she can be like me.

I will tell her that our love will be different now. I will tell her that not even death can separate us.

It will be death that brings us together at last.

Rosa, Rosa, Come Out of Your Room

By Christopher Nadeau

I KNEW ROSA was different the first night she whispered into my ear. This was, like, a week after Francine left me for that Brazilian ice cream truck driver and I was still in a pretty foul mood over it. Look, I'm not one to judge interracial dating, but to be left for someone who's not, you know, on the same level as you is a huge blow to the ego.

I took a couple sleeping pills that night and had actually gone to sleep when I felt something like mild electricity in my ear canal. Now I know it was the breath of a spirit, but then I thought I'd gotten a jolt from that old alarm clock my dad left me before he died. I knew it wasn't the clock when she said what she said to me.

"I am with you."

I couldn't open my eyes so I had to settle on asking the voice who it belonged to. She told me her name was Rosa and she was here for me.

"My spirit is undying," she said. *"My love is undying."*

A warm feeling descended, like somebody had just pulled a bunch of towels out of the dryer and allowed them to fall all over me. I felt my heartbeat increase as what felt like a very cold hand stroked my face.

"Do you pledge yourself to me?" Rosa asked.

"Fuck yeah, I do!"

Next came the lips, at least I hope that's what they were. They were cold, too, and dry. So dry. But I didn't care. I wanted her bad. It had been awhile, you know? Francine wasn't putting out the last six months of our relationship. I guess Paulo or whatever his name is was giving her what she needed.

Rosa, on the other hand, seemed more interested in what *I* needed. She did things to me and caused sensations that I only had only ever read about in *Penthouse Forum*.

When I was done and had stains on my sheets to prove it, I asked her if I could open my eyes. I don't know why I asked her permission.

"Not yet, my love."

"Well, when?" I said, sudden panic taking hold of me. "Are we going to get together again?"

"This was but the beginning. We are now pledged."

And just like that, she was gone.

I immediately felt this overpowering sense of loss, as if I was a little kid and a parent had just died. I'm not ashamed to admit I cried into my pillow until I fell back asleep.

The next morning I found myself going back and forth between periods of extreme giddiness and sadness. People at work looked at me like I was a nut and maybe I was for those few days before Rosa came back to me.

I didn't know it at the time, but apparently, it takes quite a bit of energy for her to cross over to the point where we can interact physically. Even though there's no passage of time in the after-life, it's all relative. When she's able to store up the necessary energy, she crosses back over. On our side, where time still applies, at least two days pass before I can be with her again. Sometimes it's even longer.

I've gotten used to it. After all, how many relationships involve two people seeing each other every day of the week until they get married and screw up all the chemistry they had before legal documents came into play?

It's weird, though. Because of where she exists, it's really easy for her to lose track of this reality. I guess you could say she gets…lost sometimes. She just kind of drifts away.

It's not at all like what the Jesus jumpers say it's like over there. There's no cloud city or golden mansion or any of that childish junk. She doesn't like to talk about it much, but from what she has told me, it's like a big warehouse filled with fog and drenched in the smell of rotted produce. Yeah, they can smell things there.

She told me one thing that made me so afraid of dying I stayed in the house for almost two weeks without coming out. Then I read an article online about how most deaths happen due to household accidents and I freaked all over again.

What was it she said to me? She told me about the "rooms." I asked her what she meant. We were in bed. It was so dark I could barely make out an outline of the temporary body she uses on nights when the energy is at its strongest. We still haven't figured out how I can see her face without sending her back.

"There are rooms everywhere," she said. *"Everything is separated in there."*

I told her I didn't understand.

Her voice went lower, containing a sorrow I doubt any living being could express. *"We wander from place to place, except there are no places. There are…things that follow us. They…they like to take what's left of us."*

"What does that mean?" I said. "Take what?"

Tiny sparks of electricity danced around in my neck hairs, causing them to stand up. We didn't have much time left; she was unraveling. I could feel her becoming less substantial with each passing moment.

"You're so warm," she said. *"I can never feel warm enough."*

I let what was left of her spoon me, wishing like hell I could turn over and look at her face. I knew it was beautiful. It had to be. Fate wouldn't curse me with an uggo from the after-life with all I'd already suffered.

"Rosa?" I said. "What about the rooms?"

She sighed and my body hair stood up at attention. *"You can never stay in one for long. They always come and get you."*

She started to cry. I reached back and tried to provide some comfort by rubbing whatever I could reach but she was becoming less and less physical.

"And it's so cold," she said. *"They steal our warmth."*

This was getting really hard to follow. Whenever she talked of the after-life, her words became cryptic and vague, as if ascribing physical limitations to that realm of existence was some kind of sin. She only made sense when she told me how much she loved me. Maybe that was all I needed.

Still, I wanted to help her somehow. Let's face it; I haven't led the most useful life as far as society is concerned. I was always taught you're supposed to "give back" at some point and I don't think I ever have. This would probably make up for it, if only I could find out what to do. I decided right then and there to devote my spare time to rescuing Rosa. I started with a simple question:

"Can't you stay?"

That was a question I asked a few days later when she was able to return to me. I could feel her cold, temporary flesh against me as she ran her electric fingers through my hair.

"So warm."

"Rosa, answer my question!" I caught myself before I could give in to my anger. I didn't want a rerun of what happened with Francine. The last thing I needed was for someone in the neighborhood to call the cops again.

"You know I cannot," she said.

I sighed. "Who were you? I mean, before…"

"I don't remember anymore. Is it important?"

I bit the inside of my cheek and fought off tears. "Guess not."

"Just love me now. Give me a pleasant memory to take back with me to the rooms."

I did as she asked, lying on my back and letting her do the things she did best. The things that transported me to another place and time, where only we two existed and there were no restrictions or goddam *rooms* to keep us apart. Although the pleasure was just as incredible and intense as ever, there was something missing. The whole thing felt hollow, ritualistic. I wanted more and I couldn't have it.

The coming weeks saw subtle changes develop in our relationship. I didn't always look forward to her visits anymore and I think she could sense it. It wasn't that my feelings had changed; it was because I felt like a failure again. I'd lost Francine because I spent most of our relationship openly comparing her to other women. I hadn't lost Rosa yet, but my failings as a man kept me from feeling like I had a right to be happy. I had to rescue her.

To her credit, Rosa didn't seem to mind or hold it against me. It was easy to forget her troubles when she was pleasing me but I always remembered them once she was gone.

Gone back to the rooms.

I tried to picture what they must look like. In my mind, they looked like Middle Ages prison cells without bars. I pictured just enough light spilling through to cause misshapen shadows along the walls, constant reminders that the overlords of the after-life were lurking outside to steal the warmth of those who had once lived. I wondered if they actually allowed her to leave so she could return with more warmth for them to steal. This thought filled me with an overpowering rage.

I started experiencing tantrums that would swell up inside me for no apparent reason. Anything that wasn't nailed to the floor or the wall basically went sailing across my apartment at some point during that time. The few friends I had left tried to get through to me and abandoned the project when I turned violent.

All I wanted was for the world to stop spinning us all into oblivion long enough for me to grab Rosa and jump off.

The nights she visited became awkward at times. More often than not, we would just lay there in bed, her spooning me with her cold, temporary body and me staring at the dark shapes on the walls, feeling helpless.

"Why are you so troubled?" she asked.

I laughed and shook my head. "Don't ask questions you already know the answers to."

She sighed, filling the air with electricity. *"You pledged your love to me. Has that changed?"*

"Of course not!" I started to turn around and face her and remembered the rules. The goddam rules. "It's just...will it always be like this?"

"What is always? What is forever? All there is waiting for you is the other side."

I hated it when she got all melancholy. Surely, there was more than this. If not, what was the point to anything we did? Wasn't love itself proof of a greater purpose? Or was that guy I met in college right when he said love was simply a mutation? How could a mutation survive after death?

"Do we all go there?" I asked.

"I don't understand, my love."

"When we die," I said. "Do the rooms wait for all of us?"

Silence filled the room for a long moment before she finally spoke. *"I do not know. I have heard...tales, but..."*

My head shot up sideways. "What kinds of tales?"

"They're just stories, really...folktales to comfort those that have passed on." Her hand found my groin and started rubbing it gently. *"Let's forget about this."*

I couldn't stop the erection or Rosa from stroking me until there was no longer a reason to do it. Panting like a wounded animal, I lay against my pillow and tried to recover long enough to get back to the subject of our interrupted conversation. Once my breathing returned to normal, I once again asked her about the folktales.

She sighed. *"The living are still so filled with hope."* She ran her electric fingertips through my hair. *"The tales I've heard are of some who have escaped."*

"Yeah, but you've done that."

"My escapes are temporary and probably only to replenish those lying in wait."

So, I had been right to be angry. "How did these people get out for good?"

"They had help from the living."

Now we were getting somewhere. Rumors like that tended to have some kernel of truth in them, even when they were started by spirits...at least I hoped that was the case. What did I have to lose? I decided I needed to speak with an expert.

***

Reverend Pierce looked at me like I was crazy. You'd figure a man of the cloth has heard it all when it comes to spiritual questions. I was raised Catholic but I converted to a non-denominational church when I was in my early thirties. Today I regretted it because priests seem to be better educated on this stuff.

"I'm not following you, Steve," Reverend Pierce said. "What do *rooms* have to do with the after-life?"

I shrugged and took the offered coffee mug. "I don't know. Maybe Hell isn't what we imagine it to be."

"There's no detailed description of Hell in the Bible. All we know is that it's a realm of tortured souls eternally separated from God."

"What if it's not *God* we're separated from?"

Pierce's eyebrows rose into a V. "What else could it be?"

I chuckled and shifted around in my seat. Suddenly the coffee cup was the most fascinating thing in the room to me as I took a few large gulps, wincing as the steaming hot liquid scorched my throat. "Maybe the after-life isn't what we've been taught it is?"

Pierce smirked and shook his head. "That sounds like a bunch of New Age hooey to me, Steve. Don't let Hollywood and *liberals* color your perception of God's plan."

"God's plan," I said. What kind of plan involved trapping the souls of the departed in a labyrinth of rooms where they were stalked by monsters hungry for their warmth? What kind of plan involved allowing some of them to cross back over and re-experience life before having to return to those horrible rooms? Was that supposed to be a "gift?" More likely,

God was a cruel bastard who either enjoyed our pain or didn't care.

I shuddered; I'd never thought that way before. What was happening to me?

"I always find reading the Bible to be helpful in times of doubt," Pierce said. "It certainly grounds me and keeps silly thoughts out of my head."

I felt my upper lip curl into a snarl; it was the facial expression my former boss told me about that caused so much trouble at work all the time.

If Reverend Pierce noticed, he either didn't let on or wasn't fazed by it. "Haven't seen you in church lately. Is everything okay?"

The snarl went away in a flash. "Yeah, yeah. Just, you know, recovering from the whole Francine leaving me thing but I'm cool."

He nodded. "If there's ever anything we can do…"

"Hey, thanks Rev." I got to my feet and placed the mug on his desk. "This really helped. Thanks."

I didn't bother to look back as I left his office. There was no help to be found in religion because it had no concept of what really lies beyond. It was just me and my lady against the universe.

***

I didn't receive another visitation from Rosa for almost two weeks. Each night she didn't show up was a descent into torture and despair. I started devoting my time to researching what she'd told me about the after-life to see if anyone had written about it. I found one book by some dude called Irving Standish titled, "With Black Curtains," a reference to the Cream song called "White Room." In it, he described Hell as a series of room-like realms, each one separate from the last so that the residents couldn't interact with each other. He cited those famous dark tunnel near-death accounts and said that was what waited at the end.

Some souls were actually swift enough to see the end of the tunnel and remain in the dark place between the two realms, thinking it would save them from an eternity of torment. What they didn't know, Standish wrote, was that this actually fed right into the plans of the evil source behind all this.

The only thing I could think to do was to contact him and see if there was anything else he knew that he hadn't included in his book. I figured the worst thing that could happen was he could turn out to be either an asshole or a total fraud. Instead, he turned out to be one of the most intense people I'd ever met. All I did was send one email telling him I wanted to pick his brain on the topic of Hell and that sparked off a back and forth email chain that broke only when he realized what I was planning to do.

He was a smart bastard, that Standish. He knew right off that I was only interested because of a personal stake. He said that was the only time anybody cared about Hell.

"What about God?" I wrote.

If there is a God, my friend, He's perfectly happy with the way things are.

That pissed me off even more. What kind of loving god sent us to an eternity of memory and despair? And then it occurred to me. What if Standish had it wrong? What if God wasn't happy with things? What if God couldn't affect it or wasn't willing to do so?

Anything is possible, Steve, he wrote back. *I only report what others have reported.*

"Have you ever seen it yourself?" I wrote.

Once. In a dream. A woman came to me and told me she loved me. I asked her where she was from and she showed me the Rooms. I didn't sleep for three days after that.

A *woman* had come to him? Rosa? No, it couldn't be. But I had to know if I was being used. I went for broke and asked him her name.

Her name? He wrote. *What an odd question for someone who is "just curious." Steve, have you experienced a visitation? Please tell me the truth.*

I admitted it. What did I have to lose except my self-respect, and that was gone a long, long time ago. The tone of his next email was very different from any of the others:

Why the hell didn't you tell me that before? Jesus, Steve! This is serious stuff here. Do you understand what is going on? You've become a doorway for this thing to return to the mortal world, if only briefly. Do you have any idea what that's going to do to you? Please tell me you haven't made love to it!

I didn't reply. For the rest of the day my hands wouldn't stop shaking. I think I sat in the same place for hours just staring off into nothingness. Standish's words echoed around inside my brain like bullets unable to locate their targets. But I wouldn't give them the power to change my mind. Rosa loved me. I knew she did. I felt it when we made love and there was no faking that. We would be together and I didn't care what it took at this point.

She was mine and I was hers and we would be together.

***

Standish's emails kept coming and I kept ignoring them. As he grew more and more panicky, I seemed to become calmer, more at peace with what was happening to me. Rosa's visits decreased in frequency just as I suspected they would. Although time doesn't pass on the other side, the amount of energy needed dissipates as if it does. She just didn't have enough juice left to keep crossing over.

I had to act fast, especially since I realized that I'd given Standish my home address in my first email before I knew how he preferred to communicate. Mr. Severe Intensity might decide to pay me a visit in some psycho move to save the world.

Since I could no longer predict Rosa's arrival, I had to be ready at a moment's notice. That meant little to no contact with the outside world and an almost constant state of meditation. Almost all the books I read on the paranormal said this dimension and all the others were separated by three things: Perception, vibration and ignorance. I was pretty sure

I'd eliminated all but number two, so that was where I placed all my concentration.

During the almost three weeks until I saw her again, Standish must have sent me a dozen emails. I deleted most of them without reading, but a few caught my eye before I could.

You're not the first one, Steven. I've been researching this for a few years now and it's actually the subject of my nearly completed follow-up book. There have been at least five others that I know of and they all...

I deleted the email. So I wasn't the first. So what? There's nothing new under the sun, right? Fuck it. I was going to be the first to *succeed*. I just needed my sweet Rosa to come back so I could make it happen.

***

She came back to me the same night I read Standish's email. I was asleep when she arrived, having adjusted to the fact that most of my nights were now spent alone. At first, I thought I was dreaming. If not for the sudden rush of static in the air, I might not have woken up. I often wonder how different things might have been if...no point in that, I guess.

"My love?" she said. *"Are you all right?"*

"Fine." Unable to fight the tears running down my cheeks, I allowed myself one brief glance at her silhouette in the doorway before shutting my eyes. "I'm glad you're here."

"As am I."

God, I loved the way she talked. Made me feel like I was living in some fancy Middle Ages drama. I wanted so badly for her to become physical, to walk with me in daylight, to meet people I knew, and to be at my side forever. Right then and there, I knew I was going to make that happen or shut down for good.

"It is getting more difficult to cross, my love," she said. *"It is my desire to be with you that affords me the strength to do it now."*

I could feel what she meant. Although she had a strong presence, it seemed as if there was less of her here now. Someday soon, there would be no more visitations.

"Come to me," I said.

I felt her glide across the room on mild electrical currents, the hair on my arms standing up as she approached. This was it. No take-backs, no last minute alterations in the plan. She and I were about to become...

"STEVE!"

I sat upright in bed as if a spring had been loaded into my back. It took everything I had not to look directly at Rosa as she hovered uncertainly to my right. I had no idea who belonged to the voice yelling my name but something deep inside knew before he said anything.

He rapped on my bedroom window, his face a round moon filling it as he tried to see inside. ""Steve! It's me, Irving Standish! I have to talk to you!"

"Shit," I said. "Son of a bitch!"

"What is it, my love?" Rosa sounded frightened.

I fought the urge to go to her and said nothing, frozen in place as the rapping on the window continued.

"I know what you're doing!" Standish yelled. "You have to stop!"

"Who is that man?" An edge of panic crept into Rosa's tone.

"Nobody," I said a little sharply. "Just some guy." I glared at the window, aware that Standish couldn't see me even though the asshole knew I was here. I could've kicked myself. Why hadn't I read his emails and responded to them in a way that convinced him I wasn't going to do anything drastic?

"Steeeevvvvve! You don't understand! The rooms are not what you think!"

"What does he know of the rooms?" she shrieked. *"Have you been telling people about them?"*

"What? No! Of course not!" The room spun out of control, like my life. "He-he wrote a book, and..."

"Steve, I'm giving you ten seconds to acknowledge me or I'm gonna break this damn window! I don't care if you call the cops!"

Something in Standish's tone caused me to go limp. What did he think he knew? What did he have against true love?

202

"I'm frightened," Rosa said. *"Has he come to destroy us?"*

Everything became clear then. Standish was my final test, sent here to ensure my faith was as strong as it needed to be. Maybe his heart was in the right place but he didn't see the whole picture. He was too much of an academic to understand the core of human love. I pitied him.

"They prey on the miserable!" Standish yelled. "Your unhappiness is like a beacon light to them. They don't come here for love!"

I smirked and shook my head. "Yeah, whatever," I muttered.

"He doesn't understand us," Rosa said. "He wallows in close-mindedness."

"Totally," I said.

"I'm counting, Steve! I'm counting to ten right now!"

I told Rosa to come to me right then and there. No way was this cold, unfeeling weirdo going to stop us. In my head, I started singing Starship's "Nothing's Gonna stop us Now" to drown out Standish's loud counting.

"Close your eyes, my love."

I did as she asked and instantly felt her above me, connecting with me in a way we never had before. We entered a new place, somewhere above and beyond all the pettiness and stupidity of all the people that looked down their noses at me or thought I was some kind of screw-up. Rosa lifted me higher than I'd ever been, filling me with a sweet tranquility I would do anything to maintain.

Somewhere off in the distance, the sound of shattering glass intruded upon our bliss. Someone was yelling something -- it sounded like my name – over and over like a recording. A loud gasp echoed throughout the room. A male voice sputtered something unintelligible. For a moment, I thought I could look down at the room from above and see myself surrounded by tendrils of light. The beauty of that sight made me weep.

"Fight her, Steve!" someone yelled. "Don't let her take you!"

"So warm," Rosa said. *"You're so warm."*

"Yes," I tried to say and my voice choked.

"Steve, you don't know what you're doing! They've been planning this for longer than anyone can say!"

I smirked. Who was this dork and what was he talking about? Planning what? The only plan here was mine and it was going off without a hitch. I chuckled and sang, "Nothin's gonna stop us now."

"Yes, sing to me, my love! Sing!"

I did as she asked, drowning out whatever the shouting man had to say. The room grew cold or maybe it was just me. Things faded and winked back into existence, physical reality giving way to something fluid and easily manipulated. I wanted to shape it to my whim but it was too elusive to grasp for more than an instant.

"Sing of our love!"

Rosa became a doorway, an opening into a long corridor lit only by her own residual life-force. But she had me with her this time. My own energy would be enough to light the way and pull her out of here so we could be together for eternity. I was the power and nothing was gonna stop…

The darkness remained, enfolding me like a cloak, cold and wet. It was a different kind of cold, one that seemed to come from inside. It seemed hungry, insatiable. It made me feel sick to my stomach.

"Rosa?" I yelled. There was no echo. "Where are you?"

No reply. No sense of her presence.

"We can't stay here," I said. "We've got to keep mov…"

Something grabbed my right ankle and pulled. I yanked back against it, wishing there was something I could grab onto. Whatever held onto me started purring like a cat with something thick and viscous in its mouth. I felt something long and slimy run along my ankle and wrenched myself free with a cry born of shock and nausea.

"Quickly, my love," Rosa's far away voice called out.

I saw a dull light ahead and broke into a run, stumbling forward a few times as the sound of something following closely behind nipped at my heels. After a long moment, I reached the light and felt myself enveloped into its radiance.

"Rosa?" I said. "Is this what you are?"

"Not for much longer, my love."

I smiled. She had as much faith as I did. We would be together soon.

"Follow me," she said in a singsong voice. *"We are almost there."*

I did as she asked. I would have followed that sweet voice anywhere. Once we'd arrived, however, I was a little confused. I gazed around the small area, running my hands along the edges of what felt like a damp cave wall, except the surface was more like mud in some places.

"What is this place?" I said.

Rosa looked at me, a perfect beauty in a hideous place. *"Your room."*

I told her I didn't understand but of course, I did. All of Standish's words came flooding back. I tried to say, "You wouldn't," but all that came out was a tiny croak.

"Thank you so much," Rosa said. *"I have had many loves but yours was the purest."*

I felt my arms go limp. "But I'm still alive."

She smiled and a blade plunged itself through my heart. *"Yes. They demanded seven and now we can live again."*

"Rosa."

"Farewell, my love."

And she was gone, leaving me in "my" room. It turns out the rooms scenario isn't how she described it. Those who locate more than one room are the fortunate ones. They can find a way out, even if it's only temporary. Most remain in the same room forever, while hostile parasites hover outside looking for a way in to feed on whatever warmth they have left.

I've found a few rooms. Most of those inside are completely mad, screaming lunatics begging for relief that never comes. Fools. Even when they hear about Rosa and the few that got to live again, it means nothing. But I get it. I'm still being tested. Rosa waits for me on the other side. I just need to be clever about this. I just need to convince others to care about me.

I know it's wrong in the living world but try on my existence for size before you judge me. We can't all be pure like Rosa. She truly loved me and knew I would do anything for her. I just wish she'd told me about this.

Sometimes I cry, to the amusement of the parasites outside in the long, dark corridor. Then I grow angry and they snicker even harder. Doesn't matter. I know the way out. Hopefully too much time hasn't passed; it's impossible to know here.

Lately I've crossed over looking for her. No luck so far but I did find someone else. Good old Standish tells me how sorry he is that he didn't get to me sooner. He says he wants to help me somehow.

And help me he will. After him, I'll only need six more. I'll see you soon, Rosa.

Nothing's gonna stop us now.

Caliente

By MontiLee Stormer

The Angel stood at the corner of Main and Nowhere. Feet planted at shoulder's width, rifle at eye level, butt in the hollow of her shoulder, face a grim countenance. She was willing to shoot the man at the wagon. The man's face mirrored hers. He was determined to move forward, even if it meant trampling the Heavenly Host before him. The horse hadn't moved at much more than a slow shamble since the drought, so it would be a slow trample. The dust had barely settled from the herd of early morning tumbleweeds blowing through town, and it hung in the air like a painful memory.

It was an occasional amusement to the remaining townsfolk to watch the standoff. Today a few of them, with eyes as dried as raisins, had braved the rising heat of Caliente to watch the showdown. The Angel Michaela stood in her mended gingham dress, held together with patches and bits of salvaged ribbons. It was faded brown, so far from the vibrant color it once was, she could barely remember the demure mauve and yellow roses. The petticoat, once a complimentary patchwork of green and orange, now bound her left wing, which dipped a lopsided hello to anyone behind her.

There was no one behind her, however, just the hardpan of the desert and certain death to anyone foolish enough to brave it, the very same death she was trying to prevent now, with the stare and the rifle.

"I can't let you leave, Joshua," she said. "It breaks my heart to say it, but I'd rather you died right here in front of Lucky's than out there."

She broke a nod to her left towards the empty shell of what was Lucky's General Store, before the supplies stopped coming and the people stopped shopping, and Lucky turned to ash in the desert. The Man Joshua did not look towards Lucky's. He'd probably had credit there, and with that and everything else worth buying gone, there was nothing left to keep him in Caliente. Why remind the eyes of that? He continued to hold her stare.

"Can't stay, you know that. I have a family, a boy, a wife. We can't eat dirt. We can't drink air. We need to move on."

His wife shifted on her box on the wagon. She was as gaunt as her husband, her clothes as dusty as the Angel's. She looked tired and worn out and beaten. She looked like Death had paid her a visit in the night and stole everything that made her a wife and mother and lover, and left a bag of bones to tend a husband and child.

It was cruel, this drought, and it was perpetual. Those that stuck it out over the last seven months were dying. Those that left were turned to ash in the desert. The Angel Michaela was determined to keep as many bodies on this side of the border as she could.

"You don't have faith in the rain," she asked, and looked up at a sky barren of clouds.

"I have faith that the rain takes its own time," the Man Joshua said. "But I cannot wait for it." They stood in silence a few more moments. "I'd like to leave now."

The Angel raised her rifle once more, leveling it at the man she knew, at the sun-burnt space between his eyes. One shot for him, once for the wife, and if the woman's maternal instinct didn't kick in and she begged to stay, another shell for the child. The child would be the hardest, but she wouldn't let that hesitation show. She wavered once to show mercy and was rewarded with a sucker punch and a trample beneath large heavy wheels. Her wing never would heal right, and if it set wrong, she'd bear that mark of her misstep for Eternity.

Another man stepped from behind the wagon just then, or perhaps not a man, but also not like the Angel. He was impossibly tall and he straightened as if folded to fit with the belongings under the canvas. His grin was as welcoming as a fire pit at noon on a day in midsummer as he smoothed the wrinkles from his long, black jacket. The Solicitor, as he was called in Caliente, wore a crisp, clean shirt, and his string tie lay neat upon his chest. Compared to the townsfolk, he looked fresh and bathed, and were it not for his skin color, he could almost be called in good health. Crawling from the neck of his shirt and past the cuffs at his wrists, the skin was dull and gray, and his hat sat crooked upon his head, with a spray of orange flowers tucked into the brim. When he smiled, as he did to the Angel with the leveled rifle, his teeth showed yellow and broken with red, bleeding gums. If it was meant as comforting and conciliatory, it failed.

"Now my dear," he spoke slowly as if to a child, "Mr. Oskram has made clear his intention to leave. If there been prior arrangement why that cannot be allowed, I'm afraid we may have missed that meeting. Mr. Oskram has decided to relocate to a more hospitable clime, best suited for raising his family and making a living. Surely there can be no harm in wanting what's best."

He let the last word hiss upon his tongue, and the forked tip slipped between his lips in a rude flick.

"Joshua has no place in mind," said the Michaela.

It was rude to refer to someone as if they weren't standing right there, but she needed to make a point.

"There is nothing for clicks in any direction. How can the unknown of out there be better than right here?" It was unintentional, but the Angel stomped her foot in frustration and a dust cloud drifted to her knees. It settled and the silence wrung itself out.

"It is better because it is not here," said Joshua in his quiet voice, but the Solicitor raised his hand for silence.

"What Mr. Oskram is trying to say is that he would like to have a chance in starting over. This place has a ... taint to it." The Solicitor lowered his eyes in an uneasy frown. When he raised them again, there was a flicker of delight in his hollow, flaming eyes. "Surely even you can see that?" The Solicitor was practically dancing in place.

"What I see is people giving up at the first sign of trouble. We have potential in our town and we're tossing it to the slop." She was tired of having this conversation every Blessed time, but here she was again, on the losing side of an Exodus.

"This isn't potential, ma'am. This is a death sentence." Joshua Oskram had made up his mind.

From the back of the wagon, beneath the heavy canvas, a frail voice spoke. It could have been mistaken for the wind, it was so high and so weak. "Papa? Papa, are we leaving?"

"In a bit, son. Go back to sleep." To the Angel Michaela, the Man Joshua's voice now carried the determination his face would not drop, "My boy cannot thrive here. I need to do what's best for him." He nodded to the Solicitor.

"You heard the gentleman. Mr. Oskram's intentions are clear, his mind is made up. He is leaving."

The Solicitor nodded to the Angel, slipped behind the wagon, and once again was out of sight.

"Why won't you let me save you?"

"That's not your place," said the Solicitor from beneath the canvas. "You are not here to save. Now stand aside"

Defeated, the Angel lowered her rifle and shuffled a few steps, out of the path of the wagon and its cargo. Joshua Oskram pulled the reigns of the broken animal and the wagon was moving. He stared straight ahead as he passed her, with not so much as a nod in farewell.

Joshua and his wagon, holding the contents of his family and their lives, trudged towards the boundary of Caliente. His wife wore tracks of tears on her dusty face, resigned to the decision. The Angel watched and her broken wing dipped closer to the ground. They reached the sign, "*Now Leaving Caliente, May God have Mercy On Your Soul*" and without hesitating, crossed the border.

The horse caught fire first, its screams loud and immediate as a rifle shot, then the sound was cut off as the animal was reduced to ash. The man was next, stiffening only for an instant as the flames devoured him, flesh and fabric, then the wagon, the wife, and the child inside, all ash on the other side of the border, joining other piles against the picturesque backdrop of what could be any desert, in any country, on any world.

The townspeople in their dwindling number shambled back inside to their depleted existences. A few returned to put pots or glass bottles in the streets with a weary eye to the sky. Doors were closed and the curtains were drawn. The dusty town of Caliente waited.

The Solicitor stood next to the angel on her rifle side, the threat now over. He smoothed the wrinkles from his long coat. "You can't save them all. It's not your place."

"Why can't they just wait like the rest of us?"

"Because it's been 300 years since the Great Rapture and they are tired of waiting."

"He won't have anything to reign over if they keep leaving."

"He will have Us, you and I. And the Others wherever they may be, and in the end, I think that would be best, wouldn't you say?" He removed his hat and scratched around the horns on top of his bald head. "Seven months, that one took. They just don't leave like they used to?" He replaced his hat, still crooked around on his head. "What's the score?"

"You are winning by a handful of souls, but it isn't as if we had much to begin with." The skies darkened overhead and the first drops of rain began to fall. "I don't see how they do it, just walk through the Veil like that, knowing it'll hurt beyond hurt."

"Because it's what's on the other side--they trust in a better life--and Salvation. That's why I am winning. Faith, slow faith even, will triumph over lazy complacency any day. Wait for a better day, or try and suffer towards redemption." In his brim, the spray of orange flowers with its green leaves grew a brighter with each drop of rain.

"Keeps it lively here, anyway." The Angel Michaela rested the rifle against her good shoulder and looked to her colleague, her opponent, her Eternal Kin.

"Drink, Gabriel?"

"Thank you. You accept defeat with Grace. It is admirable. Maybe you're learning something from them after all."

The two angels walked towards the center of a town whose population was recently decreased by three. They talked as the rain fell and the pots began to fill, and the wait began again.

And on the Eighth Day He... Oops

By Peggy Christie

"I'm bored."

"Me, too. What do you want to do?"

"Universe?"

"Nah."

"Galaxy?"

"Nah."

"New solar system?"

"Hmm. How many planets?"

"How about nine?"

"You don't think that's too many?"

"We can always change our minds later."

"True. How many suns?"

"Just one. And we can only put life on one planet this time."

"Oh, come on. Why?"

"Have you forgotten the Glavexion system meltdown?"

"Right. I'd almost forgotten. Okay, just one planet. How about the third one?"

"Why that one?"

"Why not?"

"Fair enough," the god replied.

"Can we make life forms that look like us again?" the goddess asked.

He shrugged. "Sure, why not? It's been a few millennia."

She clapped her hands. "Good! You work on the male form this time, though. I don't think I got it quite right on that last world."

"Yeah, putting the sex organs at mid-chest was not a good idea. They should be a little less conspicuous."

They shared a laugh as they collected the elements needed to create a brand new solar system.

***

"And so, in God's ultimate wisdom, He created the world. All the people, animals, plants, the very planet itself, exist only at His discretion."

An explosion reverberated outside the school. Mr. Anders slid his gaze toward the windows then looked back to the group of young children. He smiled to hide his fear. A young boy raised his hand.

"Yes, Alec?"

The boy pointed out the window.

"Did God do that?"

"No, that is a man-made problem. God would never hurt his creations on purpose."

Alec seemed content with the explanation and Mr. Anders continued the lesson.

"God has a purpose for everything. We may not know what it is but don't worry, children. He will provide everything when the time is right."

Another explosion rocked the windows. A high pitched scream followed by a chorus of cheers floated on the afternoon breeze. The gangs were getting closer. Soon they'd be at the school walls. God help us all if they get inside.

The children squirmed and whimpered with fear. He needed to distract them until the roving gangs grew tired of their destructive games and moved downtown to find better entertainment.

"All right everyone. Go to your desks and get your workbooks and crayons. Then come back to the circle and you can draw pictures of what you think is God's greatest creation."

The Sunday school class dispersed. Each child got his or her supplies then returned to the middle of the room, plopped down, and began to draw. A few students looked at the windows from time to time but most became absorbed in their individual drawings and forgot about the world outside.

***

"Why did you do that?"

"Doesn't he look more, I don't know, symmetrical or something?"

"I guess but they don't actually serve a purpose do they?"

"No," he answered.

"Then why put them on a male? Do they produce milk?"

"Fine. But the nipples stay."

She rolled her eyes at him then turned back to the animal she was creating. She'd already finished her sentient life form and so began to work on plants and animals.

"What's that?" he asked.

"Do you like it?"

"Sure but doesn't it need bigger wings if it's going to fly?"

"It doesn't fly."

"I don't get it."

She sighed. "I want something that's shaped like it could fly but can't. Maybe it'll be a good swimmer."

"All right but it's sort of drab. Don't you want to add a little color?"

"I like the simplicity of black and white."

"Whatever."

"Well, what are you working on, now that you've 'perfected' your sentient being?"

Her voice dripped with derision, knowing it would make him angry. He smacked her on the back of the head then turned to the creature he'd started.

"It's going to be great. See here, I've webbed its feet so it can move easily through water. The wings will allow it to fly. The beak will help it to dig through hard surfaces to get to food or defend itself."

She studied the small animal. It was rather ingenious. She was angry about the slap, though, so she laid a hand on the creature and it dissolved into a puddle of blood, bones, and fur.

"I'm making everything that can fly. Try again."

Furious, he grabbed a handful of her hair and threw her down. She tried to kick him but he side stepped her effort then

215

launched himself on top of her. As they tussled and rolled, their creations flew left and right. Limbs broke, blood spilled, and the waters sloshes around them.

By the time they'd finished fighting, not only had their life forms been destroyed but the planet itself was a ball of burning gases. As they watched, the fiery orb expanded and contracted then finally stabilized. She looked at him.

"So, sun's finished."

"Yeah, guess so. Uh, let's get to work on the planets."

"Sounds good."

***

Dr. Daly looked through the telescope eyepiece. He aimed it at a quadrant of space just the other side of Mars.

"Are you recording the data, Dr. Marrinton?"

Dr. Marrinton tapped at the computer keyboard.

"Yes, it's recording now. It's-"

She left her unfinished thought hanging in the air.

"What's wrong?" Dr. Daly asked.

"Oh my God."

Daly ran from the platform, leaped down a handful of steps, then moved to her side. He stared at the screen.

"Oh my God," he echoed.

"It's accelerating faster than we anticipated, John."

"We don't have a few years, do we?"

"No," she answered. "A few months, maybe, but that's it."

He collapsed into the chair next to her and cradled his head in his hands.

"We have to tell the president."

John snapped his head up.

"Are you fucking crazy, Sheila?"

"We have to tell someone. People need to know!"

"Why? So they can ramp up their looting, raping, and murdering?"

He held up his hands, shaking and pointing his fingers like a bad parody of a late night infomercial pitchman.

"Hey folks, remember when we said the world would end three years from now? Well, we were off by about two years and nine

months. So if you ever wanted to have sex with your neighbor, or put a big screen TV in your living room, don't wait. Act now because we'll all be dead in ninety days!"

"John, we need-"

"Sheila, shut up! There's no reason to say anything. Everyone already knows we're going to die. As far as I'm concerned, the sooner this shitty little planet blows up, the better."

She pushed her chair back as she stood.

"Well, you can be a coward, John, but I intend to inform the President."

When she turned her back on him to make the call, John grabbed the wireless keyboard off the desk. Before she could punch in a single number, he cracked the keyboard against her skull. Sheila dropped the phone, stunned, and John hit her again.

A rain of tiny black plastic squares fell to the floor as the keyboard shattered and Sheila collapsed. John threw the remains of the keyboard to the side. He spotted a heavy microscope two desks over.

He ran to it, hefted its weight then moved back to Sheila. She had managed to crawl a couple feet away. Before she could escape, John brought the scope down onto her skull, crushing her brain and all knowledge of the impending doom, to a gelatinous mass that resembled a burst overripe tomato. He slammed the scope against her head twice more before he released it. His breath came in heavy ragged gasps as spittle slipped down his chin.

John couldn't let anyone else know about the new destruction timetable and so set about the lab to destroy all the equipment. Once he was finished he would go home, eat a rare slab of sirloin steak, smoke a Cuban cigar, drink a bottle of scotch, and then blow his fucking brains out all over his living room.

***

"I think the population is getting out of control," the goddess said.

"I know. What should we do, kill 'em all?"

"What? That's where you go first? Sheesh, what kind of father figure did you have?"

The god laughed. "Ha! Good one."

The goddess smiled. "I have a few every now and again. Anyway, about the planet's population."

"What's your idea?"

"Why not throw down a plague? It's always been reliable in the past, though it's a bit irksome when the humans attribute our work to this other God."

The god rolled his eyes. "Why do you care? By tomorrow you'll be working on your next project and they'll have some other entity to worship."

She shrugged. "I suppose you're right but let's give them something nasty."

"Should we create one big plague or various forms so they won't know what's what?"

"Oh, I like where you're going with that. We can have a mild form, one severe, and a colossal vile plague. All fatal though, right?"

"We can't kill everyone. Just need to thin the herd a bit," he said.

"Fine."

She picked up a clay model of a human and pointed to different areas of its body as she thought up symptoms for the infections.

"Headache, vomiting, high body temps, aching joints. Maybe half the people afflicted with these symptoms will die."

"Sounds good."

"Coughing, blood in the lungs, blood seeping through the pores as the tissues break down. Almost every one of these will die."

He nodded then grabbed the doll.

"And the worst form where they all die?"

She paced back and forth, chewing on her fingernails.

"In addition to the others symptoms, let's screw with their blood. It clots too much, then not at all, until their organs shut down, liquefy, and they die in blinding agony."

"Wow," the god said. "You've got issues."

"Me? Have you been paying any attention to them at all? They're killing each other over perceived persecutions, religious fervor, cultural differences, if you can call their filthy little rituals and superstitions 'culture'."

"You know, they'll probably blame that other God for this plague."

"And why is that a problem?"

He sighed. "Anyway, how are we going to do this? How should we spread the disease?"

The goddess snatched the doll and threw it over her shoulder as she walked away. He stared after her, waiting for her to turn back. She never did.

"Krakken! Fine, I'll figure it out myself!" he yelled.

He picked up the doll and studied it. How was he going to pull this off? As he pondered the problem, a creature the humans had named 'rat' scuttled across his foot.

***

She pulled the blade across the man's face, slow and deep. He screamed past his rotted teeth, those that remained, and his breath brought tears to her eyes.

"Christ, pal. What have you been eating? Oh, right," she laughed. "Whatever I give you."

She'd kept the man shackled to the wall for weeks and fed him a strict diet of rotten garbage and sewer water. It surprised her that he was able to keep it down. She'd learned the hard way what feces did to him: immediate regurgitation. Same with force feeding him the steaming vomit.

Shelly never used to be like this. She'd always been the type to follow the rules, dress for dinner and church, and smile and nod as she accepted whatever crap her husband did/said/offered. Because that's what a good Christian wife and mother was supposed to do.

Once the planet fell into the meteor's path, securing its certain destruction, Shelly changed. She couldn't believe in a God that would allow such a catastrophe. That crisis of faith planted a kernel of doubt in her brain about her life's path. It germinated and grew into a giant oak tree of anger. And liberation.

Each branch of that tree pointed to a new and exciting path, each one darker and more exciting in its possibilities. By turning away from God, she turned toward a life free of rules, free from

219

consequences, and free of guilt. The world was going to end and everyone was going to die anyway. Shelly just needed to go out with bang before the world did.

First she got rid of the children. Shelly never wanted them but always felt the societal requirement to bear them. She ambushed them when they returned from school one afternoon. It was quick and painless though part of her wanted it slow and tortuous. Another part still clung to a scrap of decency, she supposed. Maybe it was maternal instinct.

Didn't matter. Once the sledgehammer crushed their skulls into strawberry jam, the last vestiges of ethics, morality, and compassion dissipated. She felt more alive with their deaths than at their births. If she'd chosen this path sooner, she could have strangled them with their own umbilical cords.

Her husband was more a challenge. She had to plan the details of his murder. It would be too easy, and less satisfying, to pummel him to death like the children. Would poison be better? Maybe just dose him up with sleeping pills. If she could knock him out, perhaps she'd be able to restrain him in some way. Then she could take her time.

Years ago, her doctor had prescribed a calming sedative because he thought she had too much stress in her life. Two sources of that stress were gone. Now for the third. Shelly crushed half of a bottle of the sedatives and mixed them in Ralph's food.

When he passed out into his mashed potatoes, it took her thirty minutes to drag his limp body from the table to the family room. His insistence on having the furniture encased in plastic came in handy for the first time in their ten year marriage. The slick surface made it easy to maneuver him into position before she stripped off his clothes.

She strapped him to the love seat with multiple bungee cords. His naked skin squeaked against the thick plastic as she arranged his limbs: legs splayed, arms extended and pulled back behind the sofa. She'd connected the restraints on his wrists to those on his ankles so his back arched and thrust his chest, stomach, and genitals forward.

Perfect.

Once the drugs wore off, Ralph's half open eyes scanned his surroundings. His speech slurred past saggy lips.

"Wha..what's going on? What happened?"

"I put drugs in your food and you passed out. Then I dragged your sorry ass here, stripped off your clothes, and tied you to the couch."

Ralph frowned. As if he didn't believe her, he tried to move his arms and legs. Panic didn't seem to set in until he looked down and realized he was naked.

"Shelly, why the hell did you do this?"

"Because I could. Because I never really wanted to be a wife and mother but I succumbed to society's expectations."

She held up an eight-inch butcher knife then ran her finger along its edge.

"Because I wanted to."

"Shelly, please don't. Think of the children."

She threw her head back and laughed until tears ran down her cheeks. When she was able to speak, she looked at Ralph.

"I'm sorry, hon. I know you're not in on the joke. Here."

Shelly put the knife on the coffee table then picked up a digital camera. She sat next to him and held up the camera so Ralph could see the view screen and every picture as she scrolled through them.

"Here's Charlie, or what's left of him. And this one is Rebecca. I know it's hard to tell but if you look at the clothing, you'll recognize Charlie's Star Trek tee shirt and Becca's charm bracelet."

Ralph's eyes filled with tears. As he wept for his murdered children, Shelly felt one last pang of horror and regret. It disappeared the moment Ralph began blubbering and trying to negotiate a way out of his predicament.

"Please, Shelly. You don't have to do this. I know the sweet gentle woman I married is in there somewhere."

She dropped the camera at her feet. She picked up the knife and dragged it across the table, gouging a thin line into the wax and wood. Ralph continued to blather on about their kids, love, and family, until she lifted the knife above her head and slammed it down.

Shelly embedded the blade a half-inch into the tabletop where it remained vertical when she released it. Ralph quieted as she stood over the knife, staring at it. Her labored breath echoed through the living room. She opened and closed her hands.

"I've always done what was expected, what a dutiful wife should do. That's what I don't have to do anymore, Ralph."

She turned to look at him and he tried to recoil into the plastic at his back. She felt a line a drool escape the corner of her mouth and she let it drip onto the floor.

"No. More."

Shelly pulled the knife free and began to slash and cut her husband into ribbons of skin and flesh. She had blacked out at some point because the next thing she knew she was slopping her husband's remains into a large black garbage bag.

That was six weeks ago.

Since then she had killed two neighbors, half of the high school marching band, a woman breast feeding her baby in the park, as well as the baby, and her daughter's former Girl Scout troupe. Today she was torturing a homeless man she'd picked up downtown, tricking him into her trust with promises of food, shelter, and sex.

She wondered how long she could make him last. How many more victims could she take before the planet died? A long ago commercial for a candy sucker popped into her head. As she carved another deep line into the homeless man's flesh, she laughed.

"It'll be a hell of a lot more than three."

***

"I'm tired of this. Wanna play a game?"

"Like what?" she asked.

"How about catch?"

"Sure. We haven't played that in eons. What have you got?"

"Um," the god said as he rummaged through an oversized trunk.

"Fireball?"

"No."

"Dwarf star?"

"Nah."

"I've got a cosmic string in here but they're a little wriggly."

"Obviously."

"Hey. There's almost a whole planet in here. How about that?"

"Perfect!"

The god picked up the rough black orb. A few cracks marred the puckered surface but otherwise it would work fine. He tossed it over to the goddess and she caught it with one hand.

"Nice catch."

"I learned from the best," she said as she threw it back to him.

They continued the easy pace, never tossing it too hard or too soft, for a few years until he decided to switch things up. He gathered an energy field around the planetoid and shot it at the goddess. She reached up both hands to grab it and it almost slipped past her.

"Ouch! Why did you throw it so hard?"

He shrugged.

"I don't know. Just 'cause."

Her forehead furrowed with anger and she whipped the planet back at him. It hit him square in the chest, knocking him down. It broke in half and a distinct red circle marked his skin. Though it didn't hurt, and faded in seconds, he felt his anger seethe inside him.

He threw one half of the planet at her, which she caught easily. But before she could ready herself for the other, the god put all his power into the second half and pushed it at the goddess. She ducked seconds before it would have smashed into her face. It sailed past her into the darkness of space.

"What is your problem? That might have actually hurt me, you know."

"Look at what you did to me!"

"Look at what? You're fine."

He looked down at his chest which was as pristine and perfect as the day he was born.

"That's not the point."

"Then what is the point? I'm dying to know."

They argued back and forth, neither one accepting the other's explanation or excuse. While she prattled on about her feelings or some such nonsense, the god stared over her shoulder.

"I think we have a problem."

"What do you mean?"

She turned around. The chunk of planet that whizzed past her was headed straight for the little blue and green world in the solar system they'd created. They stared in disbelief just as their mother approached.

"Children, what are you doing? You're not getting into trouble, are you?"

"No," they cried in unison.

"A likely story. What are you staring at? Oh, look at that lovely solar system. Did you two make that?"

"Yes," the god mumbled.

"How nice. That one little planet looks like it could have life. Does it?"

"Uh huh," the goddess answered.

"What is that little black dot? Is it...moving?"

"He threw it at me but I ducked out of the way."

"She started it by throwing it at me first."

The two pled their cases louder than the other, at the same time, until their mother held up her hands.

"So, as usual, you two create something beautiful and then make a mess of it. There are probably millions of life forms down there and now they're all going to die. Just because of your carelessness."

They begged their mother for help but she refused.

"Your father and I are tired of cleaning up after you. It's about time you learn some responsibility. Neglect equals loss. If you don't take care of something, you lose it. Simple as that. Take one last look at your creation, children, because once it's gone, it's gone for good."

They turned to watch as the planetoid hurtled through space toward their beautiful world. The god grasped the goddess' hand. She looked at him, her face covered in tears.

"I'm sorry," she said.

"So am I."

Many years later, after the little blue and green planet was nothing but a chunk of black rock, void of all life, they turned away. Their mother wiped the tears from their cheeks.

"Don't cry, my dears. Come. Your father is having trouble with the magma pockets again. Why don't you help him? It'll make you feel better."

"Yes mother," they replied and went to find their father.

ERIE TALES:
TALES OF THE APOCALYPSE/
RESURRECTION MARY

BONUS FEATURETTE
EDITOR'S PICKS 2010/2011

EDITED BY:
BOB STRAUSS
AND
NICOLE CASTLE-KOHN

Ragnarok Around the Clock

By Michael Cieslak

O f all of the places to end up when the end of the world rolled around, Dan Lindstrom ended up in New Oslo. It was a measure of the kind of luck he had been dealing with his entire life. If he had been in his tiny third story walk up he would have simply winked out of existence like the rest of New York City. He could have been in Los Angeles and drowned as the rising oceans reacted to global warming and swamped the city. Instead, he was in New Oslo listening to the other residents and visitors bicker. His life up to that point had been a series of missteps and wrong turns all of which lead him to finding himself in a tiny north woods town when the apocalypse rolled in.

He took another sip of lingonberry flavored tea and stared out of the window. Swede Anne's Coffee Shoppe was half full of 'survivors.' Their voices washed over him, the world's most monotonous wave. The same conversation had been going on for a week.

"I think we can get out on the North Road. There shouldn't be anyone there."

"The North Road doesn't go anywhere but the woods. What are you going to do, live on tree bark and deer crap? No, the thing to do is sneak down Seventh to the Old Mayal Bridge. Then we follow the Serpentine down to Chet's. There should be a couple of canoes or kayaks or something there. We pile in and let the river take us out of town."

Dan closed his eyes. A sigh escaped him. He leaned his head back against the wall, tilting the chair back on two legs. It had been like this for days. All of the dozen or so people hiding in the boarded up building had their own ideas of where they could find safety. Each one felt compelled to not only share it with everyone else, but to try and convince everyone else to go with them.

What they all failed to understand was that there was no safe haven anymore. It was the end of the world. There was no place they could go to escape the apocalypse.

The best they could hope for was a slightly different apocalypse.

"There's nothing downriver but Cooperton." The singsong lilt of the speaker tagged her as a resident. "I figure they are as bad off as we are if not worse. At least we still have power."

"You can live without power," said the first speaker. "At least I can. I've been hunting these woods since I was six."

"Great, fifty odd years and you've never bagged anything bigger than a ground squirrel. I'm telling you the river is the way to go. We don't have to stop at Cooperton. We portage right down Main Street..."

"And go where?" Dan could take no more. His chair crashed back to the floor. All eyes were on the outlander. He rose to his feet before continuing.

"Where would you go? I can guaran-damn-tee that Cooperton is just as bad off as we are here in New Oslo. Tannenbaum is going through the same stuff as we are, but they've got to deal with a crazed Santa as well. Haven't you been watching the news? It's the end of the freaking world."

Stunned silence filled the room. Dan fixed each of the people sitting there with a momentary stare before passing on to the next. There was a lot of blonde hair in this room, many blue eyes.

"Or to be more precise, it's the ends of the freaking world."

He slumped back into his chair and tried to ignore the debate which began anew. He closed his eyes when the conversation turned, inevitably, to the vikings.

Dan had a theory. It had first popped into his head when the story of Saul's Corner hit the news. This was back when there were still news broadcasts, before Los Angeles had been consumed by fires, mudslides, earthquakes, and floods of cinematic proportion. It was before cynical, agnostic New York City simply vanished.

Caleb Baxter was the preacher whose flock was being tormented by Death, War, Pestilence, and Famine. The supernatural beings killed indiscriminately yet never spoke above a whisper. Father Caleb was a grade school dropout who had received his calling late in life. He was almost completely illiterate and had never read the Scriptures. He had, however, listened to all thirty-five cassettes of The Audio Bible. He did not know about homonyms, so perhaps the misunderstanding regarding the Four Horsemen of the Apocalypse could be forgiven.

The second clue had come from the refugees from Tannenbaum, a town a few miles to the west where it was CHRISTMAS EVERY DAY OF THE YEAR. It was a great way to increase tourism, but the people who lived and worked there hated Christmas, reindeer, elves, and especially Santa. They knew that "jolly old elf" was actually a mean old drunk in a bad smelling red suit. When the end of the world came to Tannenbaum, it did so in the form of marauding elves led by an evil Kringle.

Dan's theory consisted of three simple conclusions:

It was the end of the world.

Everyone had a different idea of what this meant.

The Apocalypse was democratic.

Simply put, the dominant belief of any given area dictated how that particular portion of the world would end. Los Angeles went out like a summer blockbuster. Saul's Corner got their ridiculous Hoarse Men. Tannenbaum had psycho Santa.

New Oslo was populated by the descendants of Swedes, Norwegians, and Finns who had moved to Michigan's Upper

Peninsula and taken jobs in the mines and the mills. They had brought with them tales of Vikings and the Norse gods.

New Oslo had Valkyries.

☐

Someone began banging on the door. The people holed up in the coffee shop looked at each other for only a moment before their eyes dropped back to their laps. The frosted glass rattled in its frame.

"Someone please." The voice was quiet, pleading. "Open the door. They're almost here."

Dan had to strain to hear the words. The almost whisper was at odds with the loud knocking which had preceded it. He glanced at the furniture comprising the makeshift barricade. He turned towards the door, took one step, then swallowed hard. His throat had suddenly become dry. He sat heavily. The knocking resumed. Dan turned away from the pleas and reached for his tea. It was cold, bitter and tasted like rotted fruit and ashes. He took a long drink to wash down the acid rising in his throat.

The knocking stopped. One by one the patrons glanced back to the door. Dan thought he heard footsteps but would not have been able to swear to it. The knocking resumed a few doors down, the hardware store if Dan remembered Main Street correctly.

There was no mistaking the sound of hoofbeats clacking along the pavement. One moment it was quiet, the next the street was alive with the sound of thunder. Dan did not need to see the scene to know what had happened, what was about to happen. The episode had played out for him once already.

Once was enough.

He moved to the window despite himself.

There were two this time. When he had first witnessed the Valkyries' arrival there had been more, at least a dozen. They had descended from the clouds, their steeds running in the air. They did not break stride as their hooves touched the ground.

The two charging down the street looked much like the ones Dan had seen before. They could have even been two of the ones he had seen before. They all looked similar, long blonde braids streaming behind them. The sunlight gleamed off the brass of their breastplates and their winged helms.

The knocker had noticed the pair as well. The quiet knocking was replaced by a pounding.

"Please!" The voice pitched higher with each word. "For the love of God, please!"

From his vantage point, Dan could not see the panicked man. He had no problem seeing the Valkyries. They stormed by the window, one down the center of the street, one on the sidewalk inches from the building.

The knot of people who had gathered at the window with Dan took a collective step back.

The street bound warrior carried an impossibly long spear balanced easily in one hand. The closer one drew a sword as she rode by. The blade gleamed in the light of the setting sun. If asked, Dan would have said the the metal itself was on fire, not simply reflecting the red-orange light of the dying day.

As the pair rode by, the sword-bearer turned and looked at the coffee shop window. The people inside scattered. Dan held his ground, rooted in place by the Valkyrie's icy stare. Her eyes were the flat blue grey of a northern sea during a winter storm. As their eyes locked, she shimmered. Her edges became less defined. Her body was somehow less solid.

The brass and steel chest plate and chain mail skirt she had been wearing disappeared. Her garb was replaced by a flowing robe of white. Her blonde hair cascaded down her back in a soft wave. The two locked eyes for only a second, but in that time Dan felt a sense of love and compassion that had been missing from his life for years.

Then the screaming started.

The man who had been pounding on the shop door ran out into the street. His shriek had lost all pretense at speech. Dan could see the man. He was short, balding, carrying the sloth of his advanced years in a band which encircled his waist. He moved from the cover of hardware store entrance way to the middle of the street. He charged towards the pair, screaming, running a weaving pattern, his gut bouncing with each footfall.

It was suicide, nothing more. He had decided that he would rather his death be quick than slow. Perhaps he even entertained ideas of taking one of the Valkyrie with him or at least hurting one of them. It was an insane idea. How could a man hope to harm one of the handmaidens of the gods?

The man cut right as if to pass both of them in the street. The spear bearer shifted her weapon. She brought the shaft along the left side of her mount's head. Dan had a brief flash of a jousting exhibition he had seen at a Renaissance Festival years before.

With more agility than Dan would have credited him with, the man cut left again. In a flash the spear bearer was past him, weapon out of position, unable to do much more than turn and watch him go by.

He had a chance.

The scream turned into a cry of triumph as the little man ran between the Valkyrie. Once through he could cut through the alley at the end of the coffee shop or sprint for the tree line. Three more steps and he would be past them.

The swords-woman, the one which had held Dan's gaze for what seemed like a compressed eternity, was too fast for him. Her foot lashed out. It caught the runner in the temple and he crumpled to the street. His cry died in his throat. He raised himself to his hands and feet. He shook his head to clear it. Even from a distance, Dan could see the fine spray of blood which flew off. His scalp bore a deep gash. Blood gushed down the side of his face.

There was another scream, this one from the Valkyrie with the spear. There were no words, just an audible embodiment of rage. Dan clapped his hands to his ears, ducked his head. He was sure the window would explode inward from the force of the goddess' screech.

Her horse reared up, front hooves slicing the air. It pranced like this for a few steps until it was faced back the way it came. Perched high in the saddle, the Valkyrie and her mount appeared as one fearsome giant. She held the spear high above her head. The horse returned to all fours. As it dropped, the arm of the Valkyrie blurred. A bright flash marked the movement of the spear. It flew with all of the force of the horse's movement and the supernatural strength of its rider. If pressed, Dan would swear that he saw the spear spiraling around its midline as it flew true. One moment it was in the Valkyrie's hand. The next it was pinning the man to the ground.

He screamed once more. A crimson gout of blood accompanied the sound. The blood flew from his mouth, a spreading fan of his lost vitality. The spear had pierced his back high between the shoulder blades. It exited the front, below the ribs, and buried itself deep in the blacktop of the street.

The dead man, for this is essentially what he was at this point, still struggled to get his feet beneath him. He managed to get his left foot beneath him. He pushed up, raised himself to a half crouch before the foot slipped and he flopped back, sliding down the length of the spear shaft, hitting the ground hard.

The long column of wood was smeared with his blood and something darker, something which bespoke of death. It marked his movements as futile. He flopped against the street, boneless, twitching muscles connected to a brain which did yet comprehend its end.

The second Valkyrie rode slowly back down the street. She glanced at the coffee shop, but did not meet Dan's eyes. He desperately sought her gaze. She would not look at him. Instead she led her horse, a high stepping prance, to where the dying man lay. She leaned low, so low that she disappeared from view for a moment. There was a flash of flame red metal, a final spray of blood red liquid. She rose up again, slowly, deliberately. When she met Dan's gaze, the compassion that had once lived in her eyes was gone. Only hatred gleamed forth.

Her horse went from a prance, to a trot, from a trot to a gallop. A few paces later it was airborne, galloping across the sky. Her companion rode quickly up the street. She grabbed her spear without slowing. The still bleeding corpse was lifted into the air along with a piece of the tarmac. With a flick of her wrist, she sent corpse and concrete flying. The body hit the street and rolled until it caught against the curb. The horse whinnied as it took to the air. A trail of blood droplets marked its passing.

Dan felt his gorge rise as he looked back to the middle of the street. The man's head still sat there. Its eyes were wide, mouth a gaping hole, still screaming in silent terror.

Dan turned from the window, swallowing hard. He felt the bile burn at the back of his mouth.

He needed more tea.

☐

It was the final piece of the theory. More importantly, it was Dan's way out. He had seen the Valkyrie shimmer. For just a moment she had ceased to be the warrior woman of cartoons and bad made-for-cable movies and had looked like something else.

She had looked like a hand-maiden of Odin, someone charged with bringing the spirits of the fallen to their final reward.

The Valkyrie had become the very embodiment of the characters his Mor-Mor had told him as a child. The change had happened the moment that Dan had made eye contact with her. For just a moment they had connected and she had stopped being what everyone else thought a Valkyrie was and had become what Dan knew them to be.

There was no way to survive the coming apocalypse. He and the others in the coffee shop would not last long. Rather than suffer on earth, why not take his place among the gods? He could be immortal. The means to achieve this was right outside. All he would have to do is convince the others of this.

He looked around the room. Many of the occupants were sitting alone or in pairs. Their eyes were either wide with shock or closed in exhaustion. One table in the back held six people. Dan almost screamed when he realized they were still discussing escape options.

Instead, he stood. Most of the survivors turned towards him. He rapped on the table until he had everyones attention.

"You can stop trying to figure out where to go and how to get there. I have a plan."

Canoe guy's face hardened. He was not going to accept anyone else's ideas. That was fine with Dan. There were bound to be a few casualties. The rest regarded him with looks that ranged from cautious optimism to vague disbelief.

"The Valkyrie," he began.

"The what now?"

Dan was not sure who had asked the question. He closed his eyes and took a deep breath.

"The scary ladies on horseback with the big sharp pointy things are Valkyrie."

He could not keep the derision out of his voice. A few more expressions switched towards disbelief.

"As I am sure most of you know, in Norse mythology the Valkyrie are tasked with finding the souls of brave warriors and taking them up to Valhalla. There they live forever…"

A different voice interrupted him.

"I doubt that the guy who got impaled today would agree with you. He seems more dead than immortal."

"That is because you are not thinking about the Valkyrie as they are. You are mixing them up with all kinds of other characters. They are supposed to be peaceful."

A flurry of questions followed.

"Then how come they have swords?"

"How can a mythological character kill anyone? Those things out there are real."

"Yeah, how come they are killing everyone?"

Dan held up his hand.

"Because you expect them to do exactly that. If you all believe that they are…"

"Are you saying that this is our fault?"

Before he could answer, someone at the back table spoke up. It was the flannel clad proponent of living in the woods.

"Don't look at it as fault. Look at it as opportunity."

Dan was amazed. He had expected a lot more explaining before anyone was convinced. He had expected those seated at the back table to be among the last to accept the idea, if at all.

"What this guy, sorry son, never did get your name."

"Dan, Dan Lindstrom, my mother…"

Flannel Man waved off the explanation.

"What he is saying is that if we stop thinking of them being out to get us, they will stop being out to get us."

"That makes less than no sense at all," said the guy with the canoe plan.

"Look at Tannenbaum," Dan said. "They expected bad stuff from Santa Claus and they got just what they imagined. If you think about it, it does make sense."

"Are you saying we don't have any sense?" Canoe Guy leapt to his feet.

"Shut up and sit down, Elim. What he is saying is that if we stop thinking about these, whatchcallit, Valkyries as killers we have a chance."

"Exactly."

"What we all have to do is think about them as weak and defenseless. Once we have that image fixed in our minds, we can rush them."

"Rush them?" Dan's brow furrowed. "Why would we rush them?"

"Right, why not just escape?"

Dan turned towards the direction of the new speaker. Flannel Man would have none of it.

"Because once we stop thinking about them as weak they will come after us again."

"No, that's not it at all." No one seemed to hear Dan's protest.

"Why don't we just stop thinking about them all together? Wouldn't they just disappear?"

"You can't not think about something. Try not thinking about a purple cow. No, we imagine them weak, then we make a break for it. If we scatter we will increase the chances that some of us will get free."

Dan silently pushed his chair in. He threaded his way between the tables and back into the kitchen. He closed the door behind him. A sob escaped him.

It was hopeless. He could not get them to agree on anything. Half of them did not even know their own heritage. They might be able to think the Valkyrie into the proper shape, but it would not last. Without a fixed image of what the Valkyrie were supposed to be they would undoubtedly go back to thinking of them as executioners. His belief alone would not be enough to save him. Anyone out there at that time would be run through.

The arguing became loud enough for Dan to hear through the kitchen door. There was a shout, almost a bark of surprise. There was a loud crash.

If only there were a way to get them to all stop thinking at once.

Dan looked around the kitchen. For a coffee shop, it had a surprisingly large amount of cutlery. He started to smile as he added another conclusion to his theory.

***

Dan stepped out into the street. He dragged a hand across his brow, wiping away residual blood. His hand was still wrapped around a six inch carving knife. Hoofbeats echoed from the next block over. Dan stood in the center of Main Street. The hoof falls stopped abruptly. Dan dropped the knife and stepped away from it.

There were two Valkyrie, one at either end of the town. Dan was not sure, but he thought that they might be the two from the previous day. He focused on the closer of the two.

He concentrated on everything he knew about the handmaidens of Odin.

As the woman bore down on him she began to change. Once again the breast plate and spear disappeared to be replaced by the long flowing white robes. She smiled a beatific smile. She drew still nearer. Her horse slowed to a walk. The hand which had once held a spear was now outstretched. She leaned over the thickly muscled neck of her steed, reaching for him.

As she did, Dan could see that it was indeed the Valkyrie from the day before. Her blue eyes sparkled the way they had when she had first shimmered and then changed. Gone was the hard, angry look she had had when she drew her sword.

"I'm ready," Dan called.

Her visage seemed to flicker, just for a moment. Dan tried desperately to cling to the image of the angelic woman on horseback. He wanted only to see the kind being that was going to take him away from all of the fear and insanity that marked everyday life. He wanted to see the woman who would bear him up to the Viking heaven and not the warrior with the sword.

"No, no. I understand what you are. I am ready to be taken up to Valhalla."

"You are bloodied."

The voice of the Valkyrie sounded like winter wind.

"I...I did what needed to be done."

The Valkyrie's eyes darkened once more. Her soft features flowed. The gentle roundness disappeared. Her cheeks stood out as sharp lines on the angled plane of her face. Her eyes narrowed.

"You are bloodied, but not from battle. You are bloodied, but you are not <u>Einherjar</u>."

"No, no wait."

Dan started to move backwards, one step, then two, then half a dozen. He glanced down at the knife. She drew her flaming sword with a slow, deliberate motion. As he turned to run, Dan saw her eye flicker once more showing something, pity or glee, he was not sure which.

Then he felt the cold bite of the steel.

Across the Pond

By Christopher Nadeau

I saw the old woman when I was eleven years old. Some of my friends and I were enjoying the summer break and chasing each other through the forest in some childish imitation of a slasher movie.

I was the horribly disfigured killer getting revenge for something that happened to him when he was my age. I could identify with those guys because my father went crazy when I was five.

I was so good at finding my friends I would often pretend to wander off into the forest to give them time to think they were safe before I pounced. This time I went all the way to Judson's Pond, an area none of us were supposed to go near. I didn't know I'd reached the Pond until I felt the ground grow soft beneath my feet. I sniffed and smelled moisture that hadn't been there moments before.

I walked a bit further, wondering how close I was to the body of water I couldn't see.

"How'd you get here?" a male voice demanded.

I spun around, gasping at the sight of the stooped-over elderly man mere inches from me. He looked physically weak but my eyes fell on the shovel he carried.

"You one of them deaf ones, boy?"

I shook my head. "I think I'm lost."

The man spat something thick and brown from his nearly toothless mouth and fixed me with a quizzical stare. "You can't *think* you're lost, boy. You either is or ain't!"

I glanced around the unfamiliar area. The old man appraised me for what felt like a full minute before nodding and leaning forward a bit.

"Tell me what you see," he said.

I shrugged. "Trees and stuff… I don't know."

"Don't yank my chain, boy! I know there's trees! Hell, I pissed on one not five minutes ago! I'm askin' what you SEE."

I frowned and gazed about the area, trying to take in whatever this crazy old coot was talking about.

"I smell a pond," I said.

The old man grinned and took in a deep sniff. "Dang right, you do. *Dang* right."

I nodded and forced a smile; now that I'd given him what he wanted…

"Wanna know why you can't see it yet, boy?"

I blinked. "How come?"

The old man giggled, dropped his shovel onto the wet ground. "'Cause I ain't let you!"

At this point, it occurred to me he might be crazier than my father. Dad still battled his voices and urges and sometimes emerged victorious. This old man had succumbed to his a long time ago. I glanced around him, trying to figure out how fast to run to avoid his gnarled hands

"Takes a real special sort to make it all the way down here, boy." The old man stooped over and picked up his shovel. I'd lost my window of opportunity for escape. "Them that make the effort usually wind up… well, let's just say they don't end up too happy."

I felt my eyes widen. This was the real slasher flick come to life. But instead of an invincible killer in a mask, it was going to be a loony old man with a shovel. I fought the urge to cry.

"Well, don't just stand there like somebody planted you, boy! You come all this way."

I opened my mouth to question him and closed it as he moved closer. "Now, you be sure to hold my hand as we go or you might fall in and never come back out."

I obeyed and we headed deeper into the forest, directly for Judson's Pond.

***

Before I tell you what I saw, I should bring you up to speed on the way of things these days. Times have changed and the world has turned strange, unsettling. I'm not sure where to start but I'll do my best.

We weren't invaded or visited by aliens and we didn't discover new life out in space. In fact, space programs are non-existent; nobody feels gung-ho about finding anything else that might be as bad as or even worse than what we've got here.

We call them "newcomers. They arrived about twenty years ago, covered in a viscous liquid and speaking some bizarre foreign language that was unlike anything spoken on this planet.

Frankly, they scared the living shit out of anybody who saw them when they started showing up.

One woman in England was stepping into the shower when a newcomer seemed to emerge from her running shower head, crying and grabbing the shower curtain before stumbling and falling to the tub floor. A man in Rhode Island driving home during a horrible thunderstorm had to swerve his vehicle into a road sign when a newcomer popped out of thin air right in front of him. School children on a field trip to a swimming pool in Windsor, Canada ran screaming from the pool as not one but five newcomers suddenly appeared in the water, flailing and screaming in their odd, high-pitched language.

This type of thing happened all over the world for six months before it petered out. In most First World countries, they were quarantined and studied. In Third World countries, they were often killed on sight.

The newcomers didn't seem violent. There were a few isolated incidents of physical confrontation, but for the most part they just stood around looking frightened and shocked.

When they first arrive, they look like pink mannequins that haven't fully formed. Their faces are without lines or blemishes or even features if you don't count the hooded eyes and tiny mouths. To many of us, they look like full-grown fetuses. But that's nothing compared to how they look when they get older.

***

The old man led me by the hand deeper and deeper into the forest, the ground giving way beneath our shoes as we went. I ignored his annoying whistling and tried not to fall or stumble. The last thing I needed was to give this weirdo the idea I was too much of a burden to keep around.

"Almost there, boy, almost there," he said in a sing-song fashion.

"My mom always told me not to go to Judson's Pond," I said.

The old man stopped for a moment and cocked an eyebrow in my direction. "She ever tell you why?"

I shrugged. "She said it was dangerous."

"But did she ever tell you *why* it was dangerous?"

I frowned. I'm not sure she knew why. Maybe she was just passing along information the same way folks in church do without really understanding why they believe in what the preacher's saying.

The old man grinned. "It's only dangerous if you don't make it, boy. Look at me! I made it and I'm *just fine*!"

All those childhood lessons about not saying anything at all if I didn't have something nice to say entered my brain at the same time, a rising cacophony of propriety drowning out any and all dissent.

The old man pulled me along like a disobedient puppy, my feet momentarily leaving the floor. He told me to stop stalling because I'd "miss it" if I didn't hurry. I had no idea how someone could miss a pond, as they tended to be stationary until they dried up. Before I could give voice to this question, however, we'd reached Judson's Pond.

That's when I saw the old lady.

***

I saw my first fully grown newcomer the day I graduated junior college. It was working maintenance in the meeting hall

244

where we had our reception. I gasped when I saw it, taking a few steps back, much to the amusement of my classmates.

"First time?" Dave Marsters said.

I nodded. "Is that what they…"

"That's right," Jessica Speakman said. "In all their hideous glory."

"Jesus."

Dave said, "I doubt Jesus had anything to do with it."

I hated myself for being so close-minded but it was difficult to disagree with Dave. The newcomer looked like a burn victim, its face filled with scars and melted features. It tried to avoid my gaze as I stared but eventually it looked up from dumping a garbage can and managed a pathetic smile.

I threw up.

***

The old man placed a filthy finger over my mouth before I could say anything, his previously jovial mood now tense and annoyed.

"Don't you say nothin', boy," he whispered. "Not a dang-blamed word. Can't you see she's *thinkin'*?"

I saw the silhouette of an old woman in a rocking chair sitting a little too close to Judson's Pond. I craned my neck a bit and heard what sounded like humming but no tune I recognized. Sounded like a bunch of unconnected sounds randomly appearing in her voice box and vanishing as quickly as they'd arrived.

"Never speak until she's done thinkin'." The old man's tone was reverent; a tad frightened, as if he feared what might happen if I didn't obey.

He needn't have worried; I was too freaked out to do anything but what I was told. I stood and watched the old lady rock back and forth and hum her tuneless song for God knows how long. Once she'd stopped, I turned and gave the old man an expectant look.

"Mother, we done got us another one," the old man said.

"Already?" the old lady said. "My, it's been a good month."

"It sure enough has," the old man said.

"The boy can approach."

The old man propelled me forward. I landed on my left knee, the repulsive feeling of mud and probably feces greeting the impact. I got to my feet and took a few steps forward.

"Let me look on you, boy," the old lady said. "Come on, now."

I walked until I was close enough to be seen but still unable to see her.

"Such a handsome lad," she said. "I can smell your freshness from here."

"Go ahead now, boy," the old man said from where I'd last seen him. "Go ahead and let her get a sense of you."

I ran.

***

Rich people started hiring newcomers for menial tasks in droves. Only one problem: it wasn't legal. Newcomers were granted certain protective rights under the law but being able to work wasn't one of them. They were allowed to live in specially designated zones with their own kind. They had the right to practice their own religious beliefs which, apparently, consisted of getting together in large groups and moaning into the night sky until they passed out so that God was the last thing they acknowledged before sleep claimed them. They also had the right to maintain their own language and customs.

The segregation of newcomers lasted nearly a decade before the ACLU fought to get them integrated into society, albeit on a limited scale. Now newcomers could own homes (in specially designated areas) and move about freely as long as they kept the government apprised of their movements.

Activist groups fought tooth and nail to keep them from taking jobs from honest, hardworking Americans. But the amount of people using cheap newcomer labor was overwhelming and soon it became nothing more than an unenforced law on the books.

Then the newcomers that lived in other countries started showing up and everything went to hell.

***

I didn't get far. The old man grabbed me by the back of the shirt collar and yanked me off my feet. I went limp and allowed him to bring me back to the old lady in the rocking chair. She was once again rocking and humming that bizarre tune and we had to stand and wait until she was done.

"So disrespectful, you young people of today," she said. "When a grown-up tells you to come closer, you do as she says."

***

I cleared my throat. "Grown-ups hurt kids nowadays."

"Kids hurt grown-ups too, boy," the old man said through gritted teeth. "Always have," the old lady said. "Always have."

I wasn't sure if she was agreeing with me, him, or both of us and didn't care. I just wanted to go home.

***

"I don't know what you want from me," I said, using my scared little kid voice.

"Ain't for you to know, boy!' The old man slapped me in the back of my head.

"Let him be, Titus," the old lady said. "It's a different time."

The old man took a step back. I stepped forward as if my legs and feet were no longer fully mine to control. Whatever influence the old lady had, it was some powerful stuff.

"You should be proud you made it this far," she said.

"What does that mean?"

"It means you get to go back the way you came."

I frowned. "I don't remember which way I came in."

The old lady, still shrouded in shadow, chuckled. "Not the way you took to get here. I mean you get to still be you."

My frown deepened. "I don't understand."

"Boy's awful thick, ain't he?" Titus said.

The old lady ignored him. "Them that don't make it this far go back...changed."

I swallowed hard. "What about those who make it?"

The old lady leaned forward out of the darkness and smiled, her drawn, gray face a rictus of pure delight. "They get to *see*."

Titus grabbed me from behind and threw me into Judson's Pond.

***

The first time I saw violence committed against a newcomer, I was on my way home from the worst job I ever held. Thanks to the massive influx of cheap labor, corporations lowered what they were willing to pay for better jobs. Everybody was bitter in those days and newcomers often felt the brunt of it.

At first, only those newcomers who didn't speak any English were targeted but eventually it became commonly held belief that no newcomers were Americans. New laws granting police the ability to randomly stop them and demand documentation just seemed to fuel the fires of hatred and bigotry.

The unfortunate newcomer dressed in a landscaping company's uniform I saw getting stomped into the ground had made the decision to get something to eat at a local deli. By the time I'd rounded the corner, four guys in baseball caps and black jackets had surrounded him.

"Where the hell you think you're going, burnhead?" their leader said.

The newcomer's hooded eyes darted left and right, looking for help or escape. Eventually, they found me and lingered.

"Don't you have nothing to say?" another one of them said. "Don't you speakey the English, asshole?"

The newcomer said nothing.

"Godammit!" the leader said. "I told you I could spot one of the foreign ones a mile away."

"Let's send his ass back into the water he came from," a third man added.

In a flurry of movement, the four of them lunged at the newcomer, punching and kicking him until his horrible, high-pitched screams were silenced. Once he was down and unmoving, they lifted him and carried him to their waiting pickup truck.

I kept walking.

***

Being submerged In Judson's Pond was like being teleported to some far away world where I could only see inches in front of me and was somehow able to breathe underwater. I could see the deflected rays of sunlight above and tried kicking hard enough to aim for the surface. Something held me back. I tried to look down and see if something had wrapped itself around my ankles.

Whatever kept me from moving also dragged me down further. I kicked and flailed my arms. I opened my mouth to scream and my vision was filled with bubbles.

I felt my feet land on something solid. I forced my head to tilt downward and noticed a total lack of movement on the pond's surface. I crouched, tried propelling myself upward, only to move a few inches and then land back on the hard surface.

I looked up and could just barely make out the top of the water. There was no sunlight visible but somehow it wasn't so dark that I couldn't see.

I heard myself say, "I wanna go home. Can I please go home now?"

The surface opened up and swallowed me.

***

The first case of Newcomer's Disease took place in the Third World, in this case Brazil. The Brazilians had just begun tolerating their newcomer population when a little girl from a village just outside Rio was brought to her family doctor shivering and covered from head to upper thigh in leaking, pus-filled blisters. The small town doctor had no idea what was wrong with her. The battery of tests he ran combined with useless antibiotics and antivirals accomplished nothing.

The little girl was sent to a major hospital in Rio where she became a living experiment. Her destitute family had no ability to stop the tests, especially once she was declared infectious.

Here's where things get a little odd: no case of so-called "Newcomer's Disease" has ever officially been reported as having been passed from one individual to the next. In fact, those few who have contracted it not only failed to infect anyone in their immediate vicinity, they were never heard from again.

I'm not one to embrace conspiracy theories. I don't believe JFK was shot by more than one guy. I believe we landed on the moon. I have yet to see conclusive evidence of a cover-up at Roswell. But a supposedly infectious disease that never seems to infect anyone near the infected is suspicious.

Despite many dissenting voices, including medical professionals who debated the official story, Newcomer's Disease became the latest media sensation and government targeted "epidemic" in North America.

***

My next conscious memory was of waking up on my side in a murky, cavern-type structure. I shot up to a sitting position and winced from the pain of forcing sedentary muscles into action. How long had I been out?

I got to my feet and gazed about the place, covering my nostrils with the top of my index fingers as a pungent aroma hit them. From somewhere far off, the maddening sound of dripping water maintained a steady beat.

"What the hell?" I said, rewarded with my own words echoed back at me.

"Ain't no cussin' in this place, boy."

I whirled around, unsurprised to see crazy old Titus standing before me. "How did you get here?"

Titus hauled his hand back and slapped me. "I won't be questioned by no child!"

I placed my hand to my cheek, willed myself not to cry, hating myself for my failure and the tiny drop of urine that came out when the old man struck me. I glanced down at his withered crotch and felt a rage surging in me unlike any I'd ever experienced. Before he could react, I let out a feral snarl and ran straight for him, head-butting him in the soft spot.

The old man stumbled backward, both hands grabbing himself, a look of complete and utter surprise on his wrinkled face. His howl of pain, it sounded as if fifty animals of various types had all decided to cry out at once. The sound echoed throughout the cavern, forcing me to place my hands over my ears until it abated moments later.

"You little sum bitch!" Titus yelled. "Up to me, I'd rip your head off and whup your ass with it!"

So, he couldn't hurt me even if he wanted to. I suddenly felt a little better about the situation.

**

A man named Joey Woodstone wrote a book called *Pray for the Infected* that purported to tell the story of how an uncontained laboratory-created virus got out before the facility in which it was manufactured could be sealed off. According to Woodstone, the effects of this virus were identical to Newcomer's Disease and not at all infectious. He claimed only those in close proximity to the virus when it went airborne would contract it.

The laboratory Woodstone claimed created the virus was an American one located in a small village just outside Rio.

Had Woodstone left things at that, he might not have suffered the ramifications of his later claims, namely that the lab in question was contracted by the U.S. government to create biological warfare agents that could be specifically targeted to individuals. The intention was to create something with minimal infection risk so as to avoid any perceived violations of international law.

The American media did everything it could to erode Woodstone's credibility as a researcher and journalist. Pundit after talking head after dubious expert took their turn on him. Soon his book could only be ordered online.

The funny thing is, except for a few cases in the Southwestern portion of the nation, Newcomer's Disease never achieved any type of high-level threat status in the U.S.

But that didn't stop the millions of people waiting for a reason to take it out on the newcomers.

***

Titus pushed me along through the cavernous place, his bony fingers poking me in the back whenever I slowed down or got distracted by some far away sound or movement. Although he'd never admit it, I got the impression he'd gained a newfound respect for me since our little altercation moments ago. It was clear that he didn't believe children had the right to stand up to their elders but children eventually, hopefully, became adults one day and maybe Titus was looking towards the future.

Somewhere up ahead, I heard a creaking noise that repeated itself every few seconds as if a pattern were being established. The old man rushed me along even faster, his raspy breathing matching each step.

We entered another section of the caverns, a brighter area with less humidity but no less a pungent odor permeating the still air. I felt many eyes watching me now, following my every move as if I were the most interesting thing in their universe.

"Up ahead, boy," Titus said.

I'd already learned not to question the old man. I simply nodded and kept hoping I'd either wake up or he'd grow bored with me and let me go.

"We're here," Titus said.

I looked around the area where we'd stopped. This spot looked no different from the countless others we'd passed through to get here. There was an ammonia smell in the air, faint but detectable. It stung my nostrils and I swooned a bit, surprised when Titus caught me before I could hurt myself.

"Happens at first," he said absently. "She's waitin' on you, boy."

I took a few steps forward, once again hearing the creaking sound, and squinted into the light directly ahead. A silhouette slowly came into view until I realized it was the old woman sitting in the same rocking chair she'd been in miles above the water minutes before.

"Not too much time left, boy," she said. "They's almost born."

And I realized why I'd felt eyes watching me.

***

A strange new political party emerged from the anti-newcomer movement. It claimed to base itself around old-fashioned, traditional values and beliefs but it veered dangerously into irrational hatred territory from the moment of its inception. What scared those of us who disagreed with their various platforms was the rapid rise in acceptance they enjoyed.

The issue they used to springboard themselves into the limelight was newcomer immigration. They claimed the constant arrival of newcomers from other countries was draining the economy and destroying America

Soon state-by-state legislation was passed allowing "real citizens" to demand proof of citizenship from any newcomer they felt was engaging in suspicious behavior. Add to that the still lingering fear of the disease that never materialized and you can imagine what happened next.

They fell out of the air. At least, that's how it seemed to me. One moment there wasn't anything in front of me or behind me or to the side, the next a formless mass. I spun around like a ballet dancer, trying to take it all in while the old lady and the old man chortled and hooted like hillbillies at a hoe down.

"What's happening?" I shouted. "I don't understand!"

"Ain't nothin' to understand, boy," Titus said between guffaws. "This is somethin' to look at, not think about."

I decided he was correct. Whatever was happening made no sense to me and since the two insane senior citizens were too busy singing and acting like demented carnies to help out, there was no way for me to figure it out. I watched the lumps keep showing up until there were so many of them surrounding me, I found it difficult to move or breathe.

"Name them," the old lady said.

"Excuse me?" I said.

"You heard me, boy. Give them names."

"No way!"

"Do as you're told!" Titus screeched, taking a few steps towards me.

"I said no." I heard the tremor in my voice, but stood my ground.

The sound of the old lady going back and forth in her rocking chair filled the cavern, faster and faster until my ears were filled with the high-pitched, grinding noise. I covered my ears and screamed, felt something warm and wet come out of my nostrils and realized it wasn't mucus. My brain vibrated inside my skull, feeling as if it might explode at any moment. I tried to fall to my knees but there were too many of the lumps of flesh around me and I wound up swooning back and forth, my screams muted by the overwhelming sonic assault.

Then, just as I thought my face would melt like candle wax, the rocking sound stopped. I removed my hands from my ears,wiped the trickles of blood from my upper lip and fought back tears.

"Name them," she said again.

***

The newcomer riots were met with predictable hostility and violence. I suppose it didn't help that they were marching for rights in the middle of one of the country's worst economic recessions. It also didn't help that they were so damned ugly. Nobody could stand to look at them long enough to listen to what they had to say.

I firmly believe the nation breathed a sigh of relief when the National Guard opened fire on them. The newcomers didn't respond with like violence but they had something up their sleeves that affected us a whole lot worse than a few gunshots.

***

"Please, I don't want to name them."

Titus pushed a few of the lumps out of his way until he could make eye-contact with me. "No choice, boy. Get to it."

My lower lip quivered. "Or what?"

Titus sneered. "Or you wind up just like them."

I started crying. Each time I wiped the tears from my eyes and was again able to see, there stood Titus wearing that same goddam sneer.

I can't say why I didn't want to name those things. After all, it was my ticket out and back to my normal life. Were these things the ones who had gone before me and failed?

"*Name them, damn your hide*!" the old lady yelled. "Soon the water will be back."

"I can go home when I'm done?"

"Won't have no use for you after that," Titus said, busily picking something from his remaining teeth. "Be a pleasure to see *you* gone."

I thought "Likewise, you old bastard," but I held my tongue. Taking a deep, shaky breath, I told them I would do it.

***

255

The newcomers claimed there would be no more water falling upon the Earth until their kind was given the rights they deserved. This proclamation caused quite a stir. Religious types were unsettled, wondering if these creatures were the Lord's wrath given voice. But most people just laughed it off as the desperate ranting of a bunch of savages.

That summer was the hottest on record in well over three decades. Some areas saw no rain at all.

***

I cleared my throat and looked around at the masses of undefined flesh pulsating and shifting as far as the eye could see, Titus standing in the middle of them, an expectant look on his grizzled face. Somewhere not far off the sound of a moving rocking chair made me realize the old lady was growing impatient.

"Well?" she said. "Get to it."

"Okay." I cleared my throat again. "I've got a name."

"Gonna need more than one, boy." Titus sounded bored with the whole thing.

I smiled. "I've got more than one, all right." I placed my hands on my hips like Superman and belted out the first name. "Monsters!"

The rocking chair stopped. "What did you say?"

"Monsters. Demons. Creatures. Unwanted. R-r-repulsive!" Vocabulary was my specialty in those days.

"Stop it!" The old lady sounded hysterical now. "Titus, stop him!"

"I can't, mother! You knows the rules!"

I laughed and kept going. "Hideous! Disgusting! Ugly! Unloved!"

Eventually my twelve year old brain ran out of words and I stood in place, panting like an animal.

"You little smart-ass," the old lady said.

The masses seemed to be reducing in size, melting back into the ground and the walls of the cavern. Soon I was able to see her again, still in her rocking chair. She looked smaller, less confident.

"You got no idea what you've caused," she said. "What you've done can't be fixed."

Titus said, "Want me to kill him, mother?"

She sighed. "He made his choice. Let him live with it. The young'uns have been told what they are."

"Can I go home now?" I looked from her to him and back to her.

"Take him home, Titus." She placed her face in her hands. "Take him home."

***

It's been five years since the newcomers' threat and the rain has slowly dwindled to almost nothing. Nobody knows how they did it. It defies all rational, scientific explanation. As far as we knew, they didn't have any particular technology that could control the weather. Nobody knows what the hell happened.

Well, almost nobody.

I've been remembering things lately. All that stuff about Titus and the old lady by Judson's Pond. I can't prove this, but I'm pretty sure my memory was erased, at least for a while. However, when the newcomers made their rain threat, I was suddenly assaulted with a barrage of memories it took me months to place in perspective.

It was me. It was the stupid child who thought he'd get one over on the crazy old people. I told them what they were. I told them they were unwanted and hideous.

And that's what everybody saw when they showed up.

It's so hot these days. Judson's Pond is all but dried up and gone and I find myself journeying there often. Sometimes at night I think I hear the sound of a woman sobbing, the type of sound that can only come from a grieving, disappointed mother.

I wonder what the old lady would think about the standing execution order on all newcomers. Would she be glad they were being put out of their misery? Would she delight in the fact that the bodies of water are now at such low levels that no more newcomers have emerged to suffer into this world of hate and bigotry?

People still claim to see her on the other side where no human being can possibly walk. I never have.

I lie awake at night, wondering if there's any way to give them a new name but I made my choice and the world is dying.

Maybe someday another arrogant child will give us a name and we can cross the pond back into life.

Poems From The End

Burnt Toast

Peggy Christie

ing ball of gas.
vorld spins off its axis.

Ancient War

Peggy Christie

Time running out.
Each side trying to fill their ranks
before it's too late.
Feathery wings, pale and soft.
Touching as many as possible,
surrounding in the promise
of goodness and righteousness.
Life everlasting.
Leathery wings, dark and talon tipped.
Slashing their promises
of withheld treasures and pleasures
to those not on their side.
Eternal pain.
Love and hate.
Good and evil.
Light and dark.
Kin against kin as blood rains
from the heavens.
Flesh of the faithful,
bones of the fallen.
None are spared.
Which side will win?

The End

Peggy Christie

It's done.
Sooner or later it had to be.
Nothing lasts forever,
isn't that what they say?
The TV is barking again,
talking heads blathering about
hell.
Hell on wheels.
Hell in a hand basket.
Hell on earth.
They don't know hell.
That comes later,
after the Fall.
When the lights go out
and no one has a candle.

Erie Tales:

Tales of the Apocalypse/
Resurrection Mary

Bonus Featurette:
Editor's Picks 2010/2011

Edited By:
Bob Strauss
and
Nicola Castle-Kelly

THE END IS NIGH

Bloody Run

By MontiLee Stormer

Mary sipped.
 It tasted like hot kisses and warm touches. Long after she swallowed, she could still taste the warmth: sweet, tart, fire, memory.

She wasn't supposed to patronize with the guests, but he was shelling out cash and she was lonely. She looked a question to the bartender, her boss, her keeper, and he tipped his head with a curt bow. His eyes were smiling and that was good; George approved of the monthly regular gentleman who brought her flowers and small boxes of candy, the man who tipped his hat and pulled out her stool. One night after a show, he even kissed her on the cheek. He had a room at The Gotham. They walked the few blocks to have dinner and before too many evenings, she was in his room, kisses and touches, frantic and tender, warm and wet. She woke up tangled in his legs and with his cologne in her hair.

Whispers are cruel, and they carried rumors of dancers in other clubs in other cities. When he arrived back into town, he was evasive and closed. Mary couldn't have that. She sought out the girl who was older than her looks let on, yet wise enough to be a legend, and asked for a little something to keep him close. What the woman asked Mary to do was indecent and very personal, but she agreed with a blush. She disappeared into the bathroom and returned with a handkerchief scented with her musk. The girl told Mary to bring her beau for drinks and she would have what she wanted.

In the evening, in that bar, the Cat Dragged Inn, the girl was clear - the drink on the right was for Mary: a simple

Whisky Sour. The drink on the left was for him: the sugar so he always returned; the lemon to cleanse his mind of all other women; the cinnamon to make his love for her burn for eternity; and ginger to make her linger in his mind no matter where he was.

Mary sipped.

She looked up and she saw a man who would always travel and find a woman to keep him warm no matter where he was. She did not see a man for Mary. She knew it and it broke her heart.

Mary ran from the bar and into the streets. When the headlights cut too close she ducked into a graveyard and hid among the stones. The moon was bright and she walked, following the sound of water until she came upon the creek. Hot and thirsty, she kneeled down and leaned over the calm pool, the wet grass soaking her dress. In the water she saw the only person who would ever love her. Mary smiled and the woman in the water smiled. Her lips brushed the surface.

Mary slipped.

I've Got a Secret

By Peggy Christie

Felicia squeezed the beads of her rosary in her fist. The facets of the red glass left hexagonal imprints on her palm. Felicia found comfort in the Lord and, as a freshman at St. Katherine's high school; she had plenty of opportunity to seek solace from Him.

From her first day, Felicia became the favorite target of two upper classmen: Tammy Berkshire and Karrie Hendersen. These two seniors found perverse pleasure in making Felicia's daily life a living hell, from morning swirlies to weekly locker sabotage.

Felicia tried to appease them. She'd get them snacks or be the look out when they smoked in the bathroom. She thought it might make things better but despite her efforts, the hazing continued.

So when Tammy offered her a ride home after school, Felicia felt wary.

"Hey, Fel. You wanna ride?"

"Why?"

"Why? That's an odd question."

Karrie, who sat on the open passenger side window, giggled.

"I didn't mean anything-"

"Hey," Tammy held up her hands. "If you don't want a ride, I'm not going to force you. I was just trying to be nice."

Felicia bit her bottom lip. If Tammy was being nice and she refused her, the bullying might get worse.

"Okay. I'd love a ride home."

"That's my girl. Hop in!"

.75"

Twenty minutes later Tammy drove past Felicia's house and headed for the highway.

"Tammy, that was my house."

"I said I'd take you home, Frosh. I never said when."

Tammy and Karrie ignored her pleas to go home. For hours, Felicia sat clutching her rosary, wishing she'd never gotten in the car. Now, in the dark, Tammy drove them down Dunhill Road, a backwoods dirt lane lined on both sides with tall trees that made Felicia feel as if she were inside a coffin.

"Hey, Fel. You know about this road, right?" Tammy asked.

"No."

Karrie laughed. "You're kidding? You know don't about him?"

"Him?"

"Yeah," Tammy continued. "The Hitchhiker."

"It looks like a hitchhiker but it's not human."

"You mean like a ghost?"

Karrie laughed again. "Not everyone sees him, you understand. Only those who've been chosen."

"Ch-chosen for what?"

Karrie whispered.

"To die."

Felicia gasped and Tammy snickered.

"It's said that he looks different for everyone. Some say he looks like an old farmer, others like a Union soldier. Could be Satan himself. No matter how he looks, though, if you see him, you don't live to talk about it."

Felicia frowned. "If no one survives, who tells the stories?"

Tammy glared at Felicia in the rearview mirror.

"The point is that certain people see him and those people die. The legend says whomever sees him has a deep dark secret. Something that could ruin lives if it ever got out."

"Yeah," Karrie said. "He sees into you and can tell if you've been a bad girl."

"So, Fel. Is that whole rosary-carrying, God-loving thing real? Or are you hiding behind it?"

.75"

The two seniors laughed but Felicia stopped listening. The truth was she did have a secret.

When Felicia was growing up, the woman living down the street from her was a prostitute. No one could prove it, of course. Just watching the men come and go from her place was proof enough. They hid behind the guises of gas company uniforms or dressed as poll takers during elections. Felicia's parents stirred up the neighborhood to alienate the poor woman at every opportunity.

Melody. That was her name. Felicia wondered how someone with such a beautiful name could be a 'filthy whore'. But most of all, she wondered what it was like to be a prostitute. To have sex for money with all different kinds of men? Felicia thought it would be exciting. She thought she would enjoy it.

If her parents ever knew that, they'd kill her. Or themselves. Or both.

Suddenly a woman popped into view on the road ahead of them. Felicia could see her white nightgown shine like a star in the black sky. The wind picked up her long chestnut hair and tossed it about. As the car approached, the woman turned and looked at Felicia, who pressed her hands against the window.

"No," she whispered.

"What?" Tammy said.

"Did you see her?" Felicia asked.

"Her? Her, who?"

"It looked just like Melody."

"I didn't see anyone. Did you, Kar?"

"Nope. I think Fel's losing it."

"Who the hell is-"

Tammy looked in the review mirror. She slammed on the brakes and the Chevy skidded to a halt in a spray of rocks. While Karrie screamed at her, Tammy threw the car into park. She twisted around to get a better look at the back seat where only a red beaded rosary lay coiled on the beige leather.

Forgotten

By John Pirog

D on slowed down upon catching sight of the lonely looking figure standing on the shoulder of the road. Pulling his Chevy onto the gravel shoulder, he glanced into his rear view mirror. A petite, pale blonde female no more than 20 years old walked toward his vehicle. As she got in and turned to him with a smile, Don caught a faint smell that he could not quite describe. It wasn't "bad", but just strangely out of place.

"Hi", he spoke while extending his hand. "I'm Don."

"Clarissa she answered, extending her hand in return. Don was immediately taken back by the freezing temperature of the hand in his grasp but hoped he did not betray any sense of shock to the frail young woman. "Do you live around here, or are you on vacation?"

With a faint smile, the mysterious passenger replied, "You could say that I live around here, yes."

"Um, where are you headed ?"

"Just up the road a few miles. 453 Claymore Boulevard. Is that out of your way ?"

"No, no. I'm actually heading all the way to Pittsburgh so that's right on my way."

Several minutes of awkward silence followed before the woman exclaimed, "There, that's it!" Don pulled over onto the over grown grass by the road and put his car in park.

"Come with me!", Clarissa said as she opened the passenger door and stepped out. "I need to show you something!"

As she scampered into the darkened area partially lit by the full moon, Don looked at the immediate surroundings. An unlit brick and stone large house that appeared to be long vacant stood just up the road to the right. Miscellaneous trash, graffiti and wild weeds cluttered the area.

Don exited his Camaro and walked slowly toward the imposing structure. As he neared it, he could see that all the windows had been smashed out and the porch had partially caved in. Stepping inside, he instantly recognized the musty odor as being identical to that of the woman herself, only much stronger.

Don's instinct told him that the woman was most likely a crazy homeless squatter and that he should leave now. Yet, something was drawing him further into the decaying structure. He passed a table and chair covered in thick dust and fallen plaster as he fished a lighter from his pocket. Holding the small flame, Don saw a door in front of him. Frightened yet intrigued, he placed his hand on the door and pushed. The rusted, filthy door fell with a mighty crash, causing Don to jump back and yell.

Swallowing a lump in his throat and wiping his sweaty palms on his pants legs, he entered the room and saw something that would haunt him until his dying day.

In the corner of the room, barely illuminated by the tiny lighter, hung a tattered noose! Shreds of fabric and strands of fair blonde hair clung to it. Below the noose reposed a headless skeleton dressed in a faded yellow dress. To the right of it sat a jawless skull. Its hollow eye sockets faced the bony torso as though keeping watch over it.

Don raced from the large house. Using his cell phone, he alerted the police, who arrived within 20 minutes. After answering their questions, Don hit the road once more. As he drove, he recalled a story his grandmother once told him about her cousin who had hung herself more than 50 years earlier after her fiancé left her for another woman. When he returned home and asked his grandmother about the cousin, he was not surprised to hear the name: *Clarissa Jones*.

Don never told anyone of his experience with the hitchhiker. After all, who would believe him? Yet sometimes, when the wind whips through the trees and the moon hangs full,-he can Clarissa's voice whispering, "Thank you, Don!"

Erie Tales:

Tales of the Apocalypse/
Resurrection Mary

Bonus Featurette
Editor's Picks 2010/2011

Edited by:
Bob Strauss
and
Nicole Castle-Kelly

The Woman Next Door

By James Park

I quit smoking just before moving into the apartment at 2063 Farleigh Road. Aside from moving into the apartment itself, it was the biggest mistake I ever made. I knew it wasn't going to be easy, as I've watched friends quit, only to see them start again. They used all sorts of methods, some trying the patch, others the gum, and my more daring friends even went for hypnosis. But they all started again. I decided that my approach needed to be different, so I didn't try any gimmicks. You can chew gum or wear a patch if you want, but the best way to quit is to stop setting the ends of your cigarettes on fire. If you do that then it's impossible to carry on as a smoker.

Recently single, as of late a non-smoker, and moving into a new apartment, the possibilities felt limitless. I was ready for a new life. It didn't bother me that the apartment was most likely haunted. In fact, it fascinated me. I've read endlessly about ghosts, with a particular interest for spirits from the holocaust, and I decided that it was time to let my curiosity get the better of me. When Mr. Ackley offered the vacancy at $200 a month, I knew something wasn't right. I inspected the dwelling thoroughly, and the two-bedroom townhouse was more than habitable. The surrounding neighborhood was quaint, with a park across the street, along with an elementary school, a library, and a swimming pool. In the strip mall behind it there was a good Italian bistro, and a cozy pub where I could relax with a beer after class. It was priced $500 below the other properties in the neighborhood, so I was certain that someone had died an unfortunate death in this apartment, and their spirit remained. For $200 a month I was more than happy to share quarters with a ghost.

It was a warm July afternoon when I moved in, and it gave me the opportunity to become acquainted with my new surroundings. Traffic on the street was slow, but I imagined that might change in the fall when school started. Children came and went from the swimming pool and the library, and customers visited the diner directly behind my apartment, but other than that the neighborhood was quiet.

There was a thick layer of dust in the bottom of the mailbox, but that was no surprise. The look on Mr. Ackley's face when I signed the lease told me that I was the first person to live there in some time. I attracted attention while unloading boxes. There was a young red-headed boy riding a tricycle in the driveway, and he kept watching me from the corner of his eye. The driveway led to a row of carports, used by all of the neighbors, and I wasn't exactly certain which apartment the boy lived in. The elderly woman next door stood at her window and stared. Dressed in a wool shirt with a thick collar, hair pulled back, and a stern look across her face, she resembled Dr. Herta Oberheuser, the mad scientist of Ravensbrueck concentration camp. I waved and smiled, but didn't get a response. It must have surprised her to see someone moving into the empty apartment. When I approached her doorstep she pulled the curtains shut, and she declined to answer my knock, so I shrugged it off and returned to work.

Once settled in I fixed myself a cup of chamomile tea and rested in my favorite easy chair, a copy of David Irving's biography on Hermann Goring in hand. I taught courses on Nazi Germany to second year undergraduates. Throughout the summer I'd found myself busy reading related biographies and the published papers of my esteemed colleagues.

I wasn't disturbed by anything out of the ordinary that night, and soon discovered that my new surroundings came with a collection of annoyances that were unexpectedly human in nature. The steps in the old woman's apartment must have been just on the other side of mine, for I could hear footsteps marching up and down into late hours of the night. Other than that I couldn't hear a sound from her apartment, save for when she paced at the very top of the steps, which caused the floorboards to creak. I could hear voices in the apartment to the other side, but the voices were soft. Being that the townhouse held a family of four, I considered myself quite lucky that the noise wasn't worse. In fact, I soon learned that most of the townhouses held families, for I had selected to live on the corner of a street that dead-ended into an elementary school. The small red-headed boy on the tricycle wasn't the only child in the neighborhood, but inside the walls of my apartment I couldn't hear children at all.

It was the high school students that kept me up my first night, and many nights afterwards. I soon learned that they liked to congregate on the playground of the elementary school after dark. I imagined that they were there to smoke grass and make out, maybe even fornicate, for they were old enough to have adult desires but still young enough to be kept under their parent's watch. They needed a place to go at night, and the playground across the street from me was the place they selected. I could hear the swing set squeak in the middle of the night, accompanied by their laughing and cursing. I prayed that this would end once school started.

It didn't take long to find the spots in the neighborhood that suited me best. I spent the rest of my summer days at the library, reading about Bormann and Goebbels, and even busied myself with fine literature, for I've always been fond of the works of Poe and Doyle. Additionally, I read up on ghosts, anticipating the phenomenon I might encounter. In the evenings I tried new restaurants—the quaint diner behind my apartment, the fine Italian bistro in the strip mall—and found most places to my liking. But it was the pub where I eventually found myself most evenings. I fell in love with the atmosphere the second I walked in. The walls were adorned with prohibition era pictures, black-and-whites of men dressed in overalls huddled around large stills, holding glasses of their concocted fermentations. The booths were occupied by casual diners, but the bar made me most comfortable, for that's where the regular patrons gathered. It proved to be the best spot to make new acquaintances. Roger and Scottie were there every night, talking sports and placing bets on whatever game was shown on the big screen TV. The bartender was a young girl named Misti, and though a bit chubby, she was sweet in nature and listened to my stories. The only real nuisance at the bar was old man Wallace, for he coughed constantly, looked deathly ill, and ignored most everyone. He just sat there in his old tattered clothes, a stack of bills beside him, and a short whisky, no soda, in hand. When the glass was empty Misti would refill it and take the appropriate fee from his stack; it didn't seem necessary to ask if he wanted another. The other patrons rarely acknowledged his presence, except to joke that he resembled one of the moonshiners pictured on the wall.

The occurrences in my apartment were minor, *at first*. There were pictures that I'd straighten daily, only to find them crooked when I returned. Pieces of mail would disappear, only to reappear in other rooms. I stopped making purchases with cash, for any change left unattended would vanish. Overall, I found the presence intriguing, for the experience truly was amazing, and I assumed that it would present me with scores of stories to share with my new companions at the pub. The only real irritations came from outside my walls, for the old lady next door seemed to walk up and down the stairs endlessly, and the footsteps and creaky floorboards proved bothersome. I found that I couldn't pull into the driveway without fear of hitting the red-headed boy with the tricycle. He wasn't a very bright young lad. He'd do circles in the driveway, never paying attention to cars that came and went, and seemed inclined to jut in front of me whenever I tried to leave.

When school started I could still hear the teenagers at night, the creaking of the swing set, the laughter and the cursing. But at that point other problems proved to be more significant. The ghost became fond of hiding term papers, or getting the pages out of order, spilling liquid paper on them, and a myriad of other hijinks. I soon formed the habit of leaving papers in the car and then grading them either at the library or the diner, that is, when they were open. The obstacle proved to be inconvenient, as the library held limited weekend hours and the diner didn't open on Sundays.

As irritating as it was, it soon occurred to me that the biggest nuisance in my life was loneliness. I missed Kait. The first month apart had been refreshing, for there was no one around to criticize my way of living. She was a free spirit, a hippie, a drifter, and I was a settled intellectual, content to stay home at night with my books. It didn't matter that we both enjoyed theater and fine dining, our relationship had been doomed from the start. It was loneliness that led to my first cigarette. I'd always enjoyed a good smoke while reminiscing over the past, and thought that memories of Kait deserved a cigarette. I picked up a pack at a family-owned grocery store after leaving the pub, and didn't mind paying the inflated price that one pays for the convenience of a small grocery store near their apartment. When I lit up the taste was horrible. My palate no longer held the immunity that a pack-a-day-habit provides, and the first drag reminded me just how vile smoking is. The foul taste invaded my mouth, my lungs, and soon contaminated all of my senses. As bad as it was, I still finished the cigarette, right down to the filter, for I'd already gotten it in my mind that I deserved a smoke. When it was gone I fished out two more, for memories of Kait ran deep and I was bound to need another. I held the rest of the pack beneath the faucet and ran water over it. It was the best way I knew to prevent myself from smoking the entire pack. When I turned around both cigarettes were gone, and it made me chuckle. Perhaps the ghost was looking out for my health. I decided to retire for the evening, for I had too much pride to march back to the grocery store for a second pack of cigarettes.

The next evening I found myself at the pub talking about Kait, endlessly. Misti was such a sweet girl; she listened. It made me feel better, the way she put her hand on mine and said, "It always hurts to lose someone, but it's best to just leave the past behind and move on."

So that's what I did. I buried myself in my work, teaching classes and publishing papers, and soon found myself stranded in my office until late each evening. I didn't want to risk taking any term papers home, or even worse, losing work that I intended to publish. My little corner of the hall was cozy, so I began hiding there until it was time to meet the gang at the pub.

Late one evening I retrieved a strange letter from the mailbox. I'd left early that day for class and hadn't returned home until after the pub closed. There was no return address, but the sender, Samantha Samuelson, had signed her name. The correspondence was short and to the point: "By now you've probably learned that you're not alone. I know because I've been inside, though not in many years. You have to ignore the ghosts if you want them to leave you alone. They'll grow bored quickly. If you let on that they bother you they'll keep playing games." The letter was closed, "Kind regards."

I wasn't sure how to react. I assumed that Samantha used to live here and, out of kindness, kept an eye on the property's rental status in order to warn new tenants. She'd referred to the presence as ghosts, rather than a ghost, but I didn't care to read too deeply into this. Perhaps there were two, and each was a smoker.

After taking a few days to digest the contents of the letter, I thought it best to follow Samantha's advice. What harm was there in ignoring ghosts. I'd accrued plenty of annoyances, and of them ghosts were the least of my concerns. Kait was still at the top of my list, or better yet, I should say that loneliness topped the list, for other than Misti's kind ear I hadn't enjoyed female companionship since moving. I could hear the old woman next door marching up and down her steps at all hours of the night, and when I came and went she just stood at her window and stared. I made several attempts to talk to her, not to complain about the sound of her footsteps, but to be neighborly, and possibly get her to stop staring. But when I approached she just pulled the curtains shut and ignored my knocking.

The red-headed boy on his tricycle, the high school kids and their commotion, these were still minor irritations, and I soon discovered that the glumness of my new life by far outweighed these trivial matters. The companionship at the pub had been charming at first, but after a while I felt myself conforming to the lifestyle of a drunkard who waists his evenings away at the local watering hole. Roger and Scottie placed wagers with each other nightly, and there was a one in one chance that the winner would gloat and the loser would blame his misfortune on the official. I soon grew tired of old man Wallace's coughing, as well as the cathartic noises he released while drinking himself to death. This was no replacement for a relationship, I thought. If not for Misti, I'd have stopped visiting the pub altogether.

I had my second cigarette soon after receiving the letter. I wasn't going to start smoking again, but a letter of this magnitude deserved a cigarette. I paid the inflated price at the family-owned grocery store, and again found the taste revolting, but proceeded to puff away until the cherry rested snuggly against the filter, almost burning it. I repeated my routine, placing two cigarettes aside before running water over the rest, and I didn't let it bother me when both cigarettes went missing.

In fact, I didn't let anything ghostly bother me. The crooked pictures, the scattered mail, these were nothing, for I had real problems to contend with. And just to show the ghosts that I wasn't bothered by their silly little games I brought hand-written notes about the Nuremberg Trials back from the university. I left them on the coffee table before retiring to bed, and wasn't the least bit disturbed come morning when they were gone, even though I needed them for a paper I was writing.

The next night I didn't hide in my office after class, but brought home dinner to eat in front of the television while I watched a documentary on the Hitler Youth. I paid no concern to the fact that my napkin vanished or that the veal parmigiana purchased from a nearby café quickly turned cold. I ate it anyways, and I enjoyed it. The only frustration I revealed was directed towards the footsteps on the other side of the wall. The woman next door was walking up and down the stairs, over and over again, as if for no other reason than to annoy me.

Suddenly, it occurred to me that she might be a ghost.

I stared at my steps in shock, not quite sure what was moving on the other side of the wall. The hair on the back of my neck stood up straight as my heartbeat accelerated. The fork fell from my trembling fingers, and my eyes surveyed the apartment, wide in disbelief. I didn't know what exactly I was living with, but the presence felt real, more profound than it had ever felt before. I rose slowly, trying my hardest not to appear alarmed, and pretended to move casually as I made my way to the door.

I ignored the urge to buy a pack of cigarettes, even though I clearly deserved a smoke, and proceeded directly to the pub. Misti was working, thank God, for she was the only one with whom I could share this tale and not be ridiculed.

She listened compassionately, and then said, "Go knock on her door. That's the best way to find out if she's a ghost."

"I've tried that," I said. "She never answers."

"Knock harder," Misty said, smiling. "And don't stop knocking until the other neighbors complain. It's the only way to find out if she's a ghost or just being rude."

She warmed my heart that night, staring at me with big round eyes. The way her cheeks puffed out when she smiled was comforting, as if nothing could harm me as long as she was in a good mood.

"Ghosts are harmless," she insisted, and then offered to come home with me after closing, just to show me that there was nothing to be afraid of.

It was difficult to tell if she believed me or not, but it didn't really matter. She was looking for an excuse to invite herself over, and I leaped at the opportunity.

When we returned to the apartment I paid no mind to the footsteps on the other side of the wall, and miraculously this seemed to do the trick. The pictures hung straight, my mail was where I'd left it, and soon enough I stopped hearing footsteps from the old woman's apartment. All seemed fine until Misti excused herself to the washroom, whereupon she let out a loud shriek and came running into the bedroom, taking refuse in my arms. Her body trembled and her speech was stuttered, but she managed to tell me that she'd seen a man in the mirror.

"He was holding a butchers knife," she said, "raised above his head like he wanted to chop me up. But when I turned around there was no one there."

Misti didn't stay very long after that, and I couldn't blame her. She was scared badly, but the illusion she described didn't even resemble the type of activity that I'd experienced. Misti didn't invite me back to her place, and I didn't want to intrude. As much as we'd talked, it always seemed to be about me, and I had absolutely no idea what her living situation was like. Besides, ignoring the footsteps seemed to work — for me, at least — and I decided that I was going to hold my ground. Fleeing the apartment for the night was a surefire way to show the ghosts that they'd beaten me.

I had trouble sleeping — curled in blankets, clutching at my pillow — but I didn't sense the presence that I'd encountered at supper time. Except for the high school students on the playground, everything was quiet.

The terror didn't return until the next morning when I prepared to shave, at which point I looked in the mirror and saw the apparition that had frightened Misti. He was a ghastly looking man, with unkempt hair, face covered with stubble, bloody apron tied about his body, and a large butcher's knife held high in the air, just above my head. I turned in panic, only to find that no one was there. I looked in the mirror again, shocked to see the figure return, an expression of lunacy held within his mad face as he raised the butcher's knife. I swung around to face him, again finding myself alone in the washroom.

I dressed quickly and left, neglecting to even lock the door. It was time to take Misti's advice. The red-headed boy watched from the corner of his eye as I marched over to the old woman's doorstep. I knocked briskly, pounding my fist against the door, and didn't stop when the rest of the neighborhood began peeking out their windows, wondering who was causing all the commotion. I gave the door one thunderous pound after another, and when she finally answered my heart skipped a beat.

"I assumed that you'd come eventually," the old woman said.

"It's not the first time I've knocked," I told her.

"I know," she said. "I wanted to wait until you were persistent. This way I know you've already experienced enough that you won't think I'm crazy."

"You're not a ghost," I exclaimed.

Laughing, she invited me in, and the sight of her apartment nearly blew me away. The walls were decorated with pins and buttons from Nazi Germany, all preserved behind the glass of picture frames. I stared in astonishment, inspecting the mementos on display, badges aligned in rank to show that their owner had risen quickly within the Nazi party. There was a navy-colored chaplain's cap in the corner, and she even had Christian crosses adorned with swastikas, the ones Hitler had given to Nazi mothers.

"My father was in the war," she said. "I've taken it upon myself to preserve his trophies. But please, have a seat."

She extended a hand and I quickly followed her instruction, helping myself to a seat on the Sheraton-styled couch. Under different circumstances I could have spent hours talking to this woman, extracting as many stories as possible about her father, but given the current situation, there was only one subject that I cared to discuss.

"I assume you received my letter?" she asked.

I gave her a puzzled look and then said, "You're Samantha Samuelson?"

"Why yes, who did you expect?"

"I thought the letter was from a former tenant, not a neighbor."

"I'm sorry if I wasn't clear about who I am, but that's not really why you're here, now is it?" She took a seat across from me in an antique chair, then crossed her left leg atop the right. Her posture was excellent. Before I could answer she proceeded. "You didn't follow my instructions, did you?"

"No, I followed them," I protested. "Everyday there seemed to be new irritations, but I didn't let the ghosts bother me."

"Does the little boy on the tricycle bother you?"

I nodded.

"How about the children on the playground? Do they bother you?"

"You mean the high school kids?"

"No," she shouted, as if scolding me. "They're children."

I looked at her in wonder, and she sighed.

"I can see that you allowed the ghosts to bother you. But what about the man in the mirror? Have you seen him yet?"

"Just this morning," I admitted.

"Then it's good you came to see me. If you stare in the mirror for too long, you know, he really will kill you. It's happened to some of the previous tenants in your apartment, even though I warned them. If they'd have ignored the ghosts like I instructed, they wouldn't have even known he was there."

"Who is he?" I asked.

"His name is Christoph Braun. He lived in your apartment and used to date the woman who lived in mine. I suppose that's what gives him license to haunt both of our dwellings. He worked as a butcher at the grocery store in the strip mall, the one just on the other side of the fence, but that was way back in the 1950's. He was a good man, and quite bashful, so I've been told, but also a very hard worker. One day he went mad and butchered all of the children in the neighborhood. Then he killed his girlfriend. She was at his place when it happened, washing her face in front of the mirror. He came up behind her with his butcher's knife and chopped her into pieces. Nobody knows for sure what happened to Christoph, but you and I both know, as well as a few others, that if you stare into the mirror for too long he makes an appearance. My guess is that he chooses to hide in mirrors so that he doesn't have to face the ghosts of the children he killed. He can be quite bashful around new neighbors, and if they're not bothered by the pranks played by the ghost children, then he generally doesn't make an appearance at all. I wish I'd have known that earlier, but it's too late for me now. I too have to be careful not too look in the mirror for too long."

"Why don't you move out?" I asked, surprised that a woman of her age would choose to live in the presence of such evil. "You can't possibly feel safe here."

She laughed, as if it was a silly question, and said, "I'm an old widow with no income other than my Social Security checks. Mr. Ackley first rented this apartment to me back in 1989 for the small price of $100 a month. He hasn't raised the rent since. I've learned to ignore the children's pranks, and whenever I see Christoph Braun in the mirror I just come downstairs and finish what I was doing in front of the dinning room mirror. He's not as fast as you'd think, and it takes him a while to find me. But every once in a while he catches on, and I find myself running up and down the stairs over and over again, trying to get away from him long enough to comb my hair." She laughed after saying this, as though it were some sort of game from which she extracted amusement.

I, on the other hand, was not amused. For me there was no other choice but to spend the night at a hotel. I didn't honor the rest of my lease, and Mr. Ackley never tried to collect. I had no intention of ever going back to the apartment, regardless of the fact that it held everything I owned. It was time to start over, collect new things. As Misti had told me, sometimes it's best to just leave the past behind and move on.

I wanted to see her one last time, so I stopped by the pub that night. She wasn't there, and it surprised me, for she generally worked on Wednesdays. The bartender was someone new, so I only stayed for one drink. Roger and Scottie weren't present, and I enjoyed some peace and quiet instead of listening to them bicker over their sporting event. It wasn't until I finished my drink and was getting ready to leave that I noticed old man Wallace wasn't there. He wasn't hard to forget, for he'd only ever spoken to me once, and when he did it was to tell me that this was the only pub in town that didn't have a picture on the wall of the horseshoe-style stadium where the university played their football games. I took a look at the old black and white pictures, recalling that his observation was correct. As I admired the pictures of bootleggers, I noticed that the picture of the man that Roger and Scottie thought resembled old man Wallace was drastically altered. Instead of an old man dressed in overalls standing beside a still, it was just a picture of the still, void of any human presence. I looked at the picture beside it, and didn't recall having ever seen it before. It was a photograph of two men enjoying pints of beer over a game of chess. They looked remarkably like Roger and Scottie.

I scratched my chin and then walked out the door. I wanted to buy one last pack of cigarettes from the family-owned grocery store before leaving this phantasmal community forever, even if it meant paying their inflated price. This time I had no intention of running water over the pack. It was time to start smoking again.

The Hike

By Hall Jameson

She reached the peak of the headboard just as the man turned on the light. He jumped out of bed, a soft moan escaping his throat. She watched with eight bright eyes as he gave the blankets a shake, checked the rug, and looked under the bed. He sorted through the pile of laundry in the corner and cautiously checked the folds of the curtains. She froze as he gave the headboard a long, tired look, but knew she was practically invisible against the black lacquer finish. He shivered before slipping back into bed and switching off the light.

It took him longer than usual to settle back into sleep, but eventually his breathing became regular. He lay on his stomach, arms hooked under his pillow, head turned to the left. She studied him, selecting the best route for tonight's journey; then she moved down to the foot of the bed where she preferred to embark.

Both of his bare feet were sticking out from under the covers. Perfect. She tentatively reached out and placed a claw on the globe of his right big toe, testing the calloused skin. When he didn't stir, she pulled herself up easily using the eight wiry legs that sprouted from her thorax, the generous abdomen that followed rivaling the size of his second toe.

She began to crawl carefully along the arch of his foot, pausing when he giggled softly in his sleep, his toes curling. She continued to work the trail, venturing over his heel, reaching the edge of the covers. She found an opening and moved under the blankets towards the swell of his calf. Suddenly, he snorted and kicked the covers off. She clung to him, resisting the urge to bite down. She waited patiently for his body to become still before continuing on.

She moved over his calf and slid into the hammock that was the underside of his right knee. She selected a taut hamstring as the best route and balanced with exaggerated precision, moving slowly like an eight-legged tightrope artist, until she reached the curve of his buttock. It was covered by white boxer shorts with little green frogs on them. There was a tunnel where the fabric had bunched up and she had to decide whether to hike over the fabric or go through the tunnel.

Even though she found the darkness of the tunnel appealing, she remained on top of the fabric, carefully navigating the winding path between each frog until she reached the well of his lower back. She paused for a moment to enjoy the warmth of his skin. It smelled sweet and she considered taking a bite, well just a sip really, but resisted. She found herself drawn to the knobby route of his spine and began to work her way over the boulder of each vertebra cautiously, her bulbous abdomen dragging over his skin on each short descent.

She reached the cairn at the base of his neck — the seventh cervical vertebra. The view was spectacular from here! His back was littered with splashes of muddy freckles, and his shoulders were covered with a scree of dead, peeling skin — remnants of a recent sunburn. She took a moment to drink in the sights before proceeding down the gentle slope of his neck. She paused over his throbbing carotid, drawn by its enticing rhythm, before continuing on towards his hairline. His dark hair was cropped short, but was still wavy; she liked that — she could snuggle up in it and nap.

She took her time on every hike, taking great care not to wake him. She was sure that he had almost spotted her on the apex of the headboard tonight; that could have meant disaster for her — a crushing death would be horrible! If he only knew what an excellent housekeeper she was, he wouldn't want to squash her. She kept things immaculate in his bedroom. Thanks to her, there were no moths, houseflies, or mosquitoes in this room. If he actually cleaned once in a while, maybe he would find her web behind his headboard, but thankfully, he didn't. She was grateful for his sloppy habits; she only wished he understood her love of nocturnal hiking; perhaps then, they could be friends. She meant him no harm—honestly! She only bit on occasion, and usually only if he startled her with sudden movement. But sometimes he smelled so sweet that she simply could not resist—*scrumptious*, warm-blooded thing that he was!

She continued down the trail, following the hairline as it curved over his ear. She pulled herself up over the rim and sat quietly for a moment in the fossa near the ear canal. She then exited via the lobe, pausing when she saw a strange metal hoop that hadn't been there the night before. She tested it with her palps and gave it a tug with her fangs. She smelled fresh blood, but it was tainted with an unpleasant chemical smell, prompting her to move on.

She crossed his sideburn and paused on the apple of his cheek contemplating a fork in the trail. Did she want to explore his eyes and their delicate lashes, or examine the two caves of his nose? She decided on the latter, scaling the bridge of his nose and peeking into the right nostril. She was about to crawl into that intriguing space when he whined and swiped a hand across his face. He gave his nose a tweak, his fingers barely missing her as she rappelled gracefully off the tip. She landed in the carpet below, thereby bringing an end to that night's excursion. Perhaps tomorrow night he would fall asleep on his back; that always made for an interesting journey.

She crawled to her web behind the headboard where she had a snack waiting. Hiking always made her so hungry.

ERIE TALES:

TALES OF THE APOCALYPSE/ RESURRECTION MARY

BONUS FEATURETTE
EDITOR'S PICKS 2010/2011

EDITED BY:
BOB STRAUSS
AND
NICOLE CASTLE-KELLY

THE END IS N

Contributors

Michael Cieslak is a lifetime reader and writer of horror, mystery, and speculative fiction. A native of Detroit, he still lives within 500 yards of the city with his wife and their son, a German Shepherd/Rottweiler mix. His other interests include criminology, forensic science, photography, and nature. He would like to thank his younger brother Matt for the word "Zomboni" which was the impetus for his story in this collection.

Peggy Christie has been writing horror fiction since 1999. Her work has appeared in several websites and magazines, including House of Pain, Delirium Webzine, Sinister Tales and Appalling Limericks. Her short story, "Why Be Normal?", opened the anthology Reckless Abandon from Catalyst Press which premiered at the Horrorfind Convention in 2002. Peggy has finished her first novella and is currently working on a collection of short stories. She is also the Vice President of the Great Lakes Association of Horror Writers. Mrs. Christie lives with her husband, Robert, and dog, Roscoe P. Coltrane, in Clawson, MI.

W. S. Cwik is semi-retired from the Engineering profession. He has performed over the past twenty-five years with the Park Ridge Players, a community theatre, and has written some radio plays that have been performed with the Those Were the Days Radio Players, a group that recreates old time radio shows around the Chicago area. His published short stories have appeared in *Requiem for the Radioactive Monkeys* at Iguana Publications; *The Loyal Hannah Review*, *Crime and Suspense*, and in the anthology *Hell in the Heartland*. He has appeared as a featured reader at the Twilight Tales in Chicago.

Justin Holley is the author of two horror novels and twenty pieces of short fiction, many of which are published in various media throughout the United States, including: *Trei Literary Magazine*, *SNM Horror Magazine*, *Writer's Together Magazine*, *The Odd Mind Magazine*, and the anthologies *Atrum Tempestas* and *Satan's Wicked Refugees*.

A musician by trade, *Robert Christie* started performing at the age of thirteen on radio and television with the Duane Thamm percussion ensemble. He has recorded albums in many genres including classical, big band swing, jazz, and popular music. Always a fan of murder, mayhem, and the walking dead, he became interested in writing to exercise his Irish imagination. The power he used to create his first story, "Hook," opened a wormhole in the space/time continuum. His family hopes to see him again soon. Robert owns a school music business and advocates for school music programs in Southeastern Michigan . He lives with his wife, author Peggy Christie, and their dogs Roscoe and Dozer. They're cute.

Mary Makrias was raised in picturesque Waterford Township Michigan. After graduating from Michigan State, she moved to Houston, Texas where she spends her days as a Marketing Manager for a global building products company and her nights weaving her tales of horror. Mary has always been drawn to the magic of words. When asked why she chose horror she simply replied, "It's a nice way to work out my aggressions without hurting anyone, plus it is just plain fun!"

MontiLee Stormer writes about acts other people wish they could commit. Her interests in abnormal psychology, serial killers, and the storied Paradise Valley of Detroit are apparent in her other short stories, such as "The Suicide Bar", "And On The Seventh Day", "Flytrap" and her novels, including, *The Cat Dragged Inn* and *The Caretaker* and the highly anticipated, *Isle of Shadows* (written with Rob Callahan). She's also proud to be a regular contributor to Rob Callahan's *Nightmare Fuel Podcast*. MontiLee employs a 'well-compensated' sniper to keep the small but disturbingly dedicated legion of fanboys at bay. She lives in the Metro Detroit Area with her husband, two cats, and several knitting projects, which keep her safely off the streets. Help the authorities keep an eye on her activities at http://www.montileestormer.com.

Colleen McEuen has always been a fan of anything and everything that goes bump in the middle of the night. She works as an overnight dispatcher for a private ambulance company; which gives Colleen plenty of time to write. In fact, Colleen wrote her debut dark urban fantasy novel, Birth of a Vixen, during her first year on job. When she is not writing Colleen spends her time with her wonderful husband, four beautiful daughters, and their cat Skywalker.

Christopher Nadeau is the author of the novel *Dreamers at Infinity's Core* as well as its forthcoming sequel. He is also the author of more than fifty articles and currently writes a column on Detroit Area museums for www.examiner.com. He resides in Southeastern Michigan.

John Pirog is a lifetime Michigan resident who has traveled to 13 different countries and much of the U.S.A. John enjoys heavy metal, writing, horror comics and urban exploring. He is currently 44 years old, single and employed as a full time clerical employee.

James Park lives in Columbus, Ohio with his beautiful and articulate fiancée, Ngouanephone. He is a CPA and has an MBA from the Fisher College of Business at OSU. He enjoys writing and has had worked published in *Altered Perceptions*, *The Edge*, and *Spring Street*. He will have work featured this summer in *Do Hookers Kiss* and *Night to Dawn Magazine*.

Hall Jameson is a writer, poet, and fine art photographer. She was born in Damariscotta, Maine and lived in New England for thirty years before moving west in 1997. She now lives in Helena, Montana. When she's not writing, Hall enjoys hiking, photographing grain elevators, and cat wrangling.

As always, we appreciate your patronage of Great Lakes Association of Horror Writers, and by extension our charities, the Dominican and Siena Literacy Centers.

Made in the USA
Charleston, SC
27 June 2016